DARK OCEAN PRINCESS

NINA WALKER

ADDISON & GRAY PRESS
WWW.NINAWALKERBOOKS.COM

Ebook ISBN: 978-0-9992876-8-2

Paperback ISBN: 978-0-9992876-9-9

Dark Ocean Princess is for my author friends.

Thank you for believing in me and building this crazy amazing dream with me.

I believe in you, too.

"A RISING TIDE LIFTS ALL THE BOATS."

JOHN F. KENNEDY

ONE

IT IS TIME. MY MOTHER'S VOICE FLOATS INSIDE MY MIND like the current. The raised lilt in her inflection does little to mask her excitement. I wish I felt the same. I tell myself that the twisted emotion brandishing my chest is not fear; it is only nerves. And if I am nervous, that is okay. It is normal to be nervous on the day you are to meet your future husband.

I stand, the paper-thin fabric of my seafoam dress swaying upward along with the long dark tendrils of my hair. It's not a bother: I am used to my garments twisting about me like seaweed, but my hair, that's another story. My fingers itch to snatch at it, to pull it back to my usual crown braid, the long hair up and out of the way.

Leave it, she says, as if reading my mind. She knows me too well. *You look perfect.*

I smile and nod, still dying to fix the mess of hair. There's nothing more irritating than having unruly locks to fuss over, always drifting into my eyeline or tickling against my face. But this loose mess is the current style, a status symbol for the elite, and so it's a must for a night like tonight.

Mother swims closer, her smile bright as pearls. She is dressed in binding strips that trail out behind her, ribbons of red and yellow. Queen's colors.

And you look beautiful as well, Mother.

And it's true. Her long hair is also down, dark wispy strands of smooth black. She doesn't even flinch as one brushes her pale cheek, doesn't seem the least bit bothered. She's not like me. She's better. I'm trying to be like her. I have to be. Sapient black eyes sparkle as she looks me over, and I think if we were on the land right now, I'd be able to see her tears. Not born of sadness, but of pride. My insides squirm.

Playful schools of metallic-silver minnows swirl about her skirts, flashing in the dim light like tiny dancing mirrors. She ignores them, focused only on me.

I can't believe you're almost eighteen. She brushes a steady hand down the side of my face, cupping my cheek in her delicate palm. Her words are anchors. For a moment, I am five years old again. I ache to lean into her, to let myself be comforted, to accept her love. *You have grown into a remarkable young woman, Senra. I know you will honor our people once you ascend the throne. I just wish your father were here to see you. He would be so proud.*

A stab of guilt pierces me like a ray's barb. The mere thought of my father's death sends a wave of white-hot anger slicing through my icy blood. I suck in a breath. The cool salty water slides down my throat, steadying my lungs, and I force an agreeable smile.

Thank you, Mother. I step back, feet pushing off the black stone floor, and I glide toward my chamber's exit. I will meet my fate with the natural grace borne of my mother and the steady wisdom passed from my father. *Let's go,* I call back to her. *It would be impolite to keep my betrothed waiting.*

I stop, head tipped in reverence as she slips past me. She leads the way.

And I follow.

Willingly. Gratefully. Because if I've learned anything as the princess and heir to our vast siren empire, an empire stretching over what used to be mainland China and Tibet, it's that abiding by customs and honoring sacred agreements is critical. It's the difference between life and death.

It's why we survived when most of the human race did not.

A dull thud pounds in my chest, reminding me that I am alive. I am alive, but he is not. The thought tears at me. I'd give anything to have my father with me right now. He always knew how to smooth the edges, to give playfulness to the harder moments. But six months ago my father, the beloved Emperor, Heng Tao, was killed in a battle against sea monsters. The wretched creatures usually keep their distance. That day, they crept into our waters, hungry for our flesh, ruthless and demonic. They killed my father, feasted upon the whole

3

party of his warriors, before reinforcements arrived to fend them off. The fact that siren song didn't work to subdue the monsters is still a point of contention in the community. And to this day, it doesn't matter what anyone else says to me about those deaths, because deep down, I know I'm to blame.

That was the night I made a solemn vow, knowing I'd made a shattering, unalterable mistake. But I would never allow that same mistake to repeat itself. And so I have trained day and night, readying myself for when the monsters return, thirsty for revenge, itching to end them. I've focused only on my role as princess, what is to come, and what is expected of me. Nothing more.

Mother swims down the corridor. Our palace is a relic of the ancient China that survived under the press of ocean, human laid stone intermixed with winding coral. Guards and attendants bow as we pass, making way for their worthy empress. Since Father's death, she's stepped into the role of leading monarch well. It's wearing on her. I see it in the creases on her face and the graying of her hair, in the way her eyes lose focus as memories flood her. She deserves proper mourning for the loss of her soul mate, not to be dealing with the stress of politics. As I am nearly eighteen, she expects me to step up, to unite with my new husband, take over the title of Emperor and Empress, and relieve her of the task.

And I can't wait to do that for her, to take away even an ounce of her pain, even if I fear I don't deserve the title.

I've done everything in my power to prove my readiness and hide that fear. I'll never be the great leader that my father was. No one can. His name meant Eternal Great Waves and it fit him well. No, I won't measure up to him but I'll spend my life trying.

Eternal…

If only our siren lives were eternal, maybe we wouldn't be in this mess, maybe I wouldn't be swimming down this corridor, about to meet a fate I didn't get to choose. Just like all others on this dying planet, we sirens also grow old and die, too. That's if we're lucky enough not to be killed first. These days, more and more sirens are succumbing to early death, being taken by monsters, or worse, losing bits and pieces of our magic. I don't deserve to carry the Tao name, not after how I have failed my people, how I am still failing. I lost the privilege of the Great Waves name when I lost Father, but I am all that's left of the royal line, and so, I will prove myself. I will save my people. There is no other choice.

Introducing her Royal Empress, Shui Tao, and her daughter, Princess Senra Tao. We are announced by the Royal Entry, his voice commanding, ringing sharp between my ears. Part of our siren magic is the ability to communicate telepathically while underwater, and I know the man has been heard, simply by the dozens of inquisitive eyes that turn to face us.

We smile and glide into the vast ballroom, our muscled legs propelling us forward as we come to rest in the center. Our invited guests surround us in a semi-circle, heads bowed respectfully. They are also dressed in their finest, matching the decadence of the room that is also part ancient ruin, part carefully positioned coral and stone. There is no sunlight this far below the surface, but our eyes don't need light to see. We see everything in crystal clarity—another siren gift.

Heartbeats labor in my chest, weighted by the stares of our guests pressing into me.

A military-dressed gentleman steps forward. The wrinkles around his narrowed eyes are deep; his expression well-hidden behind closely cropped facial hair. *Empress Shui, it is a great pleasure to finally meet you,* he says humbly. *We have long awaited this day.*

He bows and kisses Mother's outstretched hand.

The pleasure is ours, Mother replies, voice smooth as it spreads to reach the minds of every guest in the room. *And how is the eastern territory?*

It's well enough. The man's smile doesn't quite reach his eyes, and I wonder how far the monsters have traveled as of late. Or perhaps it's the neighboring humans that are the problem. *We are pleased to be able to strengthen the Chinese Empire with this most advantageous marriage.* He motions behind him, hand slicing through the water and parting the crowd. *May I present my son, Lei Shen Yi.*

How many times that name has crossed my mind over the years. Hundreds? Thousands? Father sealed my betrothal when I was an infant so I grew up knowing the name of my future spouse. Lei.

But I never knew his face.

The man that is to be my husband, my lover, my partner in all things, takes a few swimming steps closer. I am frozen except for my searching eyes: they travel up and down him, taking everything in.

He is exactly as I expected.

I don't know whether to be relieved or disappointed. Dressed in the sleek black warrior suit worn by the young men of his station, he fits into his surroundings. Military are meant to blend with the ocean, so their clothing resembles whale hide. The series of small flashy adornments clipped above his heart set him apart from the others. I don't know what they all mean individually, but together they hint at battles won.

His eyes sparkle with charisma as he mimics his father, bowing low and kissing my mother's dainty hand. And then he is in front of me, smile ever so slightly teasing, gaze heavy yet open. Unlike his father, his face is bare of facial hair. It is perfectly cut with high cheekbones and wide eyes. His hair is tied back in a tight knot, accentuating the look. My breath leaves me, but not of excitement, it's something else. Something closer to worry. I push it away. Maybe he doesn't blend in so well, after all. Maybe that is exactly what I need in a partner. Someone handsome, charismatic, someone who fits the part. He takes hold of my hand and places soft lips against my flesh, lingering for a second too long.

Princess Senra. His voice is silk. *I have long awaited this moment. I am your humble servant and am honored to have been chosen for your husband. I will stand by your side and support you in all things.*

I am the most advantageous match anyone in our empire could make, so of course he feels this way. I will still lead. He will be given a tremendous amount of power as well. Logically, it all lines up. But I still can't help the flutter of mixed emotions that pull in my chest. I turn them into the playful smile that rises to my lips.

I am grateful to finally meet you and to have you at my side. It's the only response I can manage. Sending it out so everyone can hear makes me more nervous than I should be. I brush it off, turning to smile at our guests.

This is our engagement party and it's only the beginning, nothing to worry about. Lei and I will spend the next month getting to know each other better before the wedding. It's after the wedding that worries me. How am I to build a life with this man who I don't even know? Marrying for love is foolish for someone in my position, but that doesn't mean I don't long for the chance as anyone would. I can't think about that now, can't let myself dwell on matters that are out of my control. I must focus on here and now, where it all starts with a dance.

He reaches a steady hand out to me, as if none of this is new to him, as if he isn't nervous. Maybe he's not. The choir begins to sing, and it's a song that burns through me like a calming flame, grounding me, returning me to myself. Their music is ethereal and eerily beautiful. Although it is as familiar as my heartbeat, it still calls to me, still fills me with immense love for my ocean home. Lei pulls me close, and we begin to spin around the ballroom, our feet lifting off the floor several times as we dance. Some of our guests mingle around the corners of the room and others join the dance. They all watch.

I feel my mother's approving gaze on us, and I can't help my thoughts from returning to my father. Would he be equally as pleased with Lei as she seems to be? Considering Father had picked Lei for me himself, I should only assume the best of him. I should make every effort to be happy in my match.

How was your journey here? I direct the question so that only Lei can hear. His eyebrows jump, lips quirking with pleasure.

We can automatically tell when someone speaks only for us. It's meant for intimate relationships and usually considered taboo in public settings. But it's my way of letting Lei know that I want this to work as much as he does.

He lets his smile out and it's brighter than I expected, so bright it makes me even more nervous, like a spotlight is shining down on me. *It wasn't too bad,* he replies. *I haven't traveled for that great of a distance before. I must say I was a little worried. Luckily, it turned out okay.*

I'm glad to hear it.

There was a small incident with a shark but otherwise... His voice trails off into a sheepish smile. I force a laugh at his joke. He's only teasing. Sharks are the least of our worries. They're easily influenced by our magic, as are all ocean life. It's the monsters, the ones who came after the sirens, that we need to worry about.

I study his relaxed smile. His teeth are perfectly straight and as white as the full moon. They light up his face. He may be a warrior, he may be dangerous, but nothing about him is scary. I finally let my body settle, my blood and heartbeat and breath slowing enough for me to fully catch my thoughts. Although Lei is a warrior and four years older, I'm the one in the power position. I have nothing to be intimidated about. The thought makes this easier. Maybe this marriage is not only going to work, but maybe we'll become more than friends, too. Maybe we'll grow to love each other in the way my parents did. Maybe we'll be great together.

What are you thinking? he asks lightly. His eyes are eager slits.

We're so close now, our bodies barely inches apart. The water surrounding me grows hotter. I blink rapidly, no longer able to hold onto a thought even if I tried. Is this feeling attraction? Is it nerves? Something else? I wish I knew…

I can't remember, I answer honestly.

Something sparks in his eyes, and they drop to linger on my lips. If it weren't for the other people here, he would kiss me. And I'd kiss him back, if only because it would make this whole experience easier. The realization floods me with an old feeling that I haven't had since Dad's passing: hope.

I don't deserve it. Logically, I know that. But just for this moment, I let it in, let the happiness fill me up until my heart is floating.

Crash!

The sound explodes through the room, ripping us apart.

The sweet song of the choir transforms into piercing screams. I look around frantically, horror striking sharp as I catch sight of the monster jerking its way through the coral and into the room. Its gruesome mouth is open with huge bloody, razor-edged teeth. Its jaw thrashes open and shut, biting and snarling at the water. Its eyes are two red, glowing balls cut into bloodthirsty slits. The body is long, snake-like, and covered entirely in black armored scales. It's a beast bent on destruction, bent on slaying us.

I am transfixed. Is this the beast that killed my father? Lei is yelling something, but I can't hear him over the noise of voices crashing through my thoughts. He pushes me to the back of the room, farther from the monster, and then he disappears.

Why isn't the siren song working?

TWO

SIREN SONG LURES ALL SORTS OF CREATURES BUT NEVER in anger. If anything, this creature should have turned docile and would have been put to death instantly by our warriors. That's the same question I've been asking since Father's passing. Monsters shouldn't have attacked then, just as this one shouldn't be attacking now. I haven't joined the song yet, but even a child with the simplest of melodies should have been able to stop one lone monster.

It confirms everything we've feared and speculated over for months. Our magic isn't just weakening in a select few. It's across the entire empire.

And now we'll pay the price.

The beast is pinned between large shafts of coral. It will soon break free. No longer caught off guard, the people have jumped into action. Some have swam away to hide, but most have begun to sing. Lei and his father are moving toward the creature, spears ready. They're not alone. They have their party alongside them, communicating silently between the group of six men, moving in lethal harmony.

As if sensing its immediate demise, the sea monster thrashes out once more, but with much greater force. Any nearby fish scurry out of the way as pieces of coral break free. The beast uses the momentum to slam its body against the wall one more time, finally loosening itself enough to dart toward us.

Too late.

Lei thrusts his spear directly through the center of the serpent's red eye. It slumps, mouth still agape, and crashes to the floor. Since the hide of the creatures is thick as armor, the eye is the only kill point, but at least they can be killed. From the way Lei moved, I know this isn't his first kill. He's probably ended the life of many of these dangerous monsters, in turn saving the lives of countless sirens throughout the region. My approval of him rises.

I am still frozen to where Lei pushed me, against the far wall, guards surrounding me, my mother at my side.

Lei's dark gaze turns to find mine, and he looks me up and down, as if checking that I'm okay. It's a protective move that turns my stomach into a knot. I nod once and, after taking one last steadying breath, I swim over to inspect the fallen beast. It floats gently, mere inches from the floor, now dead—it's almost beautiful. Almost. The punctured eye and gory teeth are anything but pretty. I kneel before it, studying the armored scales. They're the size of my hand,

and the points are as sharp as shark teeth. The beast looks exactly like a dragon mixed with a sea serpent, like the ancient drawings from a time centuries before the seas rose. This creature should be mythology. It doesn't belong in this world.

But then again, neither do we.

I close my eyes, letting the water calm me. The smallest amount of black, bitter, coppery blood trails into my nostrils and I grimace. Will they ever stop hunting us? Demons such as this one emerged after the mages gave us our siren power. Our song *has* been an easy defense against them. The humans who choose to stay on what little land was left haven't fared as well as we have. And the mages had not only the protection of their magic, but of our people who swore to protect them through the covenant. For years, this has been our balance. We've been able to keep the monsters at bay, even as those monsters grew in number, in size, and in ferocity.

And yet...

I look up to find my mother standing over me. I take in her horrified expression and try to keep mine calm. Even still, the fears come pouring out.

How did it get all the way here? I ask her. *Why didn't the song stop it?*

And then the more obvious question cuts me deep. I'm ashamed I didn't think to ask sooner. My father would have thought of it sooner...

How many did it kill before it got to us?

She doesn't respond to any of the questions. I'm certain we're both thinking of the answers. Our palace is in the center of a highly populated city. If this disgusting thing came all the way here, what destruction was met in its path?

Pain rips through me, twisting my stomach, and I glare into the monster's remaining red eye. It's unseeing, but I don't care. I despise it. Hatred rushes through my body like a riptide and I grit my teeth, hands fisted. This isn't the first time the monsters won against me, it's the second. Guilt burns from deep within, guilt, and the question at its source. It keeps plaguing me like the lapping water above. The same question we're all asking ourselves, over and over, and over again.

Why is our magic failing?

Everyone jumps back into action as I'm whisked off to my chamber. The warriors swim away in force, weapons ready to respond to any distress happening in the kingdom. The remaining guests are shepherded to the safer innards of the palace. Lei follows close at my side. He kisses my hand again as I come to a stop outside my stone door.

Stay safe, my princess, he says. Something inside rebels at his words, rebels to be called his.

And you, too. My eyes search his. If I asked to come with him right now, how would he respond? Would he agree? Or would he insist I stay behind? And which one is the right response of the man I am to marry?

I imagine each scenario and keep the conversation locked within.

He nods once and then he's gone, disappearing around a corner, probably to go find his father. Certainly, they will go fight any monsters lurking outside. A prickly sensation akin to jealousy sweeps over me. I want to say it's worry for the wellbeing of this new man in my life, but I know that is a weak lie. Lei is powerful. He's trained. He can handle himself. No, there is only one name for the emotions I have for Lei in this moment: envy. Because I wish I could battle those monsters as much as any siren would. It's in our blood to fight them, written into our very DNA.

I rush to my chamber window and peer down, taking in the scene. I gasp, my teeth gritted to hold back the scream bursting forth. It is unlike anything I've witnessed in my life. It's horrifying.

Countless times, I have taken in this view: the view of my childhood —a vast kingdom spreading out before me like a blanket. My home. The beautiful city is comprised of ruins from the old world, from back when the buildings were above water, to coral that the first sirens brought in as part adornment and part to keep our food supply close. It's all intermixed with massive dark stone structures that my people forged with their bare hands. The ocean was not kind to the majority of the ruins, so we had to piece things together ourselves, turning chaos into accomplishment.

To me, our city has always been exceptionally beautiful. We took something that was broken, a relic from a different time, and transformed it into our own version of gold, our own kind of alchemy. Thousands of sirens reside in the city surrounding the palace, and many more beyond that. They are my people.

And now, they are dying.

Below me, more monsters battle our warriors. I count seven

monsters in total. They range in color from cobalt blue, to bittersweet yellow, to ruby red, and black as octopus ink. Their long, thin bodies move in lethal, graceful arcs as they lay waste to everything in their path. A current of screams ring through the night's water, part telepathically and part gurgling shrieks. It's when the screams are snubbed out that terror spikes my blood.

The sea monsters are utterly ravenous. But the beasts are also wildly intelligent. They should know better than to come here. Our siren magic has always been far too strong for them. They have adapted and learned to stay away from our most populated areas. Yet here they are anyway, ripping through my city, feasting on my people.

I crumple to the floor, anger and panic sweeping through me. I need to help. My mind flashes to the day my father asked me to join him, to the day he died. At the time, there'd been reports of sea monsters in our territory. Disbelieving, he'd decided to take a few of his men and go see for himself. He'd also asked me to come along as a precaution, since my song was the strongest in the kingdom.

This is my ultimate shame. The poisoning secret I keep locked up inside.

Because I had agreed, had even been excited to go. But then I'd been selfish and foolish. I'd gotten swept up in gossip and scandal, addicted to the drama of court life. And I'd lost track of the day and never showed up to our agreed upon time and place. So, he'd left without me.

And then he died without me.

I could have stopped it with my gift, had I been there. That's the truth of it. My song is the strongest in generations, and I should have been there. I may have let him down. I won't make the same mistake again. I won't cower behind these palace walls while there are helpless sirens outside needing my song. For as much as an everyday siren's song has weakened, mine is still strong. It has to be. I'm the princess.

My window is long and thin, designed to keep the outside where it belongs. I run my fingers along the edge, sticking my hand out, frustrated that's all I can manage. Unfortunately, this little window also does an excellent job of keeping me in. Doesn't matter. I won't let one small obstacle stop me from helping my people, even if I am the only heir to the throne, even if mother would die if she knew I was leaving the palace to fight off the monsters myself.

How is my life more valuable than any of theirs? It's not. Saving them won't bring my father back, it won't temper the guilt, but it will give me a purpose.

I dart back to the chamber's door, my body slicing through the water like an eel. Water might hold humans back, and I might have legs and feet like they do, but I'm anything but ordinary. Water is my home, my protector, and my tool. I'm too quick for the guards to hold me in. I bust through the door and down the corridor before they even realize I'm getting away. I know this palace better than anyone, and I swim around several corners, hiding in alcoves, and switching directions, until I am confident nobody knows where I am.

It proves to be a foolish thought.

Senra! My mother's voice blasts through my mind. *Come back here this instant!*

That was quick.

I'm sorry, Mother. I have to help, I reply, wishing I could force her out of my head. I can't stop now; I'm too close!

She must be near, but as soon as I leave the palace, I'll be able to lose her nagging voice, too. I'll need that if I'm to follow through with my plan. She'll be safe here. I don't deserve the same.

You absolutely do not have to help, she says sharply. *By leaving you are doing the opposite of helping.*

The booming crush of stone pillars crashing to the ocean floor breaks our conversation. I swim to the closest door, grateful to find it's temporarily unmanned.

I'm sorry. I stab out the half-hearted apology again, trying not to think about how her face must look right now. Twisted in worry. Disappointed eyes. *But I really have to go.*

And then I take my chance.

THREE

I FLY THROUGH THE WATER, STAYING LOW AS I RUSH JUST feet over the city streets. God willing, if I keep down, the monsters might not see me until it is too late for them to fight back. I just need to get close enough and then I can sing—that's all. Simple. I laugh silently to myself—as if anything about this is simple. But I push that doubt away and refocus. Once I entrap them with my voice, the warriors can swing in and kill them and all of this can be over. As far as I can tell, my song is the only one powerful enough for the task. It has to be me.

I swim to the top of an ancient four-story building and peek out over the worn gables and into the wash of inky darkness beyond. My eyes adjust, everything coming into crystal clarity. My gut twists. From up here, it appears there are still three monsters left. Three blood-thirsty dragons wreaking havoc on my people, and each deserving their death. One, crimson and spindly, cowers, ready to succumb to a group of siren warriors. The sight lifts a glee-filled smile to my face. I watch intently as the warriors circle the injured beast, as they get close enough to spear it straight through its black eye. Lei is in the forefront, taking point in the kill. He's got it covered, but I wish I could trade him places. Maybe killing one of these beasts will ease the guilt I've been carrying.

The thought is magnified when I spot the second monster. He is feasting on the innards of a dead body. His scales gleam metallic as he writhes over his bloody meal. The man is long dead. His mouth is stretched wide open, as if he were caught screaming before death took him. Bile rises in my throat, and I clench my fists, ready to attack. But then the third monster nabs my full attention. My body grows cold.

He is as black as the ocean floor, as dark as midnight, with rows of pointed scales shining like razors. And he's huge. His body is bigger than his companions and nearly double the size of the one that attacked the ballroom minutes earlier. Its steady eyes glow, two liquid golden orbs, illuminating his thirst, his sole focus to kill and to eat. The monster lurks, slipping through the city streets like a stretched snake, like the stuff of bedtime stories meant to scare children from straying too far from home. Its jaw slowly unhinges, a forked tongue sliding in and out between pointed teeth. Not twenty feet from where it's headed is a young girl. She can't be more than ten years old. She's crouched behind a slab of stone, curled in on her self. Her head is resting in her arms, back heaving up and down in silent sobs.

She doesn't see her death approaching.

I don't think. I rush for the monster, swimming through the water until I land in the center of the alleyway, directly in front of the gruesome creature. Now in plain view of those glowing eyes, of those gnashing teeth and forked tongue, the serpent jerks its massive head toward me. Pulsing bubbles tear from its steel-trap jaw in a watery hiss.

It charges, mouth springing open, moving as fast as a whip, and much faster than I anticipated. I am ready.

Arms outstretched, sea-foam dress billowing around me like the princess I am, I sing. The ethereal music pours from me, ghostly and celestial all at once. The monster careens toward me and for a panicked moment, my entire body clenches in fear for my life. But then the monster slows, heeding my song, caught in my trap. I raise my voice, pushing out the sweet sounds even further. The monster stops abruptly, lying at my feet and staring up into my gaze. Its head is the size of my entire body. It just blinks at me, entranced. One by one, all my flexed muscles begin to relax.

I keep singing, even though my hands shake. I keep singing, even though I don't know how to sort through the tirade of thoughts. So the siren magic still works. At least, mine does. This is proof. Not to mention, the very fact that we're all still living and breathing underwater is also proof. But this should have never happened and it's time to accept that something is terribly wrong. It shouldn't take a princess, one with the strongest siren magic in her veins, to control the creatures of the ocean. This ability to captivate our prey

22

underwater is something any siren should be able to do, noble born or not, since it's in all of us.

What's next?

I study the dragon-like creature, searching for the earlier need I had, for the need to kill. This is why I am here, isn't it? I must end this abomination. One minute it was hunting and thirsty for my blood, but now it's pawing at my feet like a pet. Up close, its golden eyes are so startlingly reflective; I can see myself staring back. Does this beast have thoughts? Feelings? Intelligence seems to be whirling behind those glittering eyes as they pull me into them, same as I am pulling him into mine.

As long as we are in water, our siren song can cause any living thing above it to willingly jump into the ocean, surrendering to a watery death. Below water, however, the song can cause anything able to survive down here, namely fish, to bend to our will. We use it to keep our bellies fed and our homes protected. For a hundred years, this is how we have survived. The land mages gave us this power in exchange for protection for their monastery. It was a choice all humans in the region were offered, back in the days when the sea rose above the land. I shudder to think what would have happened if my ancestors had chosen to refuse the magic, as many did. If that had happened, I'm positive I'd never have been born.

Senra! Where are you? Lei's voice cuts through my thoughts and I jump. For someone I've just met, his voice feels as familiar to me as the salt is to the ocean water. That realization unnerves me, as does his protectiveness. Is it too much, too soon? *Your mother said you snuck out here!*

I ignore him and keep singing to the dragon at my feet. Lei will soon hear the song and come to investigate anyway. If I really am planning to hand over this creature to his tribe of warriors, then I should reply to him.

And yet, I can't do it. I hate myself for the hesitation. If anything, I should kill this hideous thing myself, right now, before I can think another moment on it. This beast could have played a part in my father's death; maybe it was even the one who killed him. Either way, I'm sure it killed innocent siren people on its way into our city. So why am I hesitating? Why aren't I doing what I was born to do?

Something inside of me burns like the heat of land fire. Shame. Guilt. A terrible power. But also, the very sure knowledge of what I'm going to do.

My song has worked its way into the sea dragon's thick blood well enough that I could get it to do anything I command. I could ask it to impale itself on a spire, effectively killing itself, and it would follow the order without hesitation.

Again, I force myself to weigh the choice I'm about to make. Administering death is what I should do. I should kill it. It's evil. They're all evil. I know that.

But instead, I obey the mercy swelling inside and kneel down, softly placing one open palm against its cheek. The scales are much smoother than they look. For something so solid and sharp, they feel

24

as delicate as my silky dress. My hand is tiny against its massive face. The creature turns into it, as if relishing the feel of my touch.

Go. I direct the thought toward it and it alone. *Run away. Leave my people alone.*

There is no hesitation, not a moment for either of us to change the path I have set for it. It rears back and swims away, so fast, it's gone in seconds.

Senra, where are you? Lei's questioning voice pulses through my head again. This time, I answer.

I'm here. I swim up from the alley, out into the openness of ocean. *I'm fine.*

We spot each other at the same time, and he dashes forward. His mouth is set in a grim line and his eyes are narrowed on me like I'm one of those creatures he's supposed to hunt down and kill. Like out of everything that happened tonight, me leaving the palace is the worst of it. I know he wants to chastise me. The knowledge only turns my stomach sour. I fold my arms across my chest and raise my chin.

Already, he thinks he owns me. Even though I will always be ranked above him, is it possible he'll spend our lives treating me as his to possess?

Maybe I'm not being fair…

I'm fine. I press out the words again, trying to sound as strong and composed as possible. This time, my words reach any nearby Siren. I might as well defend myself to everyone. *Besides, I helped. I just sent the last one away. He won't be back.*

25

Lei's father rushes forward. *You sent it away? You should have killed it!*

I assure you, it is gone and will not be hurting our people again. It's difficult to keep my voice steady, but somehow I manage.

His reply is charged with venom and his men nod along with each word. *That's assuming your magic doesn't wear off. In case you couldn't tell, princess, our siren magic is experiencing some difficulty at the moment. Sending him away was foolish!*

I glare and rise up in the water, floating above them all. *Do not forget to whom you are speaking,* I snap. *Of course, I am well aware that those monsters shouldn't have gotten this far into our territory. But my magic is still at full strength and I am telling you, that thing is gone for good.*

Appearing censured, he bows, as do all the others in his party.

I take a few slow breaths, cooling the metal in my blood. *In any event, we must find out what is happening to our magic before it is too late,* I add.

She's right. My mother's calm voice flows into our circle, and she glides over the city toward us. She watches the aftermath of death and destruction below with a frown, then looks up to hold my gaze as she comes to a stop beside me.

Senra, what mess are you in now? She says the question so only I can hear. I keep my face still, not wanting anyone to know the shame and righteous anger warring inside, not even her. *We don't want to anger our guests so soon,* she continues. *We need their protection and alliance, lest you forget.*

I bite my lip and turn back to Lei and his father with a careful smile, a smile I have practiced a million times in my seventeen years. *I am sorry if you disagree with my choice today,* I tell them. *I was only trying to help. But what's done is done and that beast was told under the direction of my song to never return here. Now, we need to focus on restoring all siren magic to its fullest. Can we all agree on that?*

They exchange glances and nod, albeit skeptically. I wonder how many monsters they've let live? I'm sure the answer to that is zero.

Mother rests a gentle hand on my shoulder and speaks to the group. *I have spoken with the Elders. We agree. A party must be sent to visit the Tibetan monastery. Only the mages there will be able to help us regain our full power.*

We'll leave straight away, Lei's father replies.

Mother looks at me, her thin lips twisted in resolve, before she addresses the group again. *To ensure that you arrive at your destination safely, you'll need someone with full siren abilities to accompany you.*

I'm startled as I realize where she's going with this. My heart races in my chest, pure excitement crashing with each heartbeat.

You'll take Princess Senra as your guest.

27

FOUR

I WON'T EVER COMPLAIN OR HAVE THE FORTITUDE TO SAY it to the others, but my body is aching in ways I've never experienced before. My swimming legs push on, twisting shoulders continuing in their winding pattern. I've never had to move this fast for this long, and I grit my teeth against the onslaught of pain. I can do this. I have to do this.

Our party has been traveling south for three days. There haven't been any instances where I've had to use my song. No monsters. No humans. It's been an uneventful trip so far, except of course, for the screaming weakness of my overworked muscles. I naïvely thought I was strong and well-conditioned. I've spent hours in training every day since my father was killed. But this? This is different. These men are on another level of conditioning. How could I have ever thought I was ready for battle? I saw how they fought those monsters, how they didn't pause to kill. If this is what it takes, if this is the level of skill I need to survive, then I clearly have a long way to go. At least I'm not out here alone. I shudder to think what would happen to me then.

We are nearing our mark now. And the closer we get to our destination, the more a sense of foreboding falls over the group. For me, it is a bitter, nagging throb that sits dead-center in my chest. As we press through our final mile, everyone grows quiet. The constant chatter between the group is extinguished as quick as the crash of a wave.

I look around, seeing what they see. The water is different here. Lighter, somehow. Thinner. Warmer.

We are nearing the surface.

It isn't the first time I've been up and it won't be the last, and yet something about this time feels vastly different. I sense it the same as when I sense a predator is near. Awareness tightens me all the way to my core. Instinct and magic couple within. My eyesight sharpens. My breath steadies.

We swim faster, legs pushing us up. The twenty of us fan out in a well-practiced arc as we make our approach. Lei stays close to my side, as he has the last three days. I am mostly flattered by his protectiveness, but a small part of me sparks with annoyance. It's a part of me that rears its head every time he looks me over like I'm his possession to keep safe. Being the princess, I should be used to this level of scrutiny, of admiration and suffocation. After all, I've had guards watching over me since birth. My life has never been without eyes to watch it and hands to mold it. My every move has been studied, planned, and rehearsed for as long as I can remember. So why is Lei any different? I am his fiancée; he's supposed to act like this. I should be happy about his dedication. No. I am happy about this, I tell myself. We're a good match. Lei was my father's choice. I need to give him a break, even if only for the sake of the man I let down.

I cast a glance in Lei's direction, sending him an easy smile.

Everything okay? he asks.

Everything is great. Let's do this, shall we?

I grin wider and lead the way. Rushing forward, legs kicking out, my body slices through the water and I burst through the surface. The foam tickles my skin, froth rolling off my black bodysuit. I blink into the sunlight, eyes burning. It is so ungodly bright that it takes me several seconds to actually keep my eyes open without wincing. Waves kick out at my face, salty water coating my mouth, pushing up my nose and rinsing out my eyes. It's the only thing making this any easier.

I much prefer the water to the air.

The air is abrasive. Cruel. A flighty substance, so fleeting, it's nearly impossible for me to relax. Wave after wave of panic overwhelms my senses as I try desperately to replace the water in my lungs with flimsy air. I suck it in but can't seem to get enough, and it's as if my lungs are now empty. After a few more gasps, the rational part of my brain kicks in and I settle, calming my breaths into a slow canter. Sirens *can* breathe above water as well as below. I know this. I've lived this. There's nothing to worry about.

I turn to find Lei watching me, a knowing smile playing at his lips.

I take it you don't come to the surface very often? he questions with a raised eyebrow.

It's been awhile, okay? Don't judge me. I send the snarky comment back his way with a splash and a wink.

When he laughs, it's aloud. That sets me off my axis almost as much as the air does. His voice is rich and commanding. The sound is the same as what I hear inside my mind when we talk underwater, but something about it now surrounding me like this, is so different and so real. I don't know what to make of it.

Lei and I have been having a lot of one-on-one conversations this trip. Blocking all others out has been natural for us, which has helped to calm any fears I've had about marrying a stranger. We've become closer over the last few days, seeming to agree on all the things that matter. Our priorities, our values, our vision for the future, it's all the same. I'm starting to believe that maybe we can grow to love each other, maybe even as passionately as my parents did. It is fast becoming my greatest hope, even if that doubt still nags deep within. In any event, I have to try to make this work.

"Do *you* come to the surface often?" I ask. My voice cracks painfully with its audible disuse. I force out the question anyway. I will not be seen as weak, even in this. *Especially* in this.

"Not here, specifically, since the Tibetan Mages are no threat to us," he replies. "But in the northwest area where I'm from. Yes. I go to the surface as often as needed."

"To fight the humans?" I ask, already knowing the answer is yes.

The sun reflects off his black eyes like a mirror as he nods once, water dripping down his smooth cheek. We float on the surface water, each watching the other. The others in our party are busy getting into position, and if I looked, I would probably be able to see their heads bobbing above water as well. We've surrounded the island where the mages live. Long ago, before the seas rose, this was one of the tallest mountaintops in the region. Now, it's all they have left.

Lei breaks eye contact to stare at the monastery on top. I follow his lead, gazing up at the beauty. A pang of longing rips through me the moment I lock eyes on this sacred place. I've been here before, several times. All the royals have. But this is all new to him. What does he think, seeing it for the first time? Does he see the simplicity as lacking compared to the grandness of the palace and cities below? Or does he appreciate the simplicity as I do? Does he see the grace in it? The peace?

The land is dead. The sea angrily beats against the sheer cliff face anyway, as if trying to finish the job. It doesn't matter; the monastery has survived far worse than water. And the monks don't survive off the land here. It's the spoils of the ocean and the legacy of magic that keep them alive. It's that, and it's us.

"Have you ever met a mage before?" I ask Lei, out of politeness, or perhaps just something to say. I know he hasn't. Very few sirens will ever receive such an invitation.

Our bodies break through the surf as we swim toward our target.

"I haven't had the honor of meeting a mage in person," Lei responds as expected. He doesn't look at me, even though we're practically swimming shoulder to shoulder. We get closer, and he returns to our normal way of speaking, his voice carrying through my mind. *I've only met some of the regular humans that are left, but they're our enemies, and the only honor in that is to kill them before they kill us.*

I peek at him, notice his eyes, and suck in a breath. They've shifted in focus. They are two black, cold stones, lost in the memories of blood and bone and death.

The mages are different, I assure him. *They wield magic. They love our people.*

No doubt he already knows this. We all do. A century ago the world changed. The earth's people were already in turmoil when an asteroid stuck the atmosphere, breaking into thirteen pieces and pummeling the planet. The thirteen areas where the asteroid pieces hit faced varying terrors as the seas rose. And just as the world's population succumbed to the water, any land left became nothing but a scorched wasteland. Unusable.

There was no humane way to survive.

That's when the mages emerged, different sects all over the globe, and all offering a solution. They would wield their magic on human flesh, turning humans into sirens, allowing us to return to our lost cities, now underwater. Allowing us to survive.

My ancestors took the offer.

Most did not.

Our territory's mages hailed from Tibet, coming forth from deep in the monasteries where they had been secretly practicing magic for centuries. They gave us our powers, only asking for one thing in return: protection. They keep our magic alive, and we keep ocean threats away from them. They have lived in peace as they always have because of what they gave to us.

Even when the sea monsters rose from the sordid depths, we kept true to our promise. The demons crawled out from the deepest parts of the ocean like hell's retribution for our survival, but the mages never wavered and neither have we.

Just thinking about the monsters makes my skin crawl. They'll stop at nothing to feast on the living; it is their sole drive. Luckily, our song still has its hold on them. Or, it did. Mine worked well enough, but what about the others? Those eight beasts never should have been able to attack our city. I can still hear the incredible siren chorus from that night of the engagement party, can still feel it deep in my bones.

All it does is twist my gut in fear as the memory pummels me. I remember the way the creatures ravaged our city, thinking about how all those people's song failed, and I'm right back to where I started, right back to feeling helpless.

The monks should be able to offer an explanation. If anyone can fix this, it's them. It has to be. They're the ones with the magic. I hold that belief steady in the center of my heart. It's the most important one I've got right now, so I cling on tight.

We move in on the island. A rocky cliff face. No beach.

There's hardly any land left in our territory. Steps are carved into the side of the sandstone where the water meets the island. They lead up, up, up to the small buildings of the monk's sanctuary, buildings also cut into the stone, though a few freestanding structures have been added over time. The monastery curves around the crest of the island, but is mainly located at the flattened bit up top. Along the bottom is where the people live.

My eyes travel to the very peak of the monastery, and I almost feel at home.

Almost.

Every year, my parents and I travel here to meet with the mages and to enact our rituals together, to celebrate the covenant. My heart twists as I think of the last time I was here, a little less than a year ago. Our family was still intact and blissfully unaware of the death and grief looming ahead. Father's smile had been strong, proud and sure. The kind of smile that illuminated the sky.

Today, dark clouds clash with the sharp sun.

The sky is a threat of the coming storm, a stark reminder that at any moment this life can change.

FIVE

I HOIST MYSELF UP ONTO THE STONE STEPS AT THE WATER'S edge. The liquid runs down my legs and pools at my feet, creating an odd feeling that leaves me nervous. I ignore the twinge of unease always present whenever I'm completely removed from the sanctuary of my ocean home. Truthfully, I hate stepping out of the ocean. The stone crushes against my toes, another reminder of my discomfort. I blow out a slow breath and tell myself not to focus on it.

The rest of the men in our party clamber into place, and Lei's father, SunYu, leads us up the thin stairway cut into the side of the mountain. I am only a few steps behind SunYu, watching carefully as he moves from step to step. His large, lumbering feet maneuver the stairway as awkwardly as my own. It makes sense for him to be slow and careful, considering the sacred location. It's that, and the fact that he's never been here before, that makes me realize something:

the true reason why Mother sent me along on this expedition. I'm to be the bridge between these lethal siren warriors and the peaceful human monks. It makes perfect sense. This wasn't just about me getting to know Lei better or protecting the party. It's more than that.

Just before we crest the area that will put us at the opening of the first building, SunYu turns to me. His eyebrows draw together, and he runs a hand along his jaw, squinting at me in consideration.

"Are we welcome here?" he finally asks, his voice a deep, low whisper. Now that we're fully out of the water, we can't use our telepathic gift even if we want to. Our gifts are reserved only for when under the protection of water. His voice sounds much more crackly aloud, giving me pause.

"We're always welcome here," I slowly reply, standing tall and breathing in deep, salty air. I can't let these men overpower me. I am the princess. I think of my father and try to channel his strength. "Do not imagine otherwise. And do not act otherwise. The mages are our friends and this is a sacred place for them. It's not just their home; it's their sanctuary. They are monks. Do you know what that means? They're peaceful people. But do not forget, they are the ones who hold the power that keeps us in ours."

A stillness falls over the group at my words. They know it's true; it's no secret. And perhaps faced with it now, they're beginning to realize the precariousness of our situation. The last thing we need is for anyone to go rushing into the monastery like it's a battlefield. These men are used to spilling blood first and asking questions later. We can't make any enemies today, no matter how frustrated and worried we may be about our current situation, about the magic fading from our veins.

Yes, we are welcome here on this mountaintop that is now an island in the middle of a deadly sea. We are welcome, *for now*. We must keep it that way. We must.

SunYu's face has fallen, a momentary slip that tells me what I need to know. He's afraid to make a mistake. I push past him to lead us in. He doesn't fight me on it. I am the one of royal blood here, aren't I? I am the only one with personal relationships with the mages. As such, I'm the one who needs to take point.

A small thought trickles through me. Why haven't the mages sent someone to meet us yet? This visit is unexpected, but surely they would have seen us come in? And why is it still so quiet? It's never been this quiet before.

The first of the buildings is essentially the beginning of the village. The mage people have grown here and multiplied since not all the monks have taken vows of celibacy. It's tiny in comparison to our home, but they've made it work for their little tribe of people. At the top of the mountain is where the monastery sits, where they worship and the magic is performed, so I'd expect reverence up there. Down here, however? There should be the chime of children laughing and the hum of women conversing.

There should be *life*. There's nothing.

My senses kick into overdrive, and I press myself against the side of the wall, motioning for everyone else in our party to do the same. All down the line, the men push themselves against the sandy cliff face, our normally stealthy black bodysuits now stark against the light tan stone. Maybe this was a terrible idea.

"What is it?" SunYu whispers, adhering to me in a way that almost catches me off guard. Both pride and apprehension consume me, putting me on edge.

I turn to meet his gaze, Lei's too.

"It shouldn't be this quiet," I reply, my face pinching in worry. "Just around this corner is the village. I've been here every year since I can remember. It's normally bursting with life."

SunYu's black eyes flash, and he nods once in understanding. Lei shifts to the man on his right, whispering. On down the line the message is passed from siren to siren. The message of fear. The message to put up their defenses, to be ready for the worst.

It's not how I wanted to arrive.

This time, when SunYu takes the lead, I don't let my lingering pride get the better of me. I allow him to pass, but I follow close behind as we round the corner and step into the openness of the town square.

It's empty.

The village is made of small stone buildings with thatched roofs. It spreads around the side of the mountaintop like a well-loved tapestry. From home to home, we inspect all the hidden places. There isn't a single soul to be found. The place is deserted. My heartbeat drums. My eyes flicker across empty stone floors. I'm expecting to see a body, to see some kind of indication of foul play. But there's nothing. No one. It's as if the Tibetan Mages and their families simply vanished. How is that possible? Where would they even go? It's just the ocean, an endless line of horizon, sea and sky. Any land they could get to has been taken over by humans, humans who hate us for our magic, and subsequently, hate the mages.

And we all know what's lurking below. The monsters have grown too powerful, even for our kind.

I step outside the tenth empty home and shake my head. Nothing. The rest of the group meets up, all reporting the same thing. Empty.

"Do you have any idea where they could have gone?" Lei asks, coming to stand next to me. He rests the palm of his hand on my back and stares down at me like I'm supposed to know all the answers. Darkness spreads within me, a trembling sense of obligation that I'll never be able to blot out.

I shrug helplessly and clear my throat. "None. I do find it odd that there aren't any signs of struggle. It actually looks like they might have had time to pack their belongings."

"I thought the same thing," SunYu says, striding up to us and joining our conversation. His hands flex over his spear as his mouth sets into a grim line. "They left by their own volition and we need to figure out why."

That may be true, but what's more important is figuring out where they went so we can find them and demand answers, demand help. I don't say the thought, though. I don't have to. From the pained expression in these men's eyes, we're all thinking the same thing.

"Aren't there sirens nearby who could have seen this?" Lei asks his father.

When SunYu doesn't respond, I release my breath and answer for him. "The Tibetan Mages like their privacy."

"But I thought we're supposed to protect them? Isn't that part of the covenant?"

"We are," I sigh. "And we do. We have some of our warriors who live a few hours from here. The mages can summon their help with magic, if needed."

"And how often does that happen?"

I flick a glance toward SunYu, wondering how much he knows. His face remains grim and doesn't give anything away. I continue, "Not often. The monsters don't care for the magic here, as far as I know. The mages live a relatively peaceful life."

Lei twists his mouth and stares out across the water, deep in thought. It would make sense that our nearest sirens would have seen the Tibetans leave, but if that were true, why haven't those same sirens come to speak to us about it yet? We'll have to find them and question them, just in case. Still, the situation leaves me restless and worried. I'm not the only one.

We leave the lifeless village behind and trudge up to the top of the island where the monastery is housed. The building dates back hundreds of years, from long before the seas rose and the earth cracked. Every time I've been here, the monastery has been better kept than anything else. Today is no different. Below, wall edges have crumbled, caked in sea salt. The pathways are worn with centuries of families and pilgrims and endless people brimming with life and tearing away at the buildings with their daily life. But up here, the monastery is in pristine condition. It's the same sandstone color as everything else. Instead of a thatched ceiling, it's topped with a vibrant red roof with a gold-tipped ball perched at the tip. A rainbow of small, hand-sized, square flags on strings extend from the top, streaming all the way to the ground. They billow in the wind. The movement unsettles me. It is the only movement we've seen here today.

We walk inside, and still, there's nobody.

It's clear someone, probably someone besides the mages, has been here. The place has been ransacked. Papers litter the floor. Against the far wall, a chest-of-drawers lays tipped on its side, leather-bound books spilling out, many with their bindings open at awkward angles, pages bent. At my feet, a golden singing bowl lies cracked and broken. I wince, knowing the bowls, instruments with their earthy vibrations, are a sacred part of the monks' religious practice. I step over the damaged bowl, my gaze traveling to the raised altar at the center of the room.

"It's gone," I breathe, dreadful realization sweeping over me.

Lei places a warm hand on my elbow and I force myself not to step away.

"What's gone?" he asks.

I point to the empty altar, refocusing my energy. The altar is essentially a chest-level platform with a thin layer of red fabric draped across the top. Usually, the siren stone rests at its center, an item of such importance it's never moved. Right now, there's nothing but fabric.

"The stone," I reply, voice cracking. "The magic."

"What are you saying?" SunYu crosses to the center of the room in two long strides. He runs a steady hand over the empty altar, taking a bit of the red fabric between his fingers. Turning back to me, concern is etched in his brow. "What used to be here?"

I shake my head. This is sacred information. I'm not supposed to say anything. I swore to it. Or was it something else I'd sworn to? Not secrecy about the stone, but a vow to honor our alliance with the mages. I shouldn't tell, though. Just in case. My mind spins with the thought, stomach flipping. No, I have to tell. If I don't tell them the truth of the missing stone, if I don't tell them what I think has happened here, then how will we recover the magic in time?

I have no choice.

"Senra," Lei presses, "what's gone?"

I clear my throat, logic taking over. I have to do this. I send a silent prayer of forgiveness up toward the heavens, and then I speak. "The monks have been practicing magic for centuries, that's no secret to any of us. But when the asteroid hit earth's atmosphere and broke into all those pieces, one hit our part of the world. That's when the monks noticed something shift. The stone, the asteroid, it caused their magic to grow exponentially. So they found it. They retrieved the piece, brought it here, and have drawn on its magic ever since."

I turn away from the empty altar to find sunken faces and widening eyes. "That asteroid is what has allowed the monks to give us our siren magic. Every year, the royal family travels here and the monks reestablish the magic, using the energy of that stone to reseal our pact with them." I stand tall and deliver the final blow. "They give us our siren magic from the stone."

I hold Lei's gaze, witnessing as the truth sinks into his core. He breaks away from me to share a look of panic with his father, the warrior who's spent a lifetime killing humans, a lifetime secure in the knowledge of his magic. And now? Now, that could all be gone. The expansiveness of the monastery seems to close in and grow tighter around our group. The air becomes heavier, rooting me in place, pushing down on my lungs. I take a deep breath, filling them up, and then I add the final piece.

"And now that it's gone, anything could happen to us."

SIX

WE'RE BACK IN THE WATER WITHIN MINUTES. IT SURROUNDS me like a cool balm, instantly calming my nerves and grounding my spirit to my flesh. There's no reason to stay above any longer. We won't find anything more up there. There are no clues. No people. Nothing.

Our group gathers together under the sparkling surface, and SunYu gives his commands. I tune him out, worried about what's next for my people, trying to come up with a solution. But it's not as simple as to say we'll just bring everyone above water, just adapt as the land-dwellers have. There's hardly any land left. That was the problem in the first place and the entire reason why our ancestors choose to accept the gift of magic. Most of the non-magical humans live on floating cities, shanty towns forged together from whatever rubbish they could find. Floating rust piles of disease and starvation, and of things even worse than that. It's not safe up there. Not for us. And those humans? They're ruthless, stone solid in their hatred toward our siren kind. They would never accept us. Never.

The only thing we can do now is find the missing asteroid piece and figure out where the mages vanished to. If we can reunite them with the relic, they can work their magic and keep our people strong.

I peer out into the endless expanse of ocean and defeat washes over me.

Truthfully, I have no idea where the mages could have gone. It makes no sense. But maybe Mother will have an idea, or at the very least, one of the Elders.

This time as we travel, we stay close to the surface. It's not the safest choice. If any humans are lurking above, they'll try to kill us on sight. But that's just it. If humans are up there, we need to find out if they know anything. We need to question them about the mages and the stone. Most likely, a pack of desperate humans were the ones that ransacked the monastery. Who else would have something to gain besides them? Their people might even have the stone now. If they destroy it, all will be lost.

I suck in a breath, banishing the thought from my troubled mind.

From what little I heard of SunYu's directions, we're going to meet up with the closest siren groups around here and see if they saw anything. I have a strong suspicion they won't know anything, but at least it's something to focus on for now.

We're just a few miles off the coast of the island when a shadow crosses over our heads. The rush of darkness passes above our party so quickly that I almost miss it. I glance up, sighting the bottom of a small white boat against the flashing surface. It blends in so perfectly, I have to double check.

Get down, Lei yells, tugging on my arm.

A harpoon slices through the water. Fast and sure, it careens inches from my face. It plows into the chest of one of our men. Blood blossoms into the water, billowing in a cloud of death. His eyes lose focus immediately, arms and legs relaxing, and his body begins its descent to the ocean floor. I stare after him, shocked.

The warriors are no stranger to violence and battle, and it shows. Their large muscles flex as they swim into position, arcing spears drawn and at the ready. A few of the men sing, their voices a dark timbre that vibrates through the water. More harpoons shoot through the ocean from above, bubbles spinning up in their wake. They head right toward us. Most miss their mark, but a few strike true, killing our siren men in one cruel blow.

Once again, the song isn't working. I don't stop to think about it, or to let the fear get in the way, I just open my mouth as wide as I can and sing. I sing with everything inside me, with all the force I've ever known. My voice carries through the water, sweet and light and strong and pure. Beautiful, even though my intentions are anything but.

Lei still has me by the hand, swimming on the outside of the group. He watches the scene play out with a grim expression etched into his face. I continue to sing, but no men have jumped from the boat. I don't want to look, don't want to kill.

I also don't want my people to die.

Let us handle it, Senra, Lei says, tugging me further from the group. *I don't want you to get hurt.*

I flash him an incredulous look and continue to sing, even though the siren song apparently isn't working for me, either. It could just be because I'm under the water. I need to go up. If I can get my mouth above water, but still be submerged, it should do the trick and stop these humans.

Senra, you don't need to do this. We can handle it.

Call a shark, I tell him, meeting his eyes with fire in my own. I won't back down, not even for this, not even for him. *Call a shark and use it as a distraction.*

He looks at me as if I'm speaking another language but then his expression clears and he nods, opening his mouth and beginning his song. It's slightly softer than the other men, the notes long and aching as they pour through the depths. Our song is meant to calm and lure, and that it does. Especially when it comes to manipulating ocean life. Lei's song is angelic perfection.

After about a minute, the outline of a massive hammerhead shark appears in the distance. It's one of the largest predators in our sea. The sight of it fills me with both apprehension and relief. It swims towards us, all fins and gills and black shining eyes.

Bring it up to the surface, I say to Lei, keeping my voice strong with the order. *Have it attack the boat. It won't be able to do much damage but it will distract them long enough for me to lure them into the water.*

48

Even as I tell him my plan, I'm sick with the thought of it. I've never killed a human before. Looking around us, I see two more of our men fall to their graves, streams of blood curling out around the weapons speared through their splintered hearts. This is the point where normal sirens would retreat, but given the circumstances of the missing relic, we can't give up. And I have to help them. I have to be strong enough to do this, even if it results in killing. Besides, it could mean getting on that boat and figuring out if these people have any connection to our vanishing magic.

And so the fight continues, death nipping close at our heels, adrenaline racing through our veins. I'm determined to do my part.

The shark moves in, circling Lei. Unfazed, he continues his low song, directing the animal with telepathic thoughts set on revenge. The shark charges forward, pushing past us so quickly that it knocks me out of the way with its long, rubbery fin. It bursts through the water, splitting the surface, head butting against the hull of the boat, mouth open and teeth lashing.

The distraction works. The harpoons stop. We take our moment, all of us closing in. I kick up, zooming to the surface, just next to the other side of the boat. My head pops out of the water. The scuffed side of the white boat bounces on the waves. The men on board shout at each other whilst trying to shoot the shark. Water and blood fly over the edge of the vessel. I scan what I can see from down here, only my head peeking through the surface, and look for the stone or for anything familiar that I could use to help me understand what these humans might actually know. It's useless.

Should I sing now? That seems like the easiest option. My voice should be strong enough to lure them to the ocean. But then a thought startles me. I could drown them all if I do that. I'm still twisted up with the thought of killing someone, even in *this* situation, even when it's justified. If we climb on board afterward, does that guarantee we'll find anything of value? It's very possible they don't have the stone but know who does. And if that's the case, I can't question dead men.

The boat is midsized, and it looks like there are ten people on board. All men. All with long black hair tied up in a knot, worn, haggard clothing hanging off sinewy muscles, and a tinge of sunburn to their creamy skin.

I swim closer.

"Kyon! Go grab the net!" Someone yells the order, and a younger man darts closer, into my view. He's frantic, searching for something that must be lying on the deck. We're only a few feet away from each other now. His eyes flash up and then pause, meeting mine. His mouth drops open and his whole body stills. I stare at him, refusing to be the first to break the eye contact.

He's probably seen sirens before, but a female? Not likely.

Snapping from his trance, he raises his arms from below deck. But it's not a net in his hand. It's a harpoon.

I don't think. Instinct rushes in and I sing, my voice bursting forth.

And it works. Kyon drops the harpoon at his feet where it clatters. Then he places two hands on the railing and jumps into the water.

Behind him, those who are closest to my song do the same.

I ignore those men, letting them float to their watery deaths. My heart is ripped open, is blemished and black with the murder. I let it happen because I don't know what else there is left to do, not when it's this young man, this Kyon, who has my focus. There was a glimmer in Kyon's eyes before I sang and I can't help but think he knows something. I must know what that is. I rush to him, pulling him into my arms before he can fall beneath the waves. I continue to sing, allowing the music to roll over us both like a gentle caress. He gazes at me as if I'm the most beautiful thing he's ever laid eyes on— my song is still strong. Strong enough to let it break for a moment so I can ask my questions.

"What happened to the mages?"

He blinks, water rolling down his face. "The what?" he coos, a lopsided grin hanging on his mouth.

"The monks? What happened to them?"

I flex my arms; holding up a full-sized man above the water isn't as easy as I assumed. A wave crashes over his face.

"I don't know," he says, sputtering.

"Have you been to their island?"

"Yes." The answer rings so true that I'm sure my song hasn't worn off, yet.

"And what happened to them?"

"They weren't there," he answers. "We came in after everything happened. We're scavengers. Nothing else."

"And what happened before you got there?"

"I don't know."

I growl and fist his shirt tighter in my grip, figuring I might as well shove him underwater for how useful he's being right now. I squeeze him closer, anger rolling through me.

"Please explain why you went to the island. What do you mean by scavenger?"

His earthy brown eyes stare into mine, transfixed. There is mystery and darkness there, but also something that pulls to me, that sparks with electricity. We're only inches apart now. My entire body is frozen until the moment he speaks. "We went to the island to see if there was anything left. We'd heard that the Emperor sent people out there on a mission and the island was now deserted."

So that confirms it. Humans took the stone and did something with the Tibetan people. Or maybe the people left before the other humans ever arrived?

"Where are you from?"

But even as I ask it, I might already know. Only one civilization has survived up here and that's because they had some of the tallest mountains to cling to when the rest of the world washed away.

"Japan," he says.

Japan... or what's left of it, anyway.

I grit my teeth, glaring at the young man. His home is our biggest threat and not too far from where Lei and his father are from. But it's a long way to this island, an island I didn't think the Japanese even knew existed. I growl, shoving Kyon under the water. He should die. He's our enemy. They all are. I should feel no guilt over any of this.

But he's not been called to the ocean floor, has he? Really, my song has called him to me. And still, he clings to me, large hands grappling at my legs. He practically tears my bodysuit as he climbs back up me. That same twisted heart of mine can't bear to shove him down again, and so I stop fighting. His head breaks above the water, gasping for life, and I wrench myself free from his frantic grip.

Watch out, a voice yells through my head. I glance up wildly. It's too late. Something large and white and not the ocean crashes through the water. The boat. It smashes angrily against me and the whole world is washed into the darkness.

When I wake up, it's all over. The boat is gone. The humans left alive making their exit when my song wore off. They knocked me out and took Kyon with them.

But that's okay, I got everything I needed from him. Or at least, I got enough.

I rub my throbbing head, resting on the smooth sand of the ocean floor. It's colder down here and feels far better than the day spent so close to the surface. It's relaxing. It's home. I slowly peel my eyes open. Lei and SunYu huddle over me, faces matched in worried expressions. Eyebrows drawn, mouths frowning, eyes scanning for injury.

They probably thought they'd gotten the heir killed. They're men of power, the kind who are always seeking out more to feed their addiction. They both know what my death would mean for their future.

I shouldn't think such things. Father trusted them, chose Lei for me. They've only been kind to me, even if I have had to bite my tongue on more than one occasion.

I hold up a hand. *I'm all right*, I tell them, breathing in deep and slowly sitting up. I run my fingers along the back of my head and peer into the darkness, searching the outcrops and coral. I count seven bodies in all. Four of our men are dead down here, as with three of the enemies. More sharks are circling, but they won't attack, not while we're here, anyway.

I stand, letting my hands dangle next to my legs. *Let's give our fallen comrades a proper burial,* I say to the remaining men who surround me in a protective semi-circle. *And then we must return home as soon as possible. I need to convene with the Elders and my mother right away. I must tell them the news and figure out a way to save our people.*

SEVEN

SunYu, Lei, Mother and I swim to the temple together. Our guards aren't far off as the four of us maneuver through the city streets. Curious faces peek out from behind doors and windows. A few sirens caught unaware startle at our approach, bubbles dancing around them, before they bow low. In each of their eyes, I find the same things: worry and fear. And also, a steady undercurrent of trust that we'll know how to fix this. They don't need to lift a finger. We've got it under control.

But all I can think is that I *don't* know how to fix this.

And neither does my mother. Something of this magnitude must be brought before the Elders. We all agreed, quick to save further discussion until we could meet with them. My mind hums, and the world grows quiet as our group approaches the sacred site. The temple is one of the only places that survived the crush of ocean when the seas rose a hundred years ago. Some may say that's only luck. We're a superstitious people. But we're also a faithful people and so we know better than to count it as luck. God spared our temple so we could continue to worship there.

He spared it just as He spared us, and we won't disappoint Him. I won't.

The Elders are chosen to take care of the temple and counsel the people, and they're the most important advisors to the emperor and empress. There's never been a time when I didn't treat them with the utmost respect, nor was there ever a time when I saw my father not heed their advice.

They just know things. They keep our culture, our way of life, and our society together. There's no other way to explain it, except that they're all descended from a long line of families that have always kept our records, from a time before the rising seas, the asteroid, or the covenant that binds us all.

We enter the courtyard. It is vast and open, lined with statues of warriors from the old world, each still gleaming under the protection of magic. We land on the end of the long walkway and stroll as a group toward the twenty-foot golden door at the far end. We walk in silence. As a child, I would count the steps over and over again in a game. The courtyard was one of the only public spaces I was allowed to go.

The doors open for us. We don't have to knock. They must have known we were coming. Even though I am as cold as the ocean herself, an icy chill still runs down my spine. As we enter the building, we're met with a line of men and many low bows that we return in kind.

Come, a wrinkled man with knowing, ethereal milky-white eyes says, *Come now, we have much to discuss.*

I exchange a glance with Mom, and she gives me a small smile. It's as if the Elders were waiting for this day, as if they expected us to show up here tonight. It doesn't surprise me as much as it should.

We're led past the main worship halls and through a maze of corridors, then a set of stairs that goes down, down, down. It's colder than anywhere I've been in this ocean and this is the part that does surprise me. To know there are hidden depths even I haven't traveled sends a thrill through me.

I take a deep breath, letting the water settle in.

Where are we going? I direct my question to Mother so only she can hear. I know it's rude to do in the presence of others, but then again, we're royalty. Nobody would dare question us either way.

You'll see. I can tell by her tone it's the only reply I'm going to get.

We're led into an underground chamber that's larger than any of the prayer halls above. The black sheets of stone wall are engraved with carvings, images and text.

And then I know. I know exactly what this place is.

Welcome to The Hall of Records, the Elder says, his hand sweeping wide. We filter into the room, more of the Elders joining us. In all, there are ten people here. Ten people getting to see a place together that is so sacred, even I've never been here. I glance curiously at Lei, noting the shine in his eyes. His father is equally impressed, the normally stoic general, now goggling in awe. I'm certain they've never been invited down here before. I hope I don't look as impressed as they do. I keep my face and my nerve as cool as possible.

Senra knows of this place, Mother says, swimming out into the middle of the room, her voice carrying for all of us to hear. *But this is her first time coming here.* She turns to look at me. She's as beautiful and strong as ever, fitting right in with her long billowing hair and modest onyx dress. The sleeves go right down to her wrists, blending her into the shadows. *We were waiting until you were crowned Empress, but given the current situation, we decided it was time you knew the truth.*

I tilt my head, my nerves suddenly not so cool anymore. *The truth?*

Her words are like anchors, rooting me to the spot. What truth is there left to know? Is there something she's been keeping from me?

I prayed to the creator that this day would never come. Your father did, too, Mother continues, swimming back to me. Her hands cup mine and her eyes lock me in. *But the Elders always assured us it would.* She shrugs, defeated. *And they were right. I want you to know that I love you very much, more than anything. And I know you can do this.*

My mouth falls open, confusion hot on my tongue. The questions lie on the surface but I can't seem to ask them.

Come, Senra. The elder who's been directing our party takes my hand from Mother's, carefully tugging me forward. The move is so intimate and gentle that it sends a twinge of fear through me. He's old, older than anyone I know. And I can tell just by looking at him that he's also kind. The sort of person whose heart opens more and more as they grow, not the other way around like so many others. No, it's not him that scares me. It's the secret he holds, the one I know in my core is going to change everything.

He leads me to the far end of the room. This time, the others don't follow. They give us our privacy but only to an extent; because I know when the Elder speaks, he's not just talking to me. He's talking to all of us. It's like we're all in this together, only we're not. Because it's me who's been singled out.

A couple of silvery fish dash past me. We approach the wall, and I squint, trying to make out exactly what it is I'm meant to be looking at. Something odd shifts and moves against the wall, first blending with the gray stone before transforming into fleshy orange and darting away. An octopus.

The Elder chuckles. *Even all the way down here, they still find a way inside. This is their home first and they'll always remind us of that.*

Despite my nerves, a small smile cracks my face and I nod.

He points to the engravings and the text underneath. *This is why you're here, Senra. We knew this day would come. It was prophesied the moment our ancestors took the siren form.*

I take one last look into his watery eyes before turning back to the wall. And then, I read:

The water rose and the asteroids hit.

Earth Mother slumbered and Gaia recessed.

The magic swelled, the people blessed.

They became the sirens and made their bet.

And all will be well for the first century

The people will flourish in ocean's prosperity.

But magic always comes with a price,

And only a royal heir will suffice.

The ocean is cursed. The monsters are real.

But she is far worse. She is the siren heir.

Her reign is life and her song is death.

They will call her, Dark Ocean Princess.

When her people perish, the magic waning,

And her enemies take dominion, the order of Kings.

She, and she alone, will enact Gaia's retribution.

For she is the chosen one and in death she will save them.

I edge closer and run my fingers along the scrolling words. The images, too. The smooth stone curves under my fingertips, etched proof of the reason for my existence. Truthfully, the carved depictions of the princess could be my likeness, but it's the poem itself that feels true. It settles into my gut as sure as anything I've ever known.

When was this written? I ask, my voice trembling in a way that betrays me.

When the first people came to the Tibetan Monks, asking for siren magic and the exchanges were made, vows said, this prophecy was also part of the agreement. There would come a time when everything would change, and it would be at a female heir's hand. He pauses, our eyes meeting in stark understanding. *We believe that heir is you.*

I nod once. Then I take one last look at the wall in front of me, one last chance to let my eyes linger on the scrolled script, the carvings my ancestors made of a siren princess with a towering crown on her head and a pile of bodies at her feet. The familiar blemish in my heart pulses, inking black into my being. I shut it away with a quick wince. If this is my role, if this is the only way I'm to save my people, then I'll do it.

But … I'm still not exactly sure what I'm supposed to do, and that's the problem. Do I sing until all the humans are dead? Do I just retrieve the stone and find the mages? What is my task?

I can tell from looking at the Elders now, from taking in the expressions of my Mother, Lei, and his father, that they don't have a clear idea either.

You won't go alone. Lei steps forward. *We will go with you. You'll have help and protection. That's why we're here, isn't it?* He looks at the Elders. *To offer help?*

The room falls into silence for a long moment before Mother speaks. *I brought you and your father here so you would understand why she has to leave.*

I nod and cross back to them, sucking in a deep cool-waters breath, trying to think, to come from the perspective of the prophecy, because fulfilling that is what's most important, nothing else. I have to save my people, to save our magic. I couldn't save my father, and I'll never forgive myself for that. But perhaps, I can do this for him. It's what he would have wanted.

Lei looks me over. *Won't you let me protect you?*

No. The word comes out as sure as the tide. I rest my hand on Lei's shoulder and stare into his hardened eyes. *It says that it must be me and me alone. Nobody comes with me.*

And just like that, the room erupts into argument.

You will be able to do whatever needs to be done yourself but that doesn't mean you won't need an army, won't need us, SunYu speaks.

Over top of him, Mother is shaking her head at me. *You can't. It's too dangerous to go alone. Just let them go, too. They won't get in your way.*

You're going to be my wife. It's my duty, Lei argues.

And the Elders, they too seem to be in disagreement. I can't hear what they have to say; they're talking among themselves. Two of the six shake their heads while the other three nod.

I close my eyes, wishing I could push them all out of my head. I get to choose my life path, not my mother, not the Elders, and certainly not Lei. And I get to choose to fulfill this prophecy. The noise of all those voices at once is draining, pulling on me with all of their expectations, with their opinions and wants and greed.

I open my mouth and sing.

The quietest of songs, simple. Peaceful. It's not meant to entrap anyone or anything. It's just sounds on the current, vibrating magic. The power courses through me, giving me the strength needed to face my future.

My entire life up to this point flashes before my eyes. I see all the times I trained with Father, all the times he believed in me more than I believed in myself. I wasn't there for his death, but I remember in exact detail what it felt like to learn of it, where I was, that it was Mother who told me, and how my knees buckled underneath my weight, despite being weightless underwater. I remember my reaction, my grief and guilt, and how afterwards, I poured myself into my training a million times harder than ever before. It all comes together in my mind, it's all led me to this moment.

I can do this. I can carry this burden. I'm the one who's meant for this path.

They all stop at the sound of my song, dropping their guards, their arguments, their expressions so filled with opinion. After another moment, another long pull of a note, I let go of the music.

I'm going alone, I say. *There's nothing more to discuss. If you'd like to help, give me directions to Japan and send me with anything I might need. I'll be fine to hunt for my own food and I can take care of myself.*

They all stare at me, one by one understanding that I refuse to relent on this point.

Most importantly, I continue, *protect the people. The monsters will keep coming and I won't be here to help stop them from killing. The siren-kind need as many warriors as possible right now. A war has started, whether we like it or not. We're going to have to fight.*

E I G H T

THE LINE: *AND IN DEATH SHE WILL SAVE THEM*, REPEATS IN my mind. Do I have to die? Do I have to kill? Is it both? Later that night, I try helplessly to sleep, but these lingering questions haunt me, nagging my thoughts like ghosts. Images of the men on the boat shoot through my mind's eye, as clear as their harpoons that shot through the water. Besides the gentle Tibetan people, they were the first land-dwellers I've ever seen. And they were ruthless.

I think of the boy they called Kyon, reliving the way his dark eyes flashed with hatred for me, then with confusion at seeing a female siren, and then with unbound hatred once again. It was only my song that changed those raging eyes, that tempered them into two pools of dithering adoration.

The thing I can't stop thinking about is this: He looked just like a siren. Born of different parents, he could have been one of our own.

We're not so different, the sirens below and the humans above.

And yet, I saw those images in the temple and read that prophecy etched into its walls. I can't deny the truth of my birth or the reason for my existence. It's my destiny to write a new story for my people, even if it means killing more humans, perhaps ending them all. I am The Dark Ocean Princess. That is my name now. It's my duty, and mine alone, to provide a brighter future for all sirens born of my empire.

No matter what.

Is that what Father would have wanted for me? I keep telling myself it is, but truthfully, I don't have any proof. Either way, there's no turning back from the prophecy.

The night turns to morning, and with brave thoughts rooted in mind, I roll from my spongy bed and stretch to standing. My chamber is made of stone and coral, sand and water. It's been my home my entire life and the knowledge that I'm leaving it today, perhaps forever, makes me look at everything in a strange way, as if trying to memorize it.

The rainbow of colors growing from the coral and the fish that live there.

The long, thin window overlooking my empire that I've spent countless hours peering through.

My bed placed perfectly to allow the flow of energy, not under the window or facing the door, but in the far corner. The fengshui design keeps everything orderly, keeps me comfortable. What will it be like to leave that behind?

I sigh and swim to the alcove where I keep my clothing in a chest. There's a skinny floor-to-ceiling mirror hanging on one wall, not facing the actual bedroom because mirrors in bedrooms invite dark energy. I run my finger along the gilded edges and glance at my appearance.

Quick to look away, I kneel before the brass chest, pry it open, and sift through the contents. The clothing is enchanted. Another part of our magic. It allows us to keep things from disintegrating under water. Had our ancestors been sirens when the seas first rose, they could have saved so much more of our cities. They didn't make the agreement with the mages until much later, when things got so bad it was obvious not everybody had a fighting chance at survival. But that's okay, I like the coral and stone, I like the way it brings our past together with our present.

I push past the dresses neatly folded on top and slip out a fresh black bodysuit. It's the same kind of outfit I wore on my travels to the monastery. If I had it my way, I'd wear this kind of outfit daily. It's as smooth as whale hide, and I slide it over my body like a second skin. Then I go to the mirror to tie my hair back into my favorite style: an intricate braid that wraps around my head like a crown of black vines. I study myself in the mirror. My Chinese ancestry is as thick as the blood in my veins. I appreciate my raven hair, my dark, glittering eyes and my creamy smooth skin. There's perfection in the way my cheekbones sharpen in the plains of my face and my long thin neck that draws the eye to my petite frame. When I see my beauty, it's not in vanity, but in appreciation of where I come from and who I am.

To be Chinese, to be a princess, born of strong parents, of a royal line, is something that gives me strength in and of itself. But I am also siren-born and of that, I am most proud. I don't know who I would be without my magic. And that's exactly why I can't let pride cloud my judgment anymore. After what I've witnessed, I have to accept that I am not unbreakable.

None of us are safe.

We're not finned or gilled or covered in scales, we aren't evolved from the ocean or even *meant* to be here. We look just like anyone else, just like any other human, and that knowledge terrifies me. My heart thumps as I focus on the fact that it's the mages' magic and their manipulation of the siren stone that allows us to live down here, and that alone. Once that magic wears away, we'll drown and all will be lost.

I repeat the mantra that's become so strong in my heart these last few days. I can't let the magic be lost. I won't.

Taking one last hard look in the mirror, I steel myself and stare into my pupils for so long it's like peering into my very soul, a soul with as much darkness as light, a soul that's blemished with the death of her father, and now the deaths of three human men. Was it my fault? I don't have an answer. Instead, I stride from the room. No more delaying the inevitable.

The time has come to complete my mission.

There's to be a celebration. I don't get to slip away into the darkness unseen, which would be preferable. Instead, I'm to be sent away on a hero's journey and honored by my people, crowds of them. As I swim to the palace courtyard, blood quickening in my veins and watery breath catching in my throat: I take it all in. Once again, I'm struck with the idea that this might be the last time I'll get to see this beloved place, this home I have loved.

Mother joins me at the head of the palace steps, a smile on her face that doesn't quite reach her eyes. *I should have prepared you for this,* she says, running her hands down the length of her navy gown.

I frown, thinking of all the training I have had, especially over the last six months, of all the practice fighting, all the studying of our culture, our religion, our way of life. And not only ours, but the humans and mages alike. *You have,* I say in return, hoping my words can give her an ounce of comfort. *I may not be up to par with the warriors, but that doesn't mean I'm going on a suicide mission. Don't be hard on yourself, Mother. Please.*

She shakes her head once, the movement so slight I doubt anyone else noticed. But I see it, and it sends an aching pang low in my belly. *Your father and I, we should have told you about the prophecy. I was afraid. I didn't want to think it would really happen.* She pauses. *I don't think he wanted to believe it either, but he at least tried to prepare you. He was always so much better at this.*

I know exactly how she feels.

My eyes roam the courtyard, taking in the people who've gathered here. They line the path, row after row. Dressed in their finest clothing, smiles painted on their faces, they're proud to see me off. And I also know they're as taken aback by all of this as I am. They believe in me, of course. But did they see this coming? No. They expected a royal wedding, not a royal send-off.

At the head of the crowd, Lei and his father SunYu stand poised, their protective eyes fixed squarely on me. Their warriors are gathered among the crowd. Most likely of all the people here, it's these two men who are most bothered by the change in plans.

I reach out and squeeze Mom's hand. *It's okay*, I assure her. *I would have done the same thing in your position. And I'll be okay. I'm strong. I'm meant to succeed, and I will succeed.*

Her expression lightens enough to give me hope. But also just enough to know that I'd better not ask those questions that kept me awake all night. She doesn't know the answers any better than I do. Maybe I really will have to die in order to save my people. It's a sacrifice I'm willing to make, even if it's one I can't rest my mind on for long. The fear that bubbles within is too painful. It's so hot it reminds me of the ocean places we avoid, the places where the monsters live, where the earth spews into the water in streams of molten lava.

Mother steps forward, addressing the crowd, her telepathic voice now carrying for all in the vicinity to hear.

Thank you for joining us this morning. It is a special day. A day of celebration and of gratitude. This is the time to honor our God, our ancestors, and to honor Princess Senra. Her voice has changed

69

from moments before, no more fear or pain or regret cracking in the undertow of her words. It's now smooth and strong and confident. Like I need to be. *As you are already probably beginning to suspect, our magic is in grave danger.*

The statement rings across the courtyard, bodies rustling, stirring up the peace.

But we need not be afraid, Mother continues, straightening her spine. *It has been prophesied that my daughter shall save us all. In this, she must go alone to complete the task. She will meet success, that has already been foreordained.*

The crowd seems to settle. The eyes, hundreds of eyes, are heavy on me. Even though sirens should believe their Empress without question, enough of those eyes are filled with doubt, and it makes me doubt myself, too. *So with that, we must send Senra off with our love and prayers, as we would any hero.*

Shouts and song erupt, and the next bit happens so fast I barely have time to process it all.

On my bodysuit, I'm already strapped with a long spear that's cool against my back. I have that, and I have my song. I feel the presence of my two weapons now in a way I've never had to before. I've always had protection around me. This time, I'm on my own. Will it be enough? *Yes,* I tell myself, *it will.*

I'm ushered through the center of the crowd, and I'm smiling, despite the trembles racking my body, my muscles heavy with each step. Voices invade the silence of my mind, a cacophony of congratulations and well wishes. One voice rises above the rest.

You've never been more beautiful, Lei says. *I know we argued about this, but I've thought about it a lot, and I believe you can do this. And when you return, it will be my greatest honor to marry you.*

I tune out his words, nor do I look at him. He is not my path right now and I can't mitigate my feelings for him while I have so much to contend with. And then there's another voice with me, the voice of my birth, my childhood, my whole life. It's hard to imagine I might never hear it again.

I love you, my daughter. No matter what happens, always know that my love is eternal.

I grit my teeth, eyes prickling. *I love you too, Mother.*

And then, unable to bear it any longer, I push off the stone walkway and burst through the heavy water, furiously swimming up and away from the crowd.

I don't look back.

Even as the voices fade away and the quiet overwhelms me, as the landscape reshapes to nothing but the rocky ocean floor and the shimmer of surface, even as the brightly flashing schools of fish disappear and the vast, silent unknown spreads before me, *even then,* I still don't look back.

NINE

I'M TWO DAYS INTO THE FIVE-DAY JOURNEY WHEN THE
back of my neck tingles—something isn't right. The awareness
weighs heavier than even the water. It's that strange feeling of being
followed, a keen sense of being watched, or worse, stalked. And it's
different somehow from anything else I've experienced. This isn't
like the sea life, the ones I can control so easily. This is someone, or
something else entirely.

Continuing to swim on, I rotate my arms and legs the same as
before, biceps and calves flexing at all the right moments. If I appear
normal, if nothing about me changes, then maybe I can get the jump
on whoever or *whatever* this is. But the tiny hairs on my arms rise
and my spine stiffens. My breathing has grown erratic and despite
my better judgment, my right hand slowly inches closer and closer to
the long, sharp spear strapped against my back.

A whoosh of water thunders behind me, and I flip around, spear raised. It's not a someone. It's a something. A sea monster. And it's coming right for me.

It moves faster than anything I've ever witnessed down here. But I know this beast. The recognition splits me right open, panic and regret spilling out. He's the one I should have killed. The beast with the shiny black scales and the glowing golden eyes. Its long serpent body slithers through the water. Its round dragon-like face coming at me so fast I don't have time to jump out of the way.

I throw the spear, this time without an ounce of hesitation. And I miss. Panic rips through me. I should have killed him the first time! I open my mouth to sing instead.

He doesn't slow. Rather, his charge intensifies. And then the side of his massive body slams into me, hard as a rock, throwing me back through the water as if I weigh nothing. I cough, my breath and my song lost. I blink rapidly, trying to catch my thoughts. Fog rolls through my mind. It pulls me under, long thin fingers grappling to take me away. The cerulean ocean landscape narrows to blackness and my eyelids flutter shut before I can catch onto conscious thought.

But it all comes tumbling back moments later with the familiar motion of the surf. Up and down, up and down, up and down, I'm riding on top of waves. No, not riding. Resting. Floating. Unmoved in a rolling sea. Splashes of water lick at my face. And then I remember exactly what just happened.

There's something heavy wrapped around my legs. Something

slick as seaweed.

The monster. It's holding me up here, up on the surface. But why?

I squeeze my eyes shut even tighter, trying to sort the logical thoughts from the ones drenched in fear. Then I relax my face, hoping it hasn't sensed my wakefulness. Sing. That's what I need to do. I need to sing and turn this deadly beast into the one held captive instead of the other way around. It's either him or it's me. And I can't let it be me. I haven't even made it to the human island yet. To die this way would be to fail the prophecy. And all because some nasty creature has stolen me away, probably to feast on my guts with its equally disgusting littermates? Not happening.

"Princess, be calm. It's time to open your eyes. I know you're awake." The voice behind the words is grumbly and all-knowing and definitely human. It shakes me to my core. But he called me Princess....

My eyelids pop open, adjusting to the light. The sky is cloudless and red as blood with the setting sun. I was right; we're resting up here on the ocean's surface, the monster and I. He carries me on his back.

We're not alone.

Next to us is a small boat. It's not modern like the boat from before. This one is practically made from sticks; it's so rudimentary in its construction, it's more of a raft. How is the thing even floating? When my eyes travel to the man standing on board, I know.

Magic. It's a Tibetan Mage, one of the monks from the deserted island. He's peering down at me with glittering eyes and a knowing grin.

My gaze widens, the thin air blowing in my face doesn't even bother them; I'm too shocked. I know this man. He's not just anyone. He's *the* one. He's their main leader, the one with the most magic. And the most answers.

"Ah, see?" His smile grows, accentuating the wrinkles around his mouth. "You're not so alone anymore."

I can't help myself. I smile back, relief seeping from me like a sponge. He's a good man. He wouldn't hurt me.

"Your holiness." My voice comes out as a whisper, and my head falls into a bow.

The regular monks are known as trapas: the students and scholars. But he's one of the lamas, which makes him a high priest. There's the Karmapa Lama, Panchen Lama, and then the highest is the Dalai Lama. That's him. They're the three leaders of the monastery where the Tibetan Monks have lived together since the oceans rose. And they're always the ones who perform the sacred ceremonies.

"Princess Senra," he says with a joyful lightness to his voice. "How are you, my dear?"

I cough, looking up at him, taking in his shiny bald head, his dark eyes, and the long, blood red robe that blends into the sunset. I should be angry, considering his people seemingly abandoned mine. But there's a sweetness to this man that makes it impossible to harbor anger toward him. "Not the greatest," I stammer, motioning down to the writhing beast that still carries me on his scaled back. "I'm guessing you know what has happened."

75

He nods once.

"What of your people?" I can't help the question tumbling from my mouth. My father always taught me to be silent with these men, to show respect. Asking a question was never allowed. But that was before everything fell apart. "We went to your island and found the monastery empty and all of your people gone."

The Dalai Lama isn't thrown off by my question. His eyes glitter, softening with kindness. "We're safe. We fled the island before the humans arrived. No harm done."

I want to beg for answers on where they could have possibly gone, but it's not the question that slips out first. Instead, I'm drawn right back into the anger.

"If you knew they were coming, why didn't you send for our protection?" I demand, my voice suddenly filling with venom.

He breaks my gaze and turns around to stare off into the distance, watching the sun blink away behind the line of ocean and sky. After a long minute, he turns back around. "The humans needed to come in order for the prophecy to be fulfilled. Sometimes in life we must allow the darkness so we can recognize the light."

I twist my lip against my teeth, considering. "So you left because you can't fight them," I state. I'm still on my knees before this man. I couldn't bring myself to stand, even if I wanted to. He's too important. And who am I? A princess, to be sure. Beyond that? I'm just a seventeen-year-old girl trying to survive in a world mostly perished. I want to stand and challenge his words. I want to be stronger than this, but I'm drained of the confidence.

"We could fight," he replies, "but we won't. Violence is not in our nature."

I still don't understand why they wouldn't let us do it for them. They have in the past with sea monsters. It's part of the agreement for us to protect them.

None of this makes sense. Except the idea that they wanted the land-dwelling humans to intervene in our ways, they were okay with things getting worse for both of our kind. And that's an idea I certainly don't agree with. I bite my tongue, holding the accusation against my teeth.

His Holiness continues, voice as serene as the sunset, "Trust, young one. Trust in the prophecy just as you trust in the patterns of life, in the tides and the cycles of the moon. There is a waxing and waning to all things, just as there is in this."

Trust?

If only it were so simple.

It is that concept that keeps coming back to me over and over since Father's death, and still, I can't seem to hold on to the idea of trust for long. I grumble and run my hand along the scales of the monster, recoiling at the feel of him. "How did you get this thing to bring me to you?" I ask the question because I know with startling certainty that that's what has happened. Somehow, he's used magic to tame this ocean beast. Where even the siren song has fallen short, save for my own, he's succeeded with something I've never imagined possible. I simply sent the beast away, but he's done something far stronger than that. He's tamed it.

"There is more to the prophecy than what you've been told, Senra."

His words spear me, and I straighten, all focus returned to his ageless face. The red robes wrapped around his body match the sky now, a color deep and rich and, somehow, worshipful. "Tell me."

"When the timing is right, I'll tell you everything. That's a promise. But for now, you need to take the sea-dragon with you as your companion."

My mouth falls open, breath catching. "What?" Now I'm really confused. "He's my enemy. He's born of the evilness lurking in the darkest parts of the sea. I can't just take him with me."

"It's like I said before, Senra. You must learn to trust. Trust, dear one, and learn to love what you hate."

Except for the up and down of the lapping waves, I'm unmoved. Is he serious? I can't be expected to work with this beast. It's a ludicrous suggestion. But even as I think it, a part of me wonders if it's so terrible of an idea. I saw the intelligence in this creature's golden eyes for myself. And even though I meant to kill it, I chose to send it away, to save it. Could there be a higher purpose at work? Is it magic? Is it more? The prophecy at work? The Gods?

I blink rapidly, my mind spinning with the questions.

"It's not a suggestion and yes, it is something much bigger than you and me." He raises his eyebrow playfully, and I balk. Did I speak my accusations and thoughts aloud? No, I definitely did not.

One hand rises above his head, outstretched. Bright energy forms between his fingers, electricity that zaps and moves. It transforms to bright gold magic, more luminescent than a harvest moon. The same moon we've performed our ceremonies under with his people, year after year. He swirls it around his palm, expands it around him until it grows to include me and the monstrous dragon in its pulsing glow.

He chants low vowel sounds. The noise is so guttural, so earthen and grounded, and so unlike anything of the sea, that I grow transfixed. This isn't magic I've ever seen before.

The glow flashes and then disappears. The dragon lifts its head from the water, turning to study the two of us. Its golden eyes are alight, the same color as the magic moments before. Any question of the monster's enchantment is answered in that one look.

"Go now, Senra," the wizened monk orders, his voice losing its playfulness and taking on an authoritative tone. "Take the dragon as your companion. Find the missing stone, the asteroid piece that I know you're searching for. But keep your heart open, for it will take more than one lost stone returned to complete your task."

His words sink into me, deep into my rolling gut, and harden. What does that mean? Keep my heart open to what? The questions are on the tip of my tongue but I'm too awestruck to speak them. Truthfully, the idea of opening my heart terrifies me. I've already lost so much. I don't think I could bear another break.

"I'll find you when you are ready," he finishes, and then he turns, picks up a staff, and using it like a paddle, he pushes himself slowly away.

It's so unbelievable I almost laugh. He's going to row himself somewhere on that thing? We're in the middle of the ocean. And not just any ocean, one filled with terrible monsters below and even more dangerous humans above.

I stare at his back, incredulous. Taking a deep salty breath, I look to the dragon still holding me where I stand. Its eyes bore into me, and I huff.

"What am I supposed to even *do* with this thing?" I spin back to the monk.

He's gone.

Vanished into the mist, as if it was all a creation of my mind.

But it wasn't. And I'm still here, still stuck with a new pet that may as well be a venomous snake. It's just as dangerous. I let out a sigh and dive into the ocean.

Come along, you mutt, I call back to the dragon, my magic tapping into whatever primal brain is inside this thing. *I'm not letting you slow me down.* And just like a devoted pet, the black beast trails far too close for comfort. The bubbles exhaled from its gargantuan mouth tickle at my heels.

TEN

MY STOMACH TWISTS WITH HUNGER. ANOTHER DAY INTO the journey and this terrifying monster hasn't left my side. I try not to look at it behind those glowing orb eyes. Because if I focus on its gnawing teeth, its writhing body, or its black hide as sharp as knives, it's my father's face that I see. So instead, I align my thoughts on the pain in my stomach and I eye the empty expanse of blue surrounding me, careful to stay turned away from my slithering companion. All I need is an unsuspecting fish to swim nearby and dinner will be served. I could sing, lure something in, but I'm close to the surface and the idea makes me shiver. What if I have another run-in with a boat?

I push the thought away and continue to study the empty ocean around me. There's nothing out here except for water and salt and the tides that move them. I know not too far away, about twenty miles west and further down, lies the last of my siren empire. I've never been to the underwater city there, and I'm certain they'd welcome me and help me in any way I asked. But I avoid seeking any help, as I have avoided running into any sirens over the last four days. I can't get distracted. I'm supposed to do this alone. That was the prophecy, even if I now have a monster tagging along.

I wonder how my people are faring, especially the ones living all the way out here. Back home we have ample fish to go around. But here...

I grit my teeth, angry that my own people might be going hungry. The monsters keep multiplying, so there's less and less food. In this area of the ocean, it's startlingly clear there's a shortage. I hope they're okay, that I'm imagining things, or that they know a trick of which I haven't thought. This is where Lei and his father are from, and they never had complaints when we spoke of their lives here. Maybe it's because I'm much too near the surface and only a day away from the humans? I've heard lack of food was their biggest problem. Eventually, it's going to be a crisis for all people, magical or not. But for now, the sirens have been fine to use song. And as long as I succeed in returning the magical stone to the mages, the song's power will stay that way. I force my thoughts away from the opposite, the incoming possibility of widespread starvation and death.

The black monster slithers in front of me, its slimy tail lightly sliding against my arm. I bristle. Why did I save it? Why couldn't I have been as strong as the warriors instead of letting it go? There's got to be a way we can rid the ocean of all these beasts forever. I don't care how they got here or why. Balance of magical power be damned. Once all this stone business is done and I'm crowned, that will be my first task as empress. The people's needs will always come before anything else. Just as they do now.

A sharp keening rumbles from the mouth of the sea dragon, and it spins around, forcing me to meet its glowing eyes.

You're hungry, too, huh? I ask the question, not expecting to get a reply. But its head bobs up and down and its body twists agreeably. A twinge of sympathy opens in my heart, and I stab it down. *Well then, I guess we better find something before you decide to take a bite out of me.*

I try to glare, thinking of the way this creature and its friends attacked our city, but its round eyes stare back at me so innocently and unaware to my hatred that I finally let out a sigh and roll my eyes. *Whatever. I guess I'm stuck with you whether I like it or not.*

It darts ahead, moving down toward the ocean floor. I'm quick to catch up and together we swim into the deepest depths, into the silent dark places of the sea where human overfishing isn't going to be a problem. But that doesn't mean other threats won't be lurking, lying in wait, just as hungry as we are.

After a few minutes of cobalt blue water shifting to navy and then black, we slow to a stop. My eyes adjust, siren vision becoming clear with each passing second. Sure enough, there is food down here, even if much of what I see makes the tiny hairs on my arms stand on end. I've never liked coming down this deep. No siren does, not really.

Our cities are in the higher places of ocean, from before. Not these depths. The pressure of the hundreds of meters of the water above squeezes me in its metal-tight watery grip. Not to mention, it's far too cold down here to stay comfortable. I force myself to take long slow breaths, telling myself to stay calm, that I'm made for this part of the ocean just as any other. But none of that stops my heart skipping or my blood rushing.

Let's get this over with quickly, please.

My sea-dragon curls its long tail around me in response. An instant warmth of protection envelops me, reminding me of a life spent in the middle of trained guards. Is that why the mage brought us together? It's the best explanation. I shouldn't be grateful for it, but in this moment, I am.

A long eel-like creature nears, millions of years of evolution and the gnarly thing still looks as ancient as the day its ancestor bore life. Its open mouth is lined with rows upon rows of small, pointed teeth, so many they almost look like the soft bristles of my hairbrush. I know better, though. These teeth are sharp as razors. They're made to rip through the toughest of hides, tearing right into the meat. Its eyes are matte green, unmoving and unseeing, like an afterthought, probably because evolution saw no point in having eyesight down this far. Its long gray body slithers, the color reminiscent of shark-hide.

The moment it senses our presence, it attacks. Bubbles spill from its gaping mouth as it zips toward us, faster than expected. In moments, it's upon us, meeting the dragon first. A pang of fear squeezes my stomach. My hazy mind suddenly clears.

And I sing.

After only a few seconds and one long note, the creature stops, mesmerized.

The thing doesn't look very appetizing, but my stomach doesn't care what package my dinner comes in, just so long as I eat. My mouth waters and I grin, pushing pretense aside and ready to feast. Unfortunately, my monster friend beats me to it. His mighty jaw unhinges and lashes out at the creature, clomping down on its thrashing body. But it's too late. The monstrous fish is gobbled up in two quick bites.

Hey, that was mine! I gasp, placing my hands on my hips and swimming from my protector's circle of flesh.

My dragon throws me a scolded look and whimpers. I huff, grabbing the spear from its strap at my back and swim further from the protection of his curling midnight body. Guess I'm going to have to do this the old fashioned way. The idea of it sends a thrill down my spine. I always did love to hunt without magic. It wasn't something I ever needed to do, of course, but it was something I got to do occasionally for sport with my father. We bonded over the thrill of the chase, our predator instincts leading us to prey.

Once again, I sing.

The sound pours from my mouth, frothy and oceanic and ethereal as the magic from which it came. It doesn't take long for the creatures to be called to the song, lured in like fish on a line. It's not that they all have ears or can even hear as we siren can. No, it's that same telepathic connection we share. Siren magic is as strong as the ocean tide and as sure as the moon laying claim over us all.

The fish surround me on all sides. Some glow or have evolved in such a way that tells me they belong in the darkness. But others are a kind that don't belong this deep and never will. Still, they have come, and as long as I keep singing, they will continue to come.

I eye a familiar fish and a pang of homesickness strikes for the first time in these four days. I know this meal; it's the most common one back home. Many times I sat with my family to enjoy it, it was my father's favorite. The fish's round scaly-gray body hovers just in front of me. Underneath I'll find a slab of delicious white meat. Again, my stomach clenches and my mouth waters. I call to the fish, digging in the second it's within my reach. Bones crack, blood spills, and the meat fills my belly. I'm greedy and lay my teeth into one of its companion fish the moment I'm through with the first. The fish line up for me, one after the next.

Ah, that's better, I sigh, smiling at my dragon mate. His mouth seems to smile right back, curled whiskers bouncing. The moment sends guilt through my entire body at having served myself first. He's waited for too long, so I nod once. He springs forward, grabbing another fish to add to his meal, plopping it into its snarling mouth shamelessly.

We continue on like this for a few minutes, focused only on filling our bellies.

Before long, the surrounding sea life grows restless, still entranced, but base instinct starting to catch on to the trick. If I don't do something soon, I might get myself into trouble. I eye some of the uglier and deadlier fish warily, biting my bottom lip with its fresh fish taste, the taste that still reminds me of home.

Home doesn't belong in the freezing darkness surrounding me, and neither do I.

We need to get out of here…

My sea-dragon pops its head up, golden eyes staring out into the expansive blackness. The large fish caught in its mouth is released, its mangled body floating down into unknown depths. I tense, a crawling sense of unease sliding up my body. My once-empty stomach hardens into a knot. I hold my breath. My dragon seems to do the same, his instinct catching hold of my thought.

There's something else out here. Something is watching us.

They appear from the darkness, zooming toward us as fast as water snakes. There are two of them. Monsters. Dragons. Serpents. All black and cold and ready to attack. They match my companion in appearance except for their eyes, which are blood red and hungry. I begin to sing, a long dancing sound drawing out of my lungs in looping notes. They tumble in such a way that I know will subdue the beasts. The thought strikes me. Could these two be related to my dragon somehow? Does that change anything? Any sense of duty to my dragon is lost as they swim closer, unmoved by the music, and just as determined to feast.

Fear settles over me, grappling and choking me from the inside out. Why isn't it working?

My dragon rushes out, attacking the first beast that reaches us. The two screech at each other, mouths agape, short arms with long bladed claws extended. The second monster circles, bloody teeth snapping at the fish still transfixed by my song. They don't stand a chance.

Frantic, I hoist my spear into my hands and search for something more to save me. If I can spear it through its vulnerable eye, I'll kill it. But with the speed at which it's circling, the way its head is lashing about, I'm not sure I'll succeed. And then the spear will be lost to the cruel grip of the ocean.

I keep it steady in my hands, pointed outward. There's got to be more I can do. Thoughts pummel me; my mind is confused, my body stiff with fear. My years of training are failing me and if this continues, all will be lost.

I take a deep breath and force myself to think. That's when the idea comes, as clear as a ray of sunshine blazing down through a hurricane.

Stop the monsters with the red eyes, I direct the thoughts to all the creatures still under my command. *Kill them!* There's a brief moment of pause as the command sinks in. And then there's a frenzy of movement so powerful that all I see are bubbles and foam and masses of inky blood. My dragon charges into the middle of it all, fighting with a ferocity that's unlike anything I've witnessed.

Maybe this monster, this dragon, sent to me by the Mage isn't meant to be my destruction, but rather, maybe he's my salvation. I remember what the Mage said, "You must learn to love what you hate." I remember how he spoke of trust, and the lessons I needed to embrace. If there's any time to trust in something beyond my control, that time is now.

ELEVEN

MY MAGIC IS FADING. MY SONG ISN'T AS STRONG AS IT was the night the monsters first attacked the palace. I eye my companion warily, wondering if and when he's going to betray me. Because if my magic is fading, it might mean the mages' magic is, as well. As if reading my thoughts, my murderous friend shifts his head and nuzzles it against my side.

You're not my pet, I chastise. I can't help but let out a small laugh. *Hey, stop that, it tickles.*

Its golden eyes blink at me, and I swear I catch a smile turn up its mouth. I sigh and run a hand along its scaly back. Okay, maybe it kind of is my pet, as twisted as the idea may be.

We're back to swimming toward our destination, the cold darkness of our murderous meal long behind us. I can't pretend that we're not going to reach the land-dwellers at any minute. We are. This one-sided conversation is more of a distraction from the nerves jumbling my belly than anything else.

If you're mine, I muse, *then I guess I better give you a name.*

He practically purrs, his forked tongue quickly sliding in and out of his mouth.

Ancient Chinese mythology didn't always count these monsters as evil; in fact, many of them were good. Our people used to worship them thousands of years ago. We still have some of their relics. Perhaps things are changing back to that and maybe my friend is worth naming, after all. But then again, if things change back to how the dragons were centuries ago, that would mean the creatures would have power over the rain and sea, and would be the main chi energy, the epitome of masculinity. I shiver at the thought of such power in wild and untamed things.

How about we call you Mei Long?

It looks at me curiously, not understanding the reference to the dinosaur remains that looked so much like dragons—many of our ancestors called that proof enough of their existence.

But you don't really sleep, do you? I tease, thinking about our journey thus far. Anytime I've gotten tired, the beast has swept me onto its back and continued onward. We're a day early because of it.

Oh, I know, I continue my teasing. *How about Pearl?* I'm referencing the pearls many of the dragons are rumored to have embedded into their necks, but so far, I haven't seen such a thing.

The dragon balks, shaking its head, and I laugh. *Too feminine, huh?*

Yeah, I don't take you for having a lot of yin in you. You're all yang, I wink. And then I consider if that's actually true. *Are you male?*

This time, the dragon nods, catching my attention on his radiant gaze.

The thought strikes me that his eyes are as bright yellow as the sun and glow just as gold. He may be covered in black scales, but something about those eyes reminds me of the story of the ancient emperor, Huangdi. He was known as the Yellow Emperor and at his death, was transformed into a yellow dragon and taken to the heavens. After that, his entire royal line prided themselves as descendants of dragons.

Shall I honor you with the name Huanglong, then? I ask, curiosity peaking. It's the official name for the yellow dragon. My beast's eyes widen, that smile returning to its face once again. Part of me is afraid I'll be struck down for the blasphemy just at suggesting it, but the other part likes the idea that perhaps the ancient emperor has reincarnated to help me along my journey.

I sigh, knowing I can't call him that, whatever my personal beliefs may be. What if someone found out? It could be considered disrespectful and irreverent. And even if someone doesn't find out, certainly the Gods will know.

We're going to have to settle on Long, I say, patting him once on the head. *That's a good compromise. And you and I will both know that I'm really referencing the ancient dragon emperor, just in case you and him have something in common...*

My voice trails off, and he sneaks a curious glance at me, eyes as bright as fire. I stare into them for a minute, noticing the way they reflect like water, seeing my outline shining back. Repeating my earlier action, I run my hand along the curves of scales. His whole body purrs in agreement and he spins around, swimming on. At this point, I'm riding on his back again, careful not to move the wrong direction against the sharp scales.

You're not so bad. I rest my head against his side. My body has grown tired, especially after the battle we endured a few hours ago. Saving my energy for whatever is about to happen next is vital. So I try to force myself to relax, as fruitless as it may be.

The mage that brought Long to me is the highest ranked of all the mages; it's a fact I can't take for granted. I now see his wisdom in pairing me up with this dragon companion, even if I'm supposed to hate him, even if admitting to myself how grateful I am for Long's help leaves me feeling like a traitor. I can only imagine how Lei and SunYu would react if they saw me now. What would mother think? Or father? Maybe father is watching me now and disappointed in my behavior.

But they're not out here alone. I am.

So, of course, I must believe that His Holiness knew what he was doing when he magically showed up on that rickety raft and paired me with the dragon. I can see the truth in all of it now that I've been saved by him once, and I'm not even to the human island yet. I wouldn't have gotten this far had it not been for Long.

What are we going to do when we get there? I muse, speaking to my dragon as if he and I are old friends. *It's not like they're going to* have the asteroid piece sitting out in the open. The thing isn't exactly inconspicuous. It's black as onyx and twice the size of my fist. Plus, it has a slight glow with the magic it carries. If anything, they've already taken it back to wherever their king is. If they're trying to harness the magic for themselves, then I might have a shot at getting it back. But if they plan to destroy it, I have to get to it first.

Long has no answers. Of course he doesn't. Even so, having someone to talk to about all this lifts some of the weight off my shoulders.

We need to be logical about this. We can't just go storming in there until we know where the stone is located. We need to think of a plan so we don't end up in prison or killed. I can't very well just drown them all, now can I?

Long slows to a stop, and suddenly, the hairs on the ends of my arms stand on end. I glance to the surface, fear striking cold through my heart. Among the flash of sun on water, there's the unmistakable white bottom of a boat. It looks exactly like the vessel we had trouble with on our way back from the monastery. Are these the same scavengers? If they see me, they'll kill me. That's if I don't kill them first. I think of my fallen comrades and my hand immediately reaches for my spear.

Long has other ideas.

I grip tighter to his back as he slides deeper into the ocean and takes off, effectively removing us from the sight of the humans

As we move, the water whooshing past, my mind clears. Taking revenge on those men right now would only distract me from my true mission, a mission that will hopefully rid siren kind of those enemies anyway.

I'm okay, I tell Long. *I get your point. Now let's go back up to the surface. We should be close to the first of the Japanese residences. I need to get a better look at what I'm dealing with.*

We start to zoom up, and I put my hand on Long's neck, realizing my mistake with enough time to stop him. *Actually, you'd better stay low. Keep down. You're not exactly the most invisible creature, if you know what I mean.*

Long stiffens, a low keening rumbling from his gargantuan mouth. He's smart and I think he understands, considering he's massive and black, and the water is growing clearer by the minute.

I know, but at first sign of trouble you can come save me. Okay?

His head nods once, and my lips turn up into a smile. Then I stand on his back, my toes pressing into his scales, and push off.

I swim to the surface.

My head slips above the water, and I blink, trying to adjust my sight to the bright sun cascading down. The air is too soft, and I cough. I spin around, making sure nobody heard me. But I'm alone. About a mile in front of me is a tall brown mountain, much taller and wider than anything I've seen in our seas. Residences are built all throughout, though it appears not a lot grows there as far as crops, or even trees. Toward the top, a palace looms. My eyes push past the haze, bringing the building into clarity. It's undoubtedly gorgeous, and I can't help but stare at the pristine white siding, the several stories of rooms with shining glass windows, and the black roofs covering it all, swooping into ornate points.

My eyes travel down the mountain where the residences grow tighter and smaller, multiplying in number. And then where the ocean meets the land, it doesn't stop. There's at least half a mile of decks on all sides, homes built along them, and boats everywhere. As far as I can tell, they spread around the entire island; there's got to be miles and miles of people living like that.

I'll have to swim underneath the homes.

I drop down into the water and push forward, determined to get closer, even if that means facing the growing apprehension that comes with it. But as soon as I near the area where the people live, I notice the nets.

They're everywhere!

Ropes and nets of all shapes and sizes are suspended in the water. These people really must be desperate for food. Either that, or they want to deter as many of the sea monsters from venturing out here as possible.

Possibly, it's both.

The very thought of attempting to maneuver my way through that maze of traps sends me reeling. I still for a moment, bringing in a deep breath of salty cool water to settle my nerves. Then I take off, swimming around the edge of nets for a while, looking for some kind of break, maybe even a clear shot to the shore, but there's nothing. Instead, I notice several places where the nets are so tangled together it would be next to impossible to separate them. Seaweed grows up their sides and I wonder how long they've been there.

I let out a growl and swim back to the surface. There's got to be an easier way.

An idea strikes me, and I dart back to where Long is waiting.

When he spots me, he rushes forward, wrapping me with his long tail. The little arms and legs grip me in their talons, but I'm not afraid of him anymore. In fact, out here, he's the only thing left to calm me down. Besides, his frenzy is only proof that he's excited I've returned. Guilt stabs me, knowing I won't be staying with him for much longer. A prickle of something else lingers under the guilt, and I know it's a feeling much like love, not that I'd admit to it.

Listen, I say, quick to get to the point, *do not try to get on that island. You'll get caught in the nets and I'm certain they'll kill you.* And they're probably so desperate for food that they'll also eat his meat, but I don't add that last part.

His gold eyes blaze at me—he understands my order.

There are a lot of boats up there, fishing boats, but also, military of some sort. I need you to distract them for me. I'm going to get on the island and I don't know how long it will be before I'm back. It could be hours or it could be days. Can you wait here for me? Not close enough to get caught, just close enough that if I need you and sing my song, you might hear me?

It seems a foolish plan even as I say it, but it's the only one I've got.

Long's tongue slides out of his mouth and runs along my face from cheek to cheek. It's both rough and slimy, and I try not to bristle. All I can assume is it's his way of giving me a kiss, his way of offering an affectionate goodbye. I hug him back, dropping a kiss on both of his cheeks as well.

We part and head for our places.

We're two creatures of the same dark sea, Long and I. He's the masculine Yang, and me, I'm the feminine Yin. We may be opposites, but we're also two sides of the same coin, the blending of light and dark. Together, we're going to rightfully take back the magic that belongs to my people, overcoming any obstacles in our way. That might mean murder, it might mean more death and blood before this is all over, but I can't think of it now. I can't let myself back down from my destiny, no matter my feelings.

Ten minutes later, my head crests above the surface and I eye my target. Off in the distance, I hear the thunderous roar of my sea dragon.

Good boy.

I push forward.

TWELVE

IT DOESN'T TAKE LONG TO FIND THE PERFECT BOAT. I'VE
grown up studying the types of boats glossing the ocean's surface just
as I've studied all the life brimming below. All sirens are educated,
but I've been tutored beyond the norm in these matters. So when I
spot what I need bouncing up and down on slapping waves, water
crashing against the hull, I grin. The vessel is large enough that I can
stow away during the chaos, but not the kind of ship where the crew
will be rushing off to be heroes. It looks like a large fishing boat more
than a military installation, which is exactly why I choose it.

I swim closer, head skimming just below the surface, until I reach
the edge. My hand slides along the vessel. Once upon a time, it was
probably pearly white, but now its shell is gray, scuffed and grimy
from years on the ocean. I swim along the perimeter, noticing several
places where it's been repaired. Its age makes me wonder if it was

originally built in the time before the seas rose. I sneak my head above the water, foam splashing my face, to take note of the other nearby boats. Most of them appear to be just as old, if not older.

Long's screeching wail howls from the other side of the island, and I duck back under the safety of water, trying to find a way to board this boat—my escape plan. There are circular port windows at the bottom of the ship, two rows of larger, square windows above that, and first of three decks. All I have to do is get onto that first deck and hide until the boat enters the Japanese port, and I'll be free to enact the next stage of my plan: blend in.

That's the part that I'm not sure my tutoring will have adequately prepared me for.

I swim along the edge of the boat, ignoring the prickle of frustration that I didn't immediately find a way onboard. I dive back down in the water, rolling under the boat, and scurrying up the other side. A low vibration hums through the beast, the purr of the engines catching to life. The water is murky here; it seems to erupt in a cloud of mud. I must hurry else I'll lose this opportunity.

As far as I can see, there's nothing useful below the surface on this side of the vessel either, so I carefully peek my head above water. Above, men call out over each other in a frenzy, panic lacing their deep rumbling voices. It's clear they're afraid of Long. Terrified of the monster. And they should be. He's as deadly as anything lurking in our dark ocean. But I also feel a tug of worry for my dragon. The people here have survived this long, haven't they? They must know how to fight off the sea monsters. There's no other explanation, not to mention, it explains all the underwater traps they've set up close to their island home. I hope Long doesn't get too entangled in the fight or caught up in a trap. The plan is for him to create a distraction, but not to get himself killed in the process. I don't know if I can do this without him, and as much as I hated him at first, that's all changed. And it's left me more confused than ever.

In my core, a wave of guilt roars, but I push it back down, back into that ocean in me, and search for a way onboard. In the back of my mind, I'm considering the option of bailing on this boat and finding another. That would take more time and I'm not sure how much I've got. So I swim toward the hull, careful to keep clear of the massive turbines whirling in the water. I spot something sticking out from the side of the boat. It's so caked in black grime that it blends in seamlessly with the rest of the gray sludge, and I barely see it. My pulse ignites.

It's a ladder.

The engines roar, the boat lurches forward, speeding toward the shore. I dive for the ladder, gritting my teeth, kicking hard, determined to make this work. The metal is slippery as seaweed but my grip is as tight as my resolve. Muscles igniting, I haul myself up the side of the moving boat, climbing rung over slimy rung. Unease pummels me harder than the spitting wake that sprays off the water's surface. I refuse to entertain the fear building up or the persistent thought of failure spinning in my head. Staying strong is my only real option here. I can do this.

Before my hand reaches the last rung, I press myself against the slick metal and train my ears to whatever is happening above me. I wish there were a railing, something to peek over the edge easier, but there's nothing. There's only a metal siding, a ladder, and me. Well, not just me: there are men up there, men who would kill me if they saw me. The voices hit me all at once in a cacophony of angry and fearful men calling out to each other.

"Do you hear the lungs on that thing? It must be huge!"

"Move! Now!"

"You, get below deck!"

The chaos of deep voices and frantic yelling holds me back, even though it should make this easier for me if they're distracted.

"We need to speed up! I don't want to be caught out here if that thing comes this way."

"We're going as fast as we can. Just hang on."

I was right. They're not going to be joining in the battle. Under no circumstances is this boat going to be turning around. It's good enough confirmation that this boat was the right choice.

Holding my breath, I wait until I'm as sure as I'll ever be that nobody is near the ladder. But there's no way to be sure, so during a quieter moment, I swing over the edge and crouch low. I land on both feet, rivulets of salty water running down my face, my hair, my arms and legs and black bodysuit. I'm standing between a wall that runs parallel to the railing and the ocean beyond. Under my bare feet, coils of thick tan rope are piled high. They glisten in the sunlight like oily snakes.

The voices stay in the distance and I finally exhale a shaky breath.

I don't see anyone, no crewmembers to give me away, but that doesn't mean someone won't round the corner at any moment. I dive toward a small door etched into the cream wall and peer through the foggy window. Inside, it looks to be some sort of storage closet. It's empty.

Perfect.

I wrench open the heavy door and slip inside, closing it tightly behind me. Seconds later, a man comes into view on the other side of the window. My heart stalls, and I freeze. Black hair streaked with white bobs in front of the window as the man hauls rope onto his thick muscled shoulder, using his free hand to wipe the sweat from his brow. I stare at his huge back, at the weathered biceps pulsing against his stained shirt, and gulp back a breath of dizzying fear. He turns toward the storage closet.

I duck down, white-hot adrenaline coursing through my veins. The noise in my ears is as loud as crashing waves during a storm, a result of the blood racing through my body. One hand releases the spear from its place on my back, and my eyes adjust to the dim light. I take in my surroundings. There are a couple of yellow buckets with tall grimy sticks teetering out the sides. I'm not sure what they are. Some ocean sponges lie on the floor, though they're practically torn to shreds. I grit my teeth at the sight. An empty white bottle with the lid missing rolls against the side of the wall. It creates a slight tapping sound. I've seen enough human garbage in the ocean to know this waste will likely end up tossed overboard at some point. I scrunch up my nose. The place reeks of dead fish and mildew.

I hoped to find some kind of clothing that I could slip over my bodysuit, maybe even a hat to fasten over my braided hair. Anything to appear less conspicuous when we make it to port and I have to blend in with the people there. My raven hair, slanted eyes, bowed lips, and creamy skin might work out okay. But my clothes will definitely be a problem. And now that I'm thinking about it again, I'm certain I'm far too pale, having avoided the sun for my entire life. All the men I've seen are tanned from years of salt and sun, so I can only assume the women are, too.

I sigh and crouch into the corner, hoping to calm myself enough to think clearly. This is a big ship, and by the smell and appearance, I'd guess it's used for deep-sea fishing. Surely the men on board live here for days or maybe even weeks at a time. If I can find where they keep their things, then I can steal something suitable, and then—

The door bangs open. A shaft of light enters, interrupted by a dark shadow. I will myself invisible, pressing back into the darkness, praying I go unseen, my grip tightening on my spear.

The man reaches for one of the tall sticks, then stills. "Who are you?" His voice is gruff, hardened by the sea.

My mouth drops open. Fear squeezes my throat. What can I say? If I were in the water, I would sing. But I'm barely even wet and I know to sing will be to solidify my death sentence, not his.

It doesn't matter. He takes one look at my outfit and his black eyes harden. He attacks. He's faster than he looks. His fist is flying toward my face before I can blink, landing a punch against my cheek. Pain explodes along my jaw. It knocks sense into me and I strike out with my spear, gutting him through his side. He screams, a guttural screech, blood spilling down his grimy white shirt and then from his mouth.

I yank the spear out and tumble from the closet, not waiting to see if he follows me. That's if he's even still alive. It wasn't a sure kill shot, but that doesn't mean he won't die. My hands shake wildly and shock rocks me forward. I've killed before. I've killed countless fish, of course, and I even let those human pirates drown with my song, choosing only to save the young man, Kyon. But to spear a man with my own hands? It breaks me wide open. Something about it feels different, feels wrong and unnatural. I don't have time to dwell on the torrent of confused emotions battling inside.

I have to keep moving if I'm going to stay alive.

I glance around, eyes searching. There's nobody out here, and I send a prayer of thanks. Long is still making a ruckus in the distance, the engine is still grinding, men are still yelling from further up deck.

I scan the area, eager for another hiding spot. But it's just the closet, the wall and the ocean. On either side of the wall are openings to the crowded areas of the boat. I'm out of options, so I know it's time to take a risk. Spear tight in my right hand, I sprint toward the back of the boat, hoping to get lucky.

I'm not lucky.

"Isamu!" a youthful voice calls out from behind. The hairs on the back of my neck prickle. "Where did you…"

I swing around. The kid is tall and lanky, like he's not quite grown into his height yet. His eyes become wide and his mouth has dropped open into an "O" as he stares. He blinks a few times and then takes off the way he came, calling out for backup as he goes. I curse and sprint the other way to the back of the boat. It's becoming more and more likely that I'll be bailing into the ocean any minute. What a waste! This is not how I wanted this to go…

The boat is still moving toward shore, but I notice something I hadn't before. We're in a line of other boats, moving through the water in a pattern. This must be the way they're able to get to port without getting caught in all the nets and fishing lines and traps. They have a system, one the people here know by heart, or at least by following those that do.

If I can get back in the water, I can follow the boat. I should have thought of it the first time. I hiss in annoyance at my mistake. If I was worried about getting caught up under the water, then of course the captain of a massive boat has to think about these things, too. They know the way. All I have to do is follow and I can make it to the island. But now I've been seen. Stupid move!

I press myself against the steel wall, eyeing the ocean. I can do this. Nobody else has to see me. I'll jump back in.

"Hey, you!" The voice that yells at me is laced with anger, the type to kill first and ask questions later. "Who are you?"

I don't answer, nor do I look to see who's yelling at me. We're close to the island now. This will be easy. Easier than staying here, anyway.

"Are you one of them? You are, aren't you?" The voice sneers with authority. "A siren dares to step foot on my ship!"

I peel myself off the side of the wall, a slow smile playing at my lips. I step toward the edge, swing my legs over, and dive. As I'm falling toward the water, something hard strikes the back of my head.

I call out in shock but am swept below the surface before the cry can touch the air. The salt stings the wound. Blood billows around my face, the iron taste filling my mouth. My head throbs intensely, eyesight narrowing into small tunnels. I swim, panicked, needing to get away from the boat and whoever is trying to kill me before they get another blow in. Within seconds, my vision falls to complete darkness.

My mind numbs, and I'm washed away.

THIRTEEN

SOMETHING RUBS AGAINST MY ANKLE—SLICK AND ROUGH and painful. It runs up my leg, gripping against my hip, sliding up and up until it tightens over my chest. It wraps around my neck and pulls at my hair.

I jerk awake, a scream burning the back of my throat. I cough water and pop open my eyes, frantically looking about, searching for my captor. I'm caught in the grip of several slimy ropes as thick as my fist. I tell myself to settle, everything is okay. My heart races anyway, speeding faster with each second. My mind is filled with the fog of the injury. My body is anything but groggy. I try to reach my hand up to rub the back of my head, but it doesn't move. I growl and thrash, kicking out to get away from the tangle of rope. I'm stuck. I take a deep breath and force my muscles to relax.

I am made for the water. I'm a siren. I'll be fine. It's not like I'm going to drown and, as far as I know, nobody knows where I am, so if I hurry, I can get out of this mess and back on track. I peer up. A dancing ray of yellow sunlight cuts through the haze of water. About twenty feet above me are rows of decks floating on the surface. A trickle of calm settles over me like a harmony, giving me strength. I quickly orient myself and put the missing pieces of memory together. After I was hit in the head with something, I must have passed out and floated toward one of the water-logged shanty towns. I've gotten twisted in the ropes underneath but it's nothing I can't handle.

I twist my left hand. Freeing my right would be the better choice but the left is not quite as entrapped, so it gets to come first. My wrist burns in protest as I wiggle and shimmy the soft flesh against the rough rope. Finally, I'm able to wrench it free. Relief floods me. *Everything is going to be fine.* One limb down and only three to go. With my free hand, the first thing I search for is my spear. That will make quick work of this.

But it's gone.

I must not have returned it to its built-in holder on the back of my suit before I dove into the water. A foolish mistake. If I'd remembered my training, it's a mistake I never would have made. Lei wouldn't have overlooked something like that, none of the warriors would have. Am I truly cut out for this? I sigh and focus on what I can control now, which is my attitude. I need to cut myself some slack. Given the circumstances up on that ship, I shouldn't focus on what went wrong. Instead, I should focus on how I'm alive and going to move forward with my mission. I blow out a string of bubbles and watch them rise to the surface, wishing it were that easy for me to do the same.

How long was I out? Minutes? Hours? Could it have been longer?

Those men on the ship realized what I was, especially considering the first one had attacked me the moment he'd laid eyes on me, and the second had run in fear, and the third had called me a siren. Someone obviously tried to kill me when they struck me in the back of the head like that. If I'm lucky, they'll have assumed I took off and won't come looking for me. If I'm extra lucky, they won't alert whoever their authorities are to my presence on their ship. It stands to reason that if word makes way to the Japanese Emperor about me, he'll know exactly why I've come. Whoever he is. He's probably expecting an army. He won't be getting an army. Just me.

I had better be enough.

After a few minutes I'm able to get my other hand free, and then I set to work releasing my legs and torso. It doesn't take long; I'm free within seconds. I carefully swim upward, shimmying around ropes of all shapes and sizes, around long, practically invisible strings of fishing line, and even pass by a few empty cages. There aren't many fish down here, and I can see why. This place was probably over-fished decades ago.

I look up toward my destination. Going straight up will be much easier. It's only about twenty feet. Up there I can find refuge and a way to conceal myself, maybe even in one of those homes. I can strip myself of my identifying bodysuit and find human clothes. Not to mention, going up to the homes above, while intimidating, doesn't scare me nearly as much as navigating this mess of rope and wire in an attempt to swim to the island's shore. Because there's simply too much of it down here.

And because once I get to the shore, this gets real.

The back of my head throbs in violent pulses, and my breath is weak in my lungs, but I'm going to make this work. I know I can do this; it's my destiny. I come up underneath the closest dock, my head sliding above the water to get a better look at what I'm dealing with. The space between the lapping water and the deck is about four feet in height. Large round buoys bob in neat rows along the edges, and, among the fishing ropes and the traps, there are thick cables leading down to anchors that rest on the ocean floor. These docks may be old, but they're not going anywhere unless there's a strong hurricane.

Sometimes there are those terrible storms out here. What do the people do then? Do they all take shelter on higher ground? They must...

I study the nearest buoy. Once red, it's now so crusted over with ocean grime that it practically has scales. I hide in its murky shadow and smile. This cover is perfect as I sort through my plan.

"Are you all right down there?"

Okay, I clearly underestimated these humans...

I freeze, embarrassment stifling my pride. Is that person talking to me? Even as I think it, I already know the answer. I've been so foolish, so reckless. How is someone like me supposed to fulfill a life-altering prophecy? I sigh, wanting nothing more than to sink deep into the water and hide.

"Miss, you really shouldn't be down there right now," the man continues, pure concern rumbling over an aged voice. "Don't you know they spotted a sea monster not but an hour ago? It's dangerous in the water. Here, let me help you up. I can throw my ladder down to you." I almost wish I didn't understand his human language, but I do. It's part of our siren magic to speak different tongues. Considering much of the magic is connected to sound and voice, it's never surprised me. I can also speak his Japanese tongue just as well as my Chinese. So there's no sense in pretending I can't hear him, or know what he's offering.

Even still … I don't know what to do. I could sing, but that would alert the entire community of my presence. I could play along and pretend I'm one of them. I'm not sure how I would even do that in these clothes. I've studied this place, these people, and their customs. They don't wear clothes made for the sea. Rather out of options, I do the only thing that comes to mind.

I play dead.

I soften against the water, my legs floating up, my arms going limp, my head tucking to one side. My crown braid has loosened and long thick strands of my hair tickle against my cheek, spreading over my face like a net. It itches but I don't dare move.

There's a quiet curse followed by a light splash and the sound of a man huffing. Cold hands pull me out from underneath the deck. One long arm wraps around my torso and my face is fully yanked out of the water.

"Here, help me with her, will you?"

Someone else curses from above and there's another splash. More hands are on me. It takes every ounce of self-restraint not to give into fear and jump into action. This isn't what I wanted. Now there are two more people that could be a potential problem, two more humans that I might have to kill before the day's end. My gut flops. I don't want to kill anyone, I never did.

I can tell from their thick, hairy arms that they're both men. The second is much stronger than the first. He hauls me up the ladder, and I'm carefully laid out on the deck. I keep my eyes shut, trying to be gentle, to relax my mouth and my breathing, hoping it isn't totally obvious that I'm faking this whole thing. My hair is still a tangled mess over my face. My skin feels hot where these strangers just touched me.

"Has she got a pulse?"

Icy fingers press against the tender spot on my neck.

"Yes. A strong one. I think she's passed out or something. Doesn't look like she needs any resuscitation. Lucky we found her before she drowned."

There's a long pause. "Lucky you found her before the monsters did."

"Just in case," the older voice mumbles, and then hands press up and down against my chest at a quick speed. Shame burns through me. What is he doing? I should kill him right now for touching me!

"You're right." The man finally lets go. "I don't think she needs

113

CPR. Here, let's get her inside. When she wakes up we can help her find her people."

The two sets of hands are on me again, lifting and shuffling me inside one of the dock homes. I feel it the second I'm inside, in the stuffy air and the shift of shadows passing over my face, and in the way their footsteps change from an echo to a thud.

"Who's this?" a female's voice asks. Her light footsteps rush across wood floors like the pattering of rain. "Oh the poor thing, she's hurt."

"Hit her head on something," the man replies gruffly. "Maybe she fell in. Or maybe…" his voice trails off into silence.

I'm laid out on a bed, and I can feel the stares of the three of them boring down on me. Enough is enough. If these men and this woman haven't figured out what I am, it won't be long until someone else comes in here and does. I'd rather have my eyes open when that happens. I release a soft sigh, letting my eyes flutter for a few seconds before I blink them open. I reach to push my hair out of my face, pressing my hand to the back of my head and groaning. It really does hurt.

"What happened?" I ask, making sure my voice cracks, that I sound weak. But I didn't have to try, considering my lack of audible use makes it scratchy anyway.

Three humans tower above me. The woman leans over to get a better look. She is the frailest person I've ever seen. She's tiny, her limbs thin as rails, yet her hair is styled in an intricate braid that indicates she cares about her appearance. Her eyes are kind and brighten as her plump lips relax into a smile. Next to her, a man has his arm strung

114

over her shoulder. His expression seems less concerned for my health and more puzzled. He's weathered, and I can't place his age, but I'd have to guess he'd be older than my father.

It's the third person in the room, the third person standing over me, who causes my heart to race. Awareness spreads through my every cell like hot liquid. This man, is he part of the prophecy? How else could it be him? He stands a little further back, thick muscled arms crossed over his chest, dark piercing eyes taking me in like he doesn't know what to make of me, either. Like he can't understand how I ended up here, but he certainly knows who I am and knows what I can do. A short knife glints in his fist, a dagger perfectly angled for my attention. He sees me look him up and down, sees me notice the knife, and he raises an eyebrow in challenge. If he's afraid, he doesn't show it.

I know him.

I saved this man while I let his comrades drown. It wasn't what I wanted, not really. He was going to kill me and I had to defend myself. But I'd let them sink to their deaths so that I could question him. He probably doesn't see it that way. To him, it probably looked like I got what I needed and discarded him to the hungry jaws of my ocean like the others. They called him Kyon, and his name has stayed with me everyday since. His is the only non-magical human name I've ever known.

Does he believe I was going to kill him? Or does he know I spared him?

I can only hope for the latter since my life might depend on it. The entire empire depends on it, and something about that brings me right back to the prophecy. This can't just be coincidence, can it? That of all the houses I'm brought into, it's his? I gulp, my mouth dropping open slightly as I try to suck in the stale air.

"What happened?" I ask the lame question again. My throat is still raw, and I have to swallow down a cough. I already miss the water!

Kyon tilts his head, looking me up and down with an arresting gaze. A chill runs down my limbs, spine hardening, as he returns my question with one of his own. "I don't know what happened, but I'm willing to bet you do. So why don't you cut the act and tell us the truth?" He lifts the knife. "Before I slit your throat."

The blade catches the light and all words dry up in my mouth.

FOURTEEN

"KYON! THAT'S NO WAY TO TALK TO A LADY!" THE WOMAN gasps. "I raised you better than that."

He huffs, spitting his reply, "*That* is no lady."

I run my hand along the back of my head again. Blood sticks to my fingers and I wince. The woman tsks, shuffling over to a small metal box in the corner of the room where a tiny kitchen is laid out. She flicks up a lever and water pours from a spout. She uses it to quickly wet a white rag and then shuts it off. I'm still staring at the lever as she hurries back and presses it gently to my head wound.

"There, there, honey, you just relax and let me take care of this. You might need stitches."

I smile softly at her, taking the rag from her hand. "I got it. I'm sure it's not a big deal." Truthfully, I don't want her to see how quickly the wound will heal over. Another one of our siren powers grants us the

117

ability to heal fast; any cut will stitch back together by itself before the day is through.

"You shouldn't touch her," Kyon says. He's still towering over us, still staring at me like I'm a complete monster. And to him and to these people? He wouldn't be wrong. The thought of what I could do to them gives me power, but it also leaves me feeling weak. I hold my breath, not knowing what move I should make.

The old man sits on the end of the bed, his hands neatly folded in his lap as he studies me. His eyes are as kind as his wife's but that doesn't mean he isn't suspicious. I catch him glancing at my outfit, taking in the bodysuit, and I know I've been found out.

"Don't you realize what she is?" Kyon asks. I sink into myself, my fighter instincts flaring. "It's obvious she isn't one of us. We can't keep her here!"

The woman hushes him again, but the man speaks up. "Of course we know what she is, son. That doesn't mean we can't help her and treat her with human decency. Sirens are human, in case you've forgotten."

I gasp, the air lost from my lungs. *What is happening here? They know what I am and they still want to treat me with human decency?* Everything I thought I knew about land-dwellers is washed away in that moment. I expected to fight. I expected to hide. I never expected to be found out and accepted. I'm not sure I can trust it's real.

Kyon shakes his head, baring his teeth. "You don't know what you're talking about. I saw what her *people* did to ours. You know those men who died on my last outing? It was a siren attack. She was there!"

The room falls silent, and I itch to take action. Instead, I take a deep breath.

There are only a few ways I can play this, and even though Kyon deserves to be slapped right about now, making enemies with these people is not going to do me any favors. I tilt my head at him and meet his hardened gaze, making sure mine is extra soft.

"But I saved you," I say. "You were going to kill me and—"

"I was protecting myself!"

"You were going to kill me," I say again, not raising my voice to match his, "and I stopped you, and then I didn't let you drown, did I?"

He shakes his head, cheeks turning red, mouth falling into a flat line. He can't argue with the facts, even though we both know I was no friend of his that day. And I'm still not. But maybe I can make him question.

"I'm sorry about your friends," I continue. "But your men attacked us first. We were only defending ourselves. I wouldn't have used my song if I didn't need to, and I only used it as a last option."

Kyon doesn't buy it. His eyes are still fire, his exterior still ice. But he's also stopped talking, giving me the chance to continue.

I turn to his elders, knowing they're my best chance at survival. I can't tell them the truth of why I'm here. If I give them a good story, get them to sympathize with me, then maybe they'll not only let me stay here, maybe, they'll actually help me.

"I ran away," I say, willing tears to water my eyes. "I was forced into a loveless engagement, so I ran away." The story isn't true, of course,

119

but it falls so easily from my mouth that I have to stop myself from wondering if perhaps it's more true than I'd like to believe. "I didn't know where else to go. The ocean is a dangerous place, as you know. A siren can't survive out there alone, without her community."

There's a long pause as the three stare at me. Kyon lets out a growling moan, and I'm positive he's still skeptical, even as the other two flash pitying looks in my direction. They feel sorry for me. I don't know whether to rejoice in that fact or feel extreme shame.

I try to stand, but the wound on the back of my head pulses and pushes me down. Using it to my advantage, I groan and exaggerate the pain, plopping back onto the bed. "I don't want to cause any trouble for your family." My voice is weaker than before. "I'll go and find somewhere else to stay."

"You can't!" The woman rushes forward, gently pushing me down against the bed until my head is back on the pillow. Her hands are warm on my icy shoulders. She carefully peels the rag from my hair and returns to the sink to rinse it, bringing it back immediately. "You're hurt. It's not safe for you to wander around the village." Her lips pinch as she studies me. "None of your kind are safe here. Most of the people on this island hate anything to do with the sirens. There can be kindness here, but it's in the pockets of the city, it's not the norm. This is a brutal place, a hungry place. And people do crazy things when they're hungry."

My stomach twists as I wonder what kind of crazy things she's speaking of.

She continues, "Most people around here blame the siren kind for our bad circumstances. Even though the agreements were made before any of us were born, they say that siren magic has caused the sea monsters to return and our sea to be overfished."

I blink up at her, as if I've never heard this before. Truthfully, I know this is why these humans hate my people. And maybe they have a right to. It doesn't change anything for me.

My bottom lip trembles even though my insides squirm at manipulating such kind people. "Where am I to go? I can't go back home."

The older man scoots up the bed and squeezes my hand. I'm so struck by the generosity of these humans, so overcome with guilt, that tears come to my eyes for real. What am I doing? Can I really lie to these people like this? Will I have to hurt them?

"No worries, dear," the man says. "You know my son, Kyon. I'm Reo and this is my wife Hanako. You can stay with us until you're feeling better and have a plan."

I smile. "Thank you for your kindness." I pause, wondering if I should make up a false name, but something inside can't bear to do it. "I'm Senra." They won't know I'm the princess. We keep our ways and customs well guarded from ordinary humans such as these. The mages are the only ones we commune with; it's been that way for decades.

"It's a pleasure to meet you, Senra. You know, I've always wanted to meet one of your kind. I have many questions, though of course, I don't presume to think you'll answer all of them."

"It's true," Hanako adds. "We're part of a small group here on the island that wishes to extend friendship to the siren people. Though our political views aren't very popular, we believe our two civilizations could work together for the good of everyone."

"Ridiculous," Kyon scoffs. He stays back, still watching me, growing more agitated by the minute. I've been hyper-aware of his sharp eyes on me through this entire conversation. At the last bit from his mother, he throws his hands in the air and laughs bitterly, glaring at his parents. "You two don't know what it's like out on the ocean, what her people are like! She's dangerous. Deadly. She has the kind of magic that could destroy us and she wouldn't even think twice about it. We can't just let her hide out here…" His voice trails off and his jaw tenses.

Once again, the three stare at me, waiting for my response. "I promise not to cause any trouble," I say with a small frown. Kyon is right. What he's seen firsthand is completely accurate of how our people treat anyone or anything we consider a threat.

"You were forced into a loveless engagement, huh?" Kyon presses. "Somehow that doesn't surprise me coming from a filthy siren. If you're going to take advantage of my parents, you better be more specific than that, *Senra*." He says my name like it's a curse word.

My mind whirls as I hold back a spark of anger. If I give them a piece of the truth, it will be easier for me to make my story sound real. I need them to believe me. But I can't tell them of my true intentions for being here. The Dalai Lama asked me to trust. But I can't trust them. As kind as they're being, they're still human.

I sigh and nod, sitting back up. I peel the rag from my bloodied head again and return it to Hanako. "I think it stopped bleeding." She drops it in the sink and then glides over to stand next to her son.

"My father died last year in an attack," I say, stumbling through my words, the anger giving way for sadness. It's so hard to talk about it, even now. "The sea monsters got him. I'm sure you know all about those beasts?" The family nods, pain sparking in each of their eyes. I have their full attention. "That was a terrible thing for my family. My mother had no choice but to secure an advantageous betrothal for me."

"So what?" Kyon interjects, folding his arms over his chest and leaning back on his heels. "Arranged marriages are normal here, too. It's no reason to run away from home like an insolent child. There must be a bigger reason."

His mother slaps his arm, horrified. "Let the girl finish, Kyon. Show some respect!"

He grumbles and steps back, but doesn't speak up again.

"My fiancé traveled from a distant city to meet me, bringing his family with him. It was only once I met him that I knew I had to run away. You see, my mother had already accepted the betrothal and she can't afford to take care of me anymore. But once I met him, it became clear that the two of us had no love between us and never could."

My voice cracks. Humiliation grips me the second the lie escapes my lips. And yet, is it really a lie? I'd spent a week with Lei and my annoyance of him only grew. I tried to like him for my family's sake, but if I'm being true to my heart, then I have to admit, I don't love him. Part of me again wonders if I should just tell this family the entire truth. But it's a risk I can't bear to take. Making myself someone in need of rescuing is the only way I know how to gain this family's trust. Too many lives hang in the balance of my success or failure on this mission.

"Did they hurt you?" Reo asks, anger and pity rolling in his tone. His frail body is so tense, like he wants to punch someone on my behalf. I can't bring myself to let him believe that of Lei and SunYu. A tear splashes down my cheek, and I close my eyes.

"They never hurt me."

There's a long pause as my story settles into the little room.

"That settles it." Reo stands. "You'll stay here, at least until you figure out a better living situation. You'll need to keep your true nature a secret."

"Of course." I perk up. "And I can help the family. I'm an excellent fisherman."

Kyon scoffs. "Of course you are. I can't believe this," he mutters. He strides from one end of the room into the other, hands flying in the air. He halts with a stomp, the small wooden room shaking, then he turns away.

Hanako kneels before me. "I apologize for my son. His prejudice stems from his job working on the ocean."

Kyon shifts back around and meets my gaze. I bite my tongue. His job? He said he was a scavenger, but that's probably code for pirating.

Do his parents know what he's really doing out there? Somehow, I doubt it. I break his stare.

"I'm sorry. It's true, my people *can* be deadly."

Hanako's calming voice breaks the tension. "My husband and I were raised to be unassuming. We take care of our own and stay out of trouble. You already know about our feelings toward bettering relations with the siren people, but that doesn't mean we ever expected one in our home. It is a big risk to allow you to stay here."

I nod. "I know. And I will help where I can, I promise."

"It would be best if you stay out of sight and keep quiet. Of course, I'll have to find you some new clothing. We will tell our neighbors you are a cousin visiting from the other end of the island."

"How can I help?"

"Assist my wife around the home," Reo says. "I know it isn't much, but she could use the extra pair of hands. You can only fish if it doesn't draw attention. If it does, then I'll ask that you refrain."

"That sounds perfect."

I stand and follow Hanako as she gives me a tour of the humble home. Kyon's mistrusting eyes bore into me the entire time. I do my best to ignore him. The home is smaller than anything in which my people reside. Technically, it's nothing but a shack. But in her eyes, it's a palace. She beams with pride as she shows me what she calls "the bathroom" and single bedroom that are attached to the room they first brought me into. It's obvious the main room is where most of the living is done, and that the bed I've been resting on is where Kyon

125

sleeps when he's home from working on the boats. There probably isn't going to be much for me to do around here, but that will give me time to do what I'm really here for.

Despite the meager surroundings, I find myself admiring the way she's taken such care of her home. The floors are immaculately clean, the painted walls scrubbed and gleaming white. There are framed landscape paintings on the walls and hand-sewn curtains hanging in front of light-filled windows. She treats her possessions with respect, and I will do my best to offer the same respect to her.

This situation is working out perfectly for me, even if I still wrestle with guilt about it all. I'll have to use this family to get ahead, but in the meantime I can help them get some extra food on their dinner plates. It's the least I can do. In any free time I have, I'll search for information about the stolen siren stone. This dock village may be overcrowded, poor, and sad, but it's probably filled with secrets that can help me. Once I have a better idea of how to get the stone back to the mages, I'll leave this family just the way I found them.

No harm done.

If that's true, if I'm really not going to hurt them, then why do I feel like I'm exactly the kind of monster Kyon believes me to be?

FIFTEEN

JUST BECAUSE I'VE STUDIED LAND-DWELLER LIFE DOESN'T mean I actually know what I'm doing up here. I learn that lesson really quick, starting with dinner.

"Is something wrong?" Hanako asks.

I glance up from the cut of fish and some kind of fluffy substance on my plate, not sure how to answer her. This entire experience is beyond surreal. After talking for a while longer and getting changed out of my bodysuit into some of Hanako's unfamiliar human clothing, we sat down to share a meal together. We're elbow to elbow around this table and I'm sure I'm about to make a mistake at any moment, risking my favor with them.

"Do you know how to use those?" Hanako presses, pointing to the two chopsticks in my right hand. I fumble with them, trying not to drop one.

"She probably doesn't even know what they are," Kyon says in a flat tone. He's seated right next to me, the heat of his body sharp against my skin. It's unnerving.

I smack my lips, sending him an exasperated look. "I know what chopsticks are, thank you very much," I reply back. "I'm not uncivilized."

"And yet," he leans forward across the tiny space between us, "you don't know how to use them."

Heat prickles in my cheeks and I drop his challenging gaze to ponder over my plate. It's not my fault they use sticks to eat up here. Below the surface, we eat all our meals with our hands. And teeth, of course. And we certainly don't sit down for long, if at all.

"It's easy." Reo smiles. "I can teach you, if you'd like. Or if you'd rather eat with your hands…" his voice trails off as he places his own set of sticks with a neat clank on the edge of his plate. He digs into the white mushy stuff first, pinching a big lump between two knobby fingers and plopping it into his mouth. He winks and warmth spreads from my chest and outward. He's a good man.

"I'll join you," Hanako says with a teasing tone and digs into her fish.

Feeling more at ease, I decide to give it a try. I go for the fish first, since I still have no clue what the white substance could be and I'm not going to start with the unknown. The fish feels different under my fingers, not slick and oily, but dry and crumbly. I bring it into my mouth and recoil at the taste. It's absolutely disgusting. Something is wrong with it; I have no doubt. Is it spoiled? Tears spring to my eyes as

128

I chew the flaky fish and swallow the lump of horrible mangled flesh.

Three pairs of expectant eyes watch me, waiting for my reply. "Mmmm," I fake, "it's... so great."

Hanako knows something is off because she raises two thin eyebrows so high into her forehead that it makes all her wrinkles smooth out. Kyon glares, lip curling. And Reo glances from his wife, to me, and then back to his wife again. Nerves pour over me, hot and fast. I shouldn't have dishonored myself. I'm their guest and this is her home cooked meal. How could I have been so rude as to grimace over her fish? But she only laughs, her voice low and rolling and releasing all the bound tension.

"It's okay, sweetie," she says, "just tell me what's wrong so I can fix it."

I let out a sigh. "It's the fish. Why is it dead?"

"What do you mean?" Kyon scoffs. "It's cooked."

"You prefer sushi?" Reo asks, eyes sparkling.

"Sushi?" I shrug my shoulders, not knowing what a sushi is.

Light flickers in Hanako's expression and she grins with satisfaction. "Oh, I get it now. You eat raw because you're used to eating your fish under the water." Reo claps his hands and Kyon growls in disgust.

I shrug again, not getting what is so exciting or strange or wrong about any of this. Of course I eat fish under the water. I'm a siren. These people already know that about me. Why are they acting so surprised?

"I cook most of our fish," Hanako says. She points to the small

129

kitchen at my back. "On our stove."

I nod, playing along, as if I have the faintest idea what a stove is. All the faces of my tutors back home flash before my mind and I think if I could talk to them now I would reprimand them for doing such a terrible job with my education. I should know what a stove is, clearly! And sushi!

Hanako stands, shuffling to the corner of the kitchen. She opens some kind of white rounded cupboard. Another thing I should probably know about. "This one is pretty fresh," she says, pulling out something wrapped in waxy paper. "We just purchased it from the market this morning and I'm sure it was caught just yesterday." She unwraps the paper to reveal a silver fish, whole and shiny and dead. "It's not swimming," she laughs, "but it's cold and uncooked. It should taste close to what you're used to."

"Don't give her that," Kyon snaps. "That's our food. We need it!"

"Hush, Kyon," she snaps right back. "Mind your manners before I mind them for you."

My eyes grow wide at their exchange. Hanako seems unfazed by me and places the silver fish on my plate. The smell wafts into my nostrils, something I'm not used to either. But this smell, it doesn't make my stomach turn over in disgust. Rather, it creates quite the opposite effect. I squeeze my hands into fists. Maybe Kyon is right, maybe I shouldn't eat their food. They do need it more than I do. I can get myself a fish without much effort.

"Go ahead," she urges, scooting the plate even closer and then

130

returning to her seat. "Eat it because I want you to. Don't listen to my son."

I lean over the fish, inadvertently licking my lips. Maybe I could eat it, make Hanako happy. Just this once.

"She's just going to eat it whole, isn't she?" Kyon groans.

His father shushes him and I continue to stare at the fish. I need to snap it up and devour it before Hanako changes her mind. This is my opportunity to feed my stomach before I have to continue on my journey. My journey *on land*. And given the present circumstances, this is a generous gift she's offered. It would be unkind to turn it down.

"Thank you." I pick up the fish and carefully place the edge into my mouth. The familiar taste spreads over my tongue as I break off a fleshy bite and chew. She's right. It's not exactly the same as a live fish, but it's close enough. I take another, much bigger, bite. Still good. Hunger licks at my stomach and my mouth waters. I need more. I need it all. Without much thought, I finish the rest of the fish off within seconds, then I look up to find startled eyes and dropped jaws.

"What did I do wrong?"

"Wow." Reo smiles wide. "That was impressive."

Kyon frowns and Hanako beams. Did I eat it too fast? I must have. My cheeks flame but I ignore that and point to the white stuff on the plate. "What's that?"

"It's rice," Kyon sneers. "Something tells me you won't like it."

I soon run into more experiences that I'm terribly unprepared to handle. The strangest of all is learning how to use the little bathroom. Every time I think of how Hanako had to walk me through the steps of relieving myself in the toilet, I want to duck my head and never make eye contact with the woman again. We go about it a different way at home, and in my opinion, it's a much more sanitary method.

That night, I sleep fitfully and wake to a new day and a too-bright sun. It's another stark reminder that I am out of my element up here. I need to fit in so that I can venture out in search of the siren stone. After getting changed into another set of Hanako's clothes, I go through the motions of assisting her around the home.

I skip breakfast but help her wash the dishes. She teaches me how to use soap and towels. Both dry my hands and the soap stinks of something I don't even have words to describe. My eyes itch after using it.

"I'm heading out," Kyon says, kissing his mother on the cheek.

I watch them at the door, a pang of homesickness blossoming in my chest. His dark eyes linger on me, running up and down my body, taking me in slowly. He doesn't say anything, just stares at me for so long that I gulp and feel exposed. Heat rises on the back of my neck and my heart speeds.

Kyon breaks the moment and pushes his way through the door. It slams shut behind him, the little room rattling. I deflate against the counter's edge. What was that?

"He may not seem it now, but I promise, he's a good boy," Hanako says, turning back to me. "He's always been such a good boy, that Kyon." Her watery eyes hold my gaze. "Thank you."

"For what?" My eyebrows draw together and I brush my hands on the towel.

Her lips thin and she steps closer. "For letting him live."

Words choke on my throat and all I can do is nod. It would have been so simple to let him float down into the depths that day. And yet, I didn't. And somehow, I'm here now. This has to be the prophecy at work. It has to be something other than coincidence.

"My son doesn't have steady employment," she continues, drawing me from my thoughts. "He works on the different fishing boats. Every day he searches for more work and sometimes he ends up on whatever boat will take him. And sometimes, he comes back early and we don't eat."

My breath tumbles from my mouth and again, I don't have words. They just ... don't eat?

"Sometimes he goes on longer ventures," she continues. "We miss him and we worry, but it usually pays well so he does it willingly. Most days, he's home by dinner."

I hold my tongue about the pirating, knowing sometimes Kyon is doing more than just fishing out there. Who am I to judge? I haven't exactly been honest with Hanako, either.

I smile, nod again, and return to the dishes.

We spend the rest of the morning cleaning and preparing the rest of food that Kyon brought back from the market yesterday. And Reo, poor Reo, it turns out he spends most of his life in bed. He's suffering from a crippling medical condition of which I know nothing about. How would I? Sirens don't get sick. But I can tell that even though the man puts on a winning smile and fights through the pain, he's losing the battle. It's no wonder he doesn't work. He can't. What would this family do without Kyon? He is the dutiful son, providing for his parents. If I were in his position, I might resort to stealing, too. I'm so grateful that I didn't kill him the day we first met.

In the late afternoon, someone knocks on the door. I don't see who it is. Reo is there, standing on wobbly legs. He joins whoever's at the door, closing it behind them as they go.

"He's going for his walk," Hanako says over the clothing we're cleaning. "It's the only thing he can do to keep from being completely bedridden. You know, it was on his walk yesterday that he and Kyon found you."

I smile at that. It's settled. They *were* meant to find me, there's no other explanation. So much about this journey has been led by the prophecy and something much better than myself. I know that without a shadow of doubt now.

"We have a few neighborhood friends who take him," Hanako continues. "Sometimes I go with him. Sometimes Kyon does."

"Could I go?" I ask excitedly. It would be the perfect excuse to see how well I could blend in with the people outside. Plus, I could start to formulate a plan for finding the siren stone. It has to be at the palace, there's no other place that makes sense. But getting there is going to take some special planning. I need to get started.

"Maybe tomorrow," Hanako says in a tone that might as well be a "no". I sink down into the couch and hold back my tongue. This family has taken me in, they've been kind and generous. I need to be patient with them, too. I'll give it one more day here, and then take everything I've learned from them and move on.

Beneath me, beneath the floor, I can feel the pull of my ocean. Before I go anywhere, I'll need to let her restore me. I'm a siren out of water and I'm starting to feel it in my bones and in my blood and my skin and lungs. I need to get that stone so I can return to my home. I want nothing more than to feel like myself again. Looking around now, that hardly seems possible.

SIXTEEN

I PEER OUT THE SMALL, RECTANGULAR WINDOW POSITIONED high above the kitchen sink. My fingers grip the cracked wood seal, my nose inches from the warped glass. This is a view I haven't tried yet and after hours of tossing and turning in the lumpy bed, I had to take a look. Kneeling on the counter and straining my neck, I pray to catch a glimpse of the ocean. That's all I need. Somehow I believe that one look will steady my pounding heart and calm the homesick ache ripping through my body. If I can just see it, then I'll know what to do. It will give me my answers as it always has.

But there's no ocean.

There's only the full moon hanging high in a black sky, reflecting off the metal roof of the nearby home. I sigh, twist back around, and silently drop to the floor. It's steady and firm and completely unsettling. I had thought that the buoys under the decks would have bounced on the waves, even if slightly. Anything to make this city built on interlocking decks feel more like my ocean home would have been nice. The decks are anchored down into the ocean floor far better than I'd imagined. Even though I know the water's surface is but three feet below, even though I can hear the gentle lapping of waves, I don't feel close.

I stare into the darkness, taking in the room. Across it is a small metal kitchen table pushed against one wall where we've eaten our meals over the last two days. It's painted a deep green with three matching chairs tucked underneath. Hanako always keeps placemats set with a glass of fake lotus flowers in the center. I didn't know what any of those things were when I first was introduced, much like a lot of the items in the home, but she's been a willing teacher. On my other side is the front door and another window, both locked for the night. Long white curtains are drawn over the window, but they're thin enough to see if a shadow passes by outside. All day, those shadowed figures come and go. I long to meet the people they belong to, to figure out what I'm up against.

On the other side of the room are the two closed doors, one leading to the bedroom and the other leading to the bathroom. My eyes trail to the bed I've been using. It folds out from the couch and takes up the remaining space. The blue quilt draped over the top of it is rumpled from my failed attempts at sleep.

It's Kyon's bed. It even smells like him, like some foreign scent I've never known in my ocean home. It's nice, addiction-worthy, and completely unsettling. He's been sleeping on the floor of his parent's room the last two nights that I've been here. This is night three. I think it must bother him to lose any private space he had before I came here, but he doesn't complain. The boy barely even looks at me anymore, and he certainly doesn't talk to me, or even about me. He left in anger after my first night here, and he returned without saying another word on the subject of my presence.

Maybe I shouldn't think of him as a boy.

He's man enough to take care of his parents. When I inquired about his age, Hanako gave me a curious look before answering that he's eighteen. Same as me. Well, almost. My birthday isn't for a few more weeks. Does he resent having to take care of his parents at such a young age? If anyone understands the heavy responsibility, it's me. But I don't tell him that. I don't tell him anything.

Hanako is an excellent caretaker and homemaker, taking pride in making sure the food not only tastes great, but that it lasts. They eat a lot of the white fluffy substance, rice. I've tried it, trying to be polite. I don't care for something so devoid of flavor. And they still eat most of their fish cooked, leaving an extra serving raw for me. I don't know anything when it comes to tending a human home. I've helped her where I can. It's been two long days of misery, being trapped here. They're kind people, but I can't go on like this.

Not to mention, they still haven't allowed me to go fishing. They don't think it's safe for me to go out and it's killing me, being away from the water like this. I won't be able to continue hiding out for another day. Even if I wanted to, I can't handle the emotions tearing me up. I need to get back in the water. I need it like they need air. Besides, I must continue my mission. I'm not meant to be cooped up. I'm dying to move, to do something, anything. I'm used to having a whole ocean as my home; these four walls will suffocate me before long.

I lean my head back against the lower kitchen cabinets and let out a long moan. It's time to consider leaving this family. I can't do this anymore. I just can't. I blink into the darkness. Everything looks so different at night. Shadows take on new forms and entire pieces of furniture go missing. In the ocean my eyes adjust perfectly to any level of light. But up here above the water? It's an entirely different story. My eyes aren't special anymore. My siren song is useless without the water to ignite the magic. In this place, as loving as these people are to me, I'm still nothing. I'm nobody but a lost girl, a liar, and a wayward princess with no idea what she's doing.

I have to get out.

I jump up, determination pouring through my body. My night clothes stick to my sweaty skin as I lightly move about the room. My black water suit is tucked away under the bed but I don't dare wear it among humans. The clothing Hanako gave me is a little off, and I'm still not used to it. The faded denim pants are scratchy and too tight. I slip out of the cotton shorts and shimmy into the pants anyway. I know they're the smarter choice since Hanako insisted that these are common with the islanders. I keep on the dark blue sleep shirt because it's soft and not too remarkable one way or the other.

Hopefully these human clothes will help me fit in outside of these stifling walls.

One thing left to do. I grab a short stubby knife from a kitchen drawer and tuck it into my back pocket. It's not much, it's certainly no spear, but it's better than nothing. I brush my hands through my long hair, deciding to leave it loose around my face. I might need the extra cover. I glare at the shoes in the corner disdainfully. I should probably put some on, but Hanako's extra pair didn't fit well and I can't imagine trying to lumber about in the heavy things. And anyway, I won't take anything more from this family than is absolutely necessary. They've been too kind. They don't deserve this.

Taking one last look around the darkened room, I pad softly to the door, carefully unlatch the metal bolt, and slip out into the silent night. It's cooler out here. It's freeing. I can't help but smile and breath it in.

The moonlight guides me as I stroll down the dock. I know I'm meant to go toward the land, the island is my destination, with its palace perched on top. There's a call within me that's far stronger than reasonable thought. It pulls me in the opposite direction. Out toward the sea.

I need to get a look at her horizon. One look at the endless ocean, at the freedom still waiting for me, and I'll be able to settle my heart. I won't get in. I won't do anything foolish. I'll just take her in, let her calm me, and then I'll rush back through the dock city and make it to the island by morning. From there I'll be able to find the stone. Somehow.

I know it's a stupid plan even as I think it, but that rational part of me is falling further and further into oblivion as I move down the worn deck. The houses are all similar. Small, scantily built metal homes with extra wood and siding added in seemingly random places. Fortification, I suppose. They're each built right up next to the neighbor, as if to hold each other up. If one were to be knocked down, would the rest tumble after?

I keep to the shadows and move quickly. Several times I meet lines of water between decks that I know are filled with fishing line and traps, anything that might land a meal for a hungry family. I want to touch the water. To taste it. But it's dangerous. And even though it's salt, even though it's mine, it's still not the same. There is *still* no horizon.

I need the horizon. It's the only thing that will work.

The houses begin to space further apart, and that's when I catch the first glorious glimpse of flashing water, of that steady line where the sky kisses his sea.

I run.

All my thoughts release except for one. And it's stronger than anything I've ever known. Stronger than family. Stronger than prophecy. Or curse. Or duty.

This is blood. This is instinct. Magic. At least, it's whatever is left of my magic. And it's telling me one thing: get in the water.

Something catches my ankle, and I stumble, falling flat on my face. Pain burns at my knees and chin but I don't bother to check what it was that tripped me, don't even care when a ruckus of metal

141

clattering echoes through the night. None of that matters. I jump back up and keep running.

And then she's there. My ocean. My home. The second mother I didn't even realize I had. I need her embrace.

I sprint further, feet pounding against the weathered deck, an echo of the whooshing in my ears. Bits of salt and mud stick to the bottoms of my feet. The musky odor of human life gives way to the familiar. A caressing wind blows through my hair. A peaceful smile spreads over my face, smoothing it out for the first time in days.

I'm almost there.

A body slams me to the ground. I cry out, losing the last breath in my lungs. Raw panic hooks on tight, and I jerk back, ready to fight my assailant. He's much bigger than me, pinning my arms down behind me.

"Get off me!" I hiss the moment my breath returns. Sharp fear is etched in my voice, a reminder of the trouble I've put myself into tonight.

"Shh," he hisses back. "It's Kyon."

Anger burns through me and I wrench back, trying to slam my head into his face.

"Will you cut it out?" he growls. "I'm trying to help you! You were about to jump in!"

"So?" I counter, rage still rolling.

"So? It's booby-trapped. You go in there and you're as good as dead."

The thought sobers me, icy calm that extinguishes the fire. I take a deep breath. "Please let me go. I promise not to jump in."

Slowly, he rolls off of me. But he's close as I sit up. I run a hand though my hair and meet his dark gaze, barely making out any of his features, except for the sharp angles lit by the moon. I blink a few times, focusing in on what little I can.

"You followed me?"

His face is still for a moment and then he sighs heavily. "You aren't as inconspicuous as you think you are. Yes, I followed you. I don't trust you. Remember?"

I nod, licking my lips and closing my eyes for a minute. It's a good thing he followed me. If he's right about the traps, I could have been killed.

"Not to mention, you should be grateful it's me who found you and not someone else. People aren't accepting of your kind and there's a rumor going around that a siren was trying to stow away on a ship a few days ago." My eyes pop open. "Why do you think my parents have been so careful to keep you inside? The siren attacked a man and *almost* killed him. You wouldn't have anything to do with that, would you?"

So he's alive? Relieved, I bite my lip but don't answer.

"That's what I thought. Damn, Mom and Dad are too kind for their own good."

"They said there are others here who feel the way about my kind," I hiss.

A weighted pause fills the space between us with heavy air as I wait for his reply. "Let me just put it this way, Senra. There aren't many people like my parents. You got extremely lucky when Dad found you."

I suck in a deep breath, steadying my thoughts. He's right. And it's another reason I know there's so much more at work here than just myself. I need to be grateful. I send a silent prayer up toward the stars twinkling above. *I am grateful.*

"Thank you, Kyon." I'm still looking to the sky when I point to the round moon. "It's hard to be away from my home. The last few nights I handled it, but tonight, with the moon full, I guess I just couldn't stay away." My voice catches. I hate that I'm so vulnerable, a spiked puffer fish, cut open for him to see all my fleshy soft insides. Shame hardens in my throat and I swallow it down, continuing to speak the truth. "I don't know what to do. I don't know how to be a normal human. And I can't go home."

Not yet.

He sighs again. This time, it's not annoyed. It's resigned. "Come on." He stands and reaches out his hand. "I know a place where you can swim in peace. But we need to be quick about it. I don't want anyone seeing you."

We both glance around, suddenly aware of how exposed we are out here.

"Don't make me regret this," he mutters, then he takes off, running back the way we came, tugging me after him. His hand is warm and solid and unnerving. Having to trust him creates a deeper vulnerability than before. I know he doesn't like me. I see the way he looks at me, the distrust that's always there in his hooded gaze. Am

I really going to let him lead me somewhere? Can I trust him to help me? This would be the perfect opportunity for him to turn me in to the authorities.

And yet, I follow. I'm not sure I have a choice. I let him lead me because it feels like being led by something bigger than just him or I.

So I go.

And with Kyon as my guide, with his hand holding mine, my prickling fear strangely begins to melt away. But it does little to replace the need to jump into the water, to be welcomed home. That desire speeds my heart and overwhelms my mixed-up emotions, growing infinitely stronger with each running step.

SEVENTEEN

"WE'RE ALMOST THERE," KYON WHISPERS. HIS VOICE IS A low timbre that brushes against my ear and makes me shiver. I'm again struck with the questions born from my fear. Why is he being so nice to me? This man is supposed to hate me. Could all of this be an elaborate trap? I keep my eyes wide and gaze searching, just in case.

"We need to keep quiet," he continues. "We don't have much time before people are going to start waking up. Maybe an hour or two."

I nod, taking in his tall form, his broad shoulders and the way his clothes fit tightly against his strong body. My muscles grow tense as we turn another corner. I'm dying to question Kyon, but my need to be in the water outweighs even that, so I go along with him, following this person who could be leading me to my death.

In front of us is a long stretch of dock. Gone are the familiar shanty homes of wood and metal. Instead, we're standing in the middle of what appears to be a long line of vendor booths. It reminds me of the market back home where sirens come from all over the city to barter over clothing, goods, and services. I smile just thinking of the lively place. I often went to admire the jewelry, the pearl items being my favorites. These booths are all locked up tight for the night. I try to imagine how this place will look in the light of day. I see the people rushing about, in a hurry to find exactly what they're looking for. I smell both fresh and cooked fish. And I hear the people as they call to each other over the crowd. Each vendor is eager to empty their carts, unafraid to holler about the merits of their items. I wonder if they have jewelry here too, and if so, what it would look like. Would it shine as ours does? Do land-dwellers covet pearls as my people do?

We hurry through the market. The mountainside looms up ahead. I'm much closer than I've ever gotten before, and I eye the rocky top—on the other side is the palace. And the stone.

"Are we going up there?" I ask, pointing. Anticipation zaps through my blood at the idea. This could be my chance.

"Not even close," Kyon replies gruffly. "There are a lot of restricted areas on the island and the palace is by far the most off limits to us. However, that doesn't mean there aren't public zones here. There's the evacuation centers, plus a few beaches and coves open for swimming. That's where we're headed now."

I want to ask about the evacuation centers but stop myself, the questions bitter on my tongue. No need to remind Kyon of why he should hate me. The evacuations must be for when the docks aren't safe, like when a dragon shows up, or a siren, or a bad storm.

I stare out into the darkness, trying to figure out this place. Everything is so different from my kingdom. We may look similar to these people, but that's where it ends. Our cities have room to spread out. This entire place is overrun with too many people, probably a hundred thousand packed into four or five square miles. No wonder this entire place carries an undercurrent of body odor. Being a siren, all our senses are enhanced under the water, except for smell, which is blocked by the water. I've decided it's not a hindrance not to smell. It would be an advantage up here. But then I catch another hint of the unknown spicy aroma coming off Kyon and I question myself.

My eyes flick across the homes on the mountainside. Forged from stone, they look nicer than the ones on the docks, but they're still small and stitched close together. The best of these homes don't compare to the worst of ours. And even in the darkness, I can tell the land is pretty barren. The people must really struggle to survive in such wicked conditions. Our cities are beautiful, abundant, and lush. These people are starving, fighting for every meal, while all we have to do is sing and food comes to us.

It's no wonder the humans hate us.

"Does anything grow in the soil here?" I ask.

Kyon stops to look at me, his eyes hidden in the shadows, but I hear it when he clicks his tongue. "A bit. Not enough. The land has been tarnished for a century. Nobody has enough to eat, if that's what you're asking." He turns away at that last part. Is it because he blames the sirens for this, too?

We make it onto the rocky shore and follow a winding footpath along the edge. A light breeze catches my hair and the odor changes, letting way to dirty earth and salty ocean. We pass a few armed guards and keep our heads down. The guards don't seem to care about us either way. They stand, still as statues, large black guns in their arms. It's the first time I've ever seen a gun, and it sends a ping of fear running down my spine. I know what it is and I know what it can do to me, to anyone. But maybe it's like Kyon said before: the public areas are safe for trespassers, no matter the time of night.

Safe...

That word tumbles around inside my mind like a stone in need of polishing. Is anything *really* safe for me here? In my core I've allowed myself to relax into the feeling of safety. I must remember that it's a façade. I'm not safe with Kyon. I'm not even safe with his parents. Reo and Hanako have shown me nothing but kindness and I have every reason to trust them, except for the biggest reason of all: I'm different. I'm certain that if the right person found out about me staying here, I'd be thrown in prison or worse.

I brush the thought away for the present moment.

The moon has moved further in the sky now, but it still dares me to make a break for water. My skin itches so badly I could scream. If I could crawl out of my body, I would. I would crawl right out and dive into the water and never resurface. The gentle swooshing of waves brushing up against the rocky land loosens the hot tears burning my eyes.

149

"I need to be in there. I need…" My voice cracks, a tear breaking loose and splashing down my cheek. Has a siren ever been away from water this long? It's not right. I can't do this.

"The swimming area is just right here." Kyon squeezes my hand tighter and pulls much harder than before, as if he can sense how strong my struggle has become. "Just hang on for one more minute."

A minute stretches into an eternity.

We push past a couple of scraggly trees, the only ones I've seen up close on the island so far. We stumble out onto a small stretch of pale sandy beach. A black ocean cove of water dances under the moon. Another tear falls.

I strain to break free of his grip. I must dive into that water.

"Let go," I hiss.

But Kyon's grip is far stronger than mine. Since my magic is useless above water, I don't have my added strength to break free of his prison.

"Hold on, Senra," he chastises. "We need a few rules before you get in."

I glare but face him, my dry lips pressed into a thin line and little bursts of breath pulsing from my lungs.

"You can't get your clothes wet, especially not the jeans. They'll be terrible to walk back home in and will take ages to dry," he says, moving in closer. He looks over my shoulder at the water and doesn't directly meet my gaze. "You're going to have to take them off."

My eyes widen, blood rushing to my cheeks. I sputter for a reply but can't get a word out. He wants me to get *naked*?

"It's not like that," he growls, snapping his gaze back to mine. The moon reflects off the water, lighting his face. "I'm not going to *look* at you, Senra. You can keep your underwear on for all I care. I still know what you are, in case you forgot, and believe me, I'm not interested in *that*. I'm only trying to keep you from getting questioned by the guards. Nobody swims in jeans."

My breath is heavy, my blood tingling my cheeks. I bite my lip and look away.

"Okay, fine," I agree reluctantly. Maybe he has a valid point.

"Second rule, no singing and absolutely no magic stuff. I don't want you drawing attention to me. That could get back to my parents and land them in a ton of trouble. You have to promise me you're just swimming and nothing else, okay?"

I'm not sure this is a rule I can agree to, let alone a promise I can make. But I nod because I'd do just about anything right now to get into that water.

There's a long pause before he adds the next part, "And the third and final rule is that you owe me a favor."

I raise an eyebrow, trying to make out the intricacies of his expression in the darkness. He's pretty unreadable in full light, let alone with only the moon to shine a light on what he could be thinking.

"What kind of favor?" I ask slowly, suspicion in every word.

He shakes his head. "I don't know yet. I'll tell you when I do."

I grit my teeth, wanting nothing more than to punch him square in the nose for this. He's taking advantage, isn't he? I can't be making promises and agreeing to mysterious favors. I twist to glance at the ocean again, feeling her call to me. Her pull is stronger than anything I've ever felt before. It's like a rope squeezing my chest the longer I stand here. Maybe he's helping me and maybe I should be thankful. I am *here*, aren't I? This cove looks safe.

Kyon's grip tightens on my slender wrist, nearly bruising me. I tug but he doesn't relax. I think of the knife in my back pocket. I could use my free hand to kill him right now, slit his throat and be done with his stupid rules. But I can't. I'm not the monster he thinks I am. At least, I don't want to be. The very thought of hurting Kyon makes my stomach twist into a knot.

"Okay fine," I huff. "I agree to your rules. Now please, release me."

"Be my guest. You've got thirty minutes." He drops my wrist and points. "Be careful of the perimeters. You'll see the netting in the water once you're out there. If you go beyond the safety of the swimming area and get caught, you're on your own."

I'm already running toward the water, stripping off the layers of heavy clothing as I go. I toss the blue shirt carelessly to one side. It drifts on the wind before falling to the sand. I slide my legs from the clunky pants so fast I nearly topple over. Once free, I leave them in a crumpled pile. Steps from the water, I discard the measly human undergarments Hanako insisted I wear, not caring a bit for where they land.

Nor do I care if Kyon actually turned away, though I'm assuming he kept his word on that. I should care, but I've lost all sense of propriety. It happened the second he let go of my wrist. Somewhere inside there's got to be a bubble of shame, knowing that to strip naked in front of a man who's not my husband is not the princess my parents raised me to be. Even though we're sirens, we're still a modest people; honor runs deep. Magicking our clothing and always keeping our private bits covered has been the custom for generations.

I no longer care about any of that.

I dive into the welcoming foam, relishing in the cold water as it surrounds my naked body. I'm bare to the darkness of that same wonderful water and for the first time in days I can breathe. For the first time in days I'm not drenched in hot sweat and my skin isn't as dry as the scales of fish left to rot in the sun. I'm free. My limbs fire up with the movement of swimming. My entire being sparks to life, and I can't imagine ever wanting to be anything but a siren.

Everything feels right again.

This is where I'm meant to be.

I swim as close to the nets as I dare and then sit on the ocean floor, lying back on the fine sand, staring up at the ocean surface nearly fifteen feet above. The moon is still flashing down at me, but it's no longer a dare. It's a welcome home.

I've been weak. I've been fearful and complacent, and I've lost my nerve to the tides of these humans' lives. That is no more. I'll do anything in my power to make sure my people never ever lose this magic.

Breaking one of Kyon's rules, I call out to my dragon. I'm not sure if the telepathy is strong enough but I have to try. Long disappeared and the humans think they're safe again. I know he's close. I can feel his presence the way I feel the ocean. He's waiting for me.

Long, it's Princess Senra. Stay close to the island. I'm here and I'm safe. I'll be needing your help soon. I'll call for you when it's time to come get me.

After a few seconds, a keening rumble vibrates through the water. It's high pitched, animalistic, and as primal as the ancient folklore from which he hails. I'm sure it's Long calling back to me. He's received the message. He's ready.

I take a final breath, letting the water fill my lungs and restore me, and then I push off the sandy bottom. On my way to the shore, I spot one long flash of wiggling silver. A fish.

No singing, I promised, and that really could get me into trouble.

So I don't sing, but I don't need song to capture the fish. I've had a lifetime of practice. I dart toward it and snap its squirmy body in my fist. This will be my gift to Kyon's family before I leave them today. I must leave them.

I pop my head out of the water, scanning the beach for Kyon. I'd like privacy to dry off and change back into those clothes.

I spot him standing under the trees, leaning against the trunk of the taller of the two. My eyes squint and my ears prick. Kyon's low voice rolls over the landscape, a whisper and then a hearty laugh. He's talking to someone.

We're not alone.

EIGHTEEN

SHOULD I DROP BACK UNDER THE SAFETY OF WATER? CALL out to Kyon? Every choice feels like the wrong one, like the difference between life and death. I don't know what to do! The seconds race by as I consider my options. Hiding in the water might make me more suspicious but so might announcing myself. I inch back down, instinct pulling at my racing heart.

"Are you almost finished?" Kyon calls out. His voice is conversational and calm, like how he speaks to his parents, but certainly not how he speaks to me.

I freeze, my head barely above the water's surface. I feel so much better than I did twenty minutes ago. Renewed. Even with the adrenaline swimming through my body at this newest situation. To answer Kyon's question, no, I'm not ready to face whatever is next and whoever he's talking to. My toes dig into the sand.

"Yes," I call back. My voice cracks, and I clear my throat. I guess I'm getting out, after all. The thought sends a pang of regret through me, and I sigh.

The person to whom Kyon is speaking turns to face me. I suddenly feel barer than ever. Except for my head, I'm hidden under the black water, thankfully, so it's not like he can see much of me. It's still too dark to make out the new person's features but my siren magic kicks in, drawing the scene into perfect clarity. The man has wide shoulders and floppy black hair. The rumble of his voice is youthful and happy. "Who's that?" he asks, one corner of his mouth pulling into a conspiratorial smile. "You got a new girl you haven't told me about, Kyon?"

A new girl? I squeeze my hands tighter over my chest.

"That's my cousin, you idiot," Kyon replies, quieter this time. "Now turn around so she can get out and get dressed without you ogling her."

The two forms shift to face the other way, and I tentatively step from the water. The breeze is cold against my skin, raising little bumps across my exposed flesh. I don't mind. Actually, I love it. The cold is my preference. I hate this muggy, overcrowded island, even if I have seen little of it. It's way too hot up here, too crowded, too everything that isn't *me*.

"You don't have a cousin," the companion responds, his voice challenging but still a bit playful.

"You don't know everything about me, Asahi," Kyon snaps in a way that doesn't sound like anger. "I *do* have a cousin. She's from the other side of the island. She's staying with us for a while, while her dad is out at sea."

Asahi doesn't react to Kyon's sharpness the way I'd expect, the way I would. Instead, he chuckles heartily and doesn't press the issue.

I ditch the fish still squirming in my right hand and scan the beach, finding my clothing folded and stacked nicely only a few strides from the shoreline. My cheeks burn to think that Kyon took care of these for me while I was busy uniting with my ocean. The image of him flashes through my mind, picking up each piece, shaking the sand away, folding them... Even the two undergarments Hanako insisted I wear are here, draped on top of the pile. We don't layer our clothes like this underwater but I know I must wear them, know they've been closest to my most intimate parts, and am embarrassed that Kyon has touched them.

Why does it matter? It doesn't. I'm leaving Kyon and his family anyway. I grit my teeth and get dressed, caring very little that I'm dripping wet and the clothing is sticking to my skin. Once finished, I run my fingers through my long tangled hair as I stride up the beach to the two men whose backs are still to me.

"All right, I'm done," I say, but add nothing else. I don't want to mess this up and say the wrong thing. My heart pounds hard against my ribcage as they turn to face me. I'm struck with the thought that Asahi will instantly recognize me to be a siren and kill me on the spot.

He doesn't.

"Senra, this is my friend, Asahi," Kyon says, his voice is smooth as the inside of a clam shell. I catch the hardness in his eyes and I know it's a ruse. He's worried. He's begging me to play along with those pleading eyes.

I know the feeling.

Asahi looks me up and down, a wicked grin forming on his full mouth. He's shorter than Kyon and quite stocky. His defined muscles pop as he folds his arms over his chest. There's a glint to his eyes hinting of mischief and lightheartedness. Something about him makes me want to relax, to trust that he's a good person. But I have to be smart. Staying on edge could mean staying alive.

"Hello, Senra." He tilts his head and studies me with curious brown eyes. "I didn't know Kyon had a cousin."

I nod once, meeting his sparkling eyes with a challenge. "Yes, he does."

"That's funny, because I've known Kyon all my life and never once has he mentioned you."

I shrug and raise an eyebrow. "So he's supposed to tell you every single thing, is he?"

There's a pause, and then Asahi laughs, breaking the tension. He winks at me and pats Kyon on the back. "How long is she staying with you? I like this girl. You've been holding out on me, man." He grins back at me. "Do you have a boyfriend?"

Blood rushes to my cheeks. To speak so casually, to be so forward, it's unheard of back home. My mouth drops. I don't know what to say.

"Shut up, Asa, she's off-limits."

Asahi only laughs again as the three of us turn and walk toward the docks again. The air has changed, and the sun will be peaking above the horizon soon. I watch the dock city, wishing I could see past the masses of homes to the actual ocean. I'm sure the ones up on the mountain have that luxury.

"I'm glad I ran into you," Asahi says, patting Kyon on the back. "I have news. Big news, man." He glances at me. "But I guess it'll have to wait."

"Aren't you on your way to work or something?" Kyon replies, unfazed.

Asahi grins. "I am. But that's just it. Something happened at work yesterday. I have the best secret ever."

Kyon shakes his head. "You're an idiot, Asa. How they even let you into that place is beyond me."

"You and I both know they love me."

"They love your uncle, actually. This job of yours is called nepotism, in case you don't know the correct term for it. Say it with me, nep-ot-is-m."

I laugh. I've never seen this side of Kyon, this light-hearted teasing. But that's not what matters. What matters is that Asahi mentioned a secret. I peek over at him, getting a better look now that the sun is beginning to rise. He's about our age, late teens if I had to guess. Unlike Kyon, his hair is combed perfectly to the side and he's wearing nicer clothes than what I've seen of Kyon's family: black slacks and a white button down shirt with shiny shoes and a red tie. Based on the old texts I studied with my tutors, the ones preserved through magic, this is the style of dress I guessed *all* land-dwellers would have looked like today. I can see now how wrong I was.

"Where do you work?" I ask the well-dressed young man, curiosity getting the best of me.

Asahi shoots me a charming smile, eyes running from my lips, to my body, then back up to my eyes. It takes everything in me not to smack him for that, but I feign innocence, blinking through my thick lashes. His attraction toward me is rather obvious. It might be wise to use it to my advantage.

"I work in the palace," he says, waggling his eyebrows. "The royal family *loves* me. I actually work with Emperor Hiroto himself. Impressive, huh?"

Impressive, indeed. I become hyper-aware of Asahi, my every sense attuned to him and what he might be able to do for me.

"Actually, he's an apprentice for his uncle." Kyon laughs at his friend without an ounce of bitterness or envy. "His uncle is the one who works for the royals. The family probably doesn't even know Asa's name."

I smile. I couldn't care less how close Asahi is to the family; the fact is, he has what I need. Access. *This is it.* He could be the answer I've been looking for. This big-mouthed kid with the light-hearted spirit, with swollen pride, and his newest interest set on me.

I smile openly, one meant to dazzle. "That is very impressive, Asahi."

I say his name slow, rounding out each letter like it's important. I don't let myself hold back or feel shame in practicing the years of feminine charm I learned as princess. "I wish I could do something like that. I'd love to be privy to the secrets of the royal family. It's wonderful to even think about." I look back at Asahi, tilting my head as I gaze at him. "You must be very special."

He blushes, his chest popping out as he nods. "Thank you," he chokes out, then he clears his throat and says it again. From over his shoulder, Kyon's glare on me smolders. I pay him no attention. Now is not the time to back down.

"Do you think I could get a tour?" I ask Asahi, glancing down at my bare feet then quickly back up at him. I hope he didn't notice that I'm not wearing any shoes. I can't imagine that's normal around here, but then again, I don't know for sure. "Sorry, I shouldn't have asked that. Kyon agreed to take me swimming because I couldn't sleep. We need to get back. I don't even have my shoes!"

My cheeks pink at the pathetic attempt to cover for my mistake.

Asahi laughs, playing right into it and placing a hand on my shoulder. His warm smile only grows. He's practically glowing when our eyes meet again. "I'll take you on a tour, sure. We won't be able to go everywhere but I can get you on the grounds. How about tonight? Is that too soon? We can make it a date."

I beam back at him, my lips parted just slightly as I smile. "That would be amazing," I finally say. "I'd love to go on a date and get to know you better, Asahi."

161

He quirks the side of his mouth, his deep brown eyes triumphant. "You can call me Asa, all my friends do."

Kyon throws up his hands. When neither of us pay him attention, he growls and stalks away, calling out over his shoulder, "Come on Senra, we have to get back before my parents wake up. Bye, *Asahi*, have a good day working for your uncle."

I giggle and wink at Asahi before chasing after Kyon.

"I'll pick you up at seven," Asahi calls out after me.

I whip around to give him another dazzling smile and a coy wave of my fingers. When I catch up to Kyon, he doesn't look at me, but I feel the anger radiating from him. It's obvious I've just used his friend to get a tour of the palace. He knows what I am, after all. He must know there's more to this than just a girl trying to get close to the royal palace for a measly tour.

"Kyon," I reach out, placing a hand on his shoulder. "I don't know what to say to thank you for taking me to the cove."

He spins on me, brushing my hand away and grimacing at my touch. Hatred burns in his dark gaze. It locks me in. He steps close, his face only inches away. "You're exploiting my best friend *and* my family."

I bristle. If he only knew the reasons why, maybe he would understand, maybe he wouldn't despise me so much. But I'm too scared to tell him the truth. I know the risks. They're too big to take. Too many lives are at stake. Feeling uncomfortable faced with this truth, I do the only thing I can think of and turn it back on him. "You're a pirate, Kyon. You steal and exploit. How is that different?"

He shakes his head. "I do what's necessary *to survive.*"

"Exactly."

He steps back and spins away, stalking down the deck. I hurry after him but we fall into silence. And it stays that way. We don't speak about it again.

For the rest of the day, as we go about our duties, him readying for another boating expedition that leaves in a few days' time, and me helping Hanako with more laundry and meals, Kyon and I don't exchange a single word. It hurts, knowing he hates me. I can't figure out why the pain is there or how to make it go away. His silence cuts so deep that it almost makes it possible to hate him back. Almost.

NINETEEN

"DON'T GO," KYON FINALLY BREAKS THE SILENCE BETWEEN US.

I'm standing by the window, waiting for Asahi. And I don't turn to Kyon, not yet. After fighting the inner demons and eventually lying to Hanako and Reo that this was only meant to be a fun date, an attempt to acclimate to human life, they offered their approval and hugs and well wishes. Hanako even helped me get ready into a form-fitting black dress that she insisted upon, and did my hair in the current style, pinning it to the top of my head in a wispy bun.

A date. I've never been on a date before. But *that's* not what this is really about. There's no use in pretending my lies are truth when it comes to Kyon. He sees right through me. I feel him standing at my back and I can no longer resist.

"You don't want me to see your friend?" I turn to smirk up at him. The smirk is my way of ignoring the real issue. That Kyon knows

I'm up to something. And that the two of us are alone in this family room, that there's an undeniable attraction between us, even if we both refuse to acknowledge it. The air grows heavy with the tension.

"That's not what this is about and you know it."

He steps even closer and I gulp.

"I have to go," I finally whisper, letting slip a tiny piece of the truth.

"Why?"

Everything inside me burns with the desire to tell him what's really going on. But I can't. "You wouldn't understand," I finally say. My voice trails off and the back of my neck prickles with the heat. What I really mean to say is that I don't know if I can trust him. And that I want to. So badly. And he must understand that's exactly what I'm thinking because his reply tilts me off my axis.

"I might understand," his voice is low and hushed. "If you gave me a chance, if you were honest with me, I might even be able to help you. It's called trust, Senra. You should try it."

My lips part and the air is knocked out of my lungs. Why are we talking about trust again? Everything keeps coming back to that concept, no matter how hard I try to avoid it. Ever since the Dalai Lama asked me to trust, it's been one thing after another. My journey has been wrought with twists and turns that can't be coincidence, but fate. The very fact that we're even standing here right now attests to that.

But there's still that nagging doubt. What changed for Kyon to be saying these things to me? He went from hating me to wanting to help me in the space of a single day? I bite my lip, unsure of what to think or believe. My fear demands I tread carefully. My heart kicks out in protest and all I can think about is how good Kyon smells, how close he stands, the way his eyes carry all the mysteries I'd die to discover, and that I do want to trust him. I really do.

Knock, knock! The two solid pounds on the door break us apart. I jump back, returning to the reality of the moment and of my life.

I am Senra, the Dark Ocean Princess. I can't lose focus.

I brush past Kyon to open the door for Asahi, to leave for my date and my destiny without another look back.

On the outside, I'm giddy, a wide smile spread across my face, a typical teenage girl on a date with a boy she's excited about. On the inside, however, I'm tormented with nerves. Kyon was right. I am using Asahi. In fact, I'm using everyone with whom I've come into contact since landing on this miserable island. His parents for their generosity, him for his knowledge, and now Asahi for his connections. But it's the price I have to pay, the price of duty, of choosing life for my people. I'll pay it and more in a heartbeat if it means my empire is safe and I can return home victorious.

And so as Asahi leads me up the stone steps to the palace, I slide my arm through his and grin up at him. "This is amazing, Asa," I sigh, making sure to use his nickname. "Thank you for bringing me here. I'll be honest, I'm surprised you're allowed to do this."

Asahi clears his throat, a flash of pride playing at his lips. "Well, truthfully, I'm pulling some strings to do this. And we won't be able to go near the royal family's living quarters, of course."

"Of course," I agree, though I'm a mix of disappointment and relief.

I take in the grounds, where despite the lack of vegetation on the island, gardeners have worked the soil here into bitter submission. There are manicured lawns and perfectly trimmed bonsai trees lining pathways of white stone. Still, granite rocks jut out in places, reminding me that this was the highest peak in Japan. *Was it the highest?* I'm struck with the thought that they might have more islands in the area. The entire country was made up of mountains before the seas rose. I should know the answer to this, it's my job to know, and I want to kick myself for not paying better attention to my tutors during our geography lessons. If anything, this is the main inhabited island. And if this is the best they have, this poverty and overcrowding, then Hanako and Reo are right to want to open relations with the siren people. We could help them, but as it stands right now, the prejudices between our two peoples runs so deep, the interactions always end in bloodshed.

The night sky spreads out, cloudless and black, lit with a scattering of distant stars, the moon a floating orb at my back. I resist the urge to turn and stare, to gape at the endless ocean. Instead, I blink up at the palace, taking it in up close, breathless at its beauty. The long, white walls glow in the darkness, the black, swooped roofs blend into the night, seemingly stacked on top of each other. A few of the glass windows are lit from behind, shadows occasionally crossing. A warm breeze picks up, brushing a lock of hair across my face. I breathe in the deep scent of something wonderful and unknown. Could it be the plants? Perhaps the flowers? My eyes flutter closed for a second, relishing in something so incredible, I can hardly believe I've lived nearly eighteen years without it.

My eyes pop open and I return my focus to the palace. I'm convinced that somewhere inside is the siren stone and if I had to bet, I'd say it's wherever the Japanese emperor is. If he has any idea what he's stolen, then surely he's not taking his eyes off his treasure. My gaze travels upwards to the top of the palace and I count six stories. The top floor is smaller than the rest, sitting to one side, with balconies and tall windows. Something about it screams royalty, even if just for the fact that my family lives at the top of our palace back home. The emperor is probably up there now, maybe even holding the stone in his greedy hands at this very moment, plotting ways to use it. Again, I pray he doesn't figure out how to access the magic, or worse, destroy the stone.

If only Asahi could get me up to that sixth floor, I could take over from there…

"You look so serious," Asahi says, leaning to speak into my ear. "Don't worry. I already got the approval from my uncle. We're just going to go into a few of the areas. It'll be fun."

I rework my expression to the one of giddy, clueless teenager on a date with a cute boy and nod. "Thanks, Asa. You're the best."

I make good use of his nickname again because I know it makes him trust me more, makes him feel like we're closer than we actually are. *I hate it.* The guilt is ripping me to shreds, but I can't stop. I won't stop. He beams at me and leads me down a side path to the back side of the palace. We pass more armed guards here than anywhere else I've been on the island, and I'm reminded of my warriors back home with their sharp spears and deadly voices. I'm struck with a pang of guilt, missing their protection, wishing I'd taken the time to truly thank them for the stability they've provided to me for so many years. Only now do I see how I took them for granted.

"This way. We're going through the crew member entrance," Asahi says, pulling me after him. We walk up to a door where two guards stand on either side. They nod at Asahi, granting us immediate entrance.

We step inside and are immediately separated. A woman in a beautiful silk outfit ushers me toward what appears to be a ladies' dressing area. She's silent, elderly, her face lined with deep wrinkles, knuckles knobby as the bonsai trees outside, and skin as translucent as a jellyfish. She takes my hand and smiles at me with watery blue eyes.

"It's okay," Asahi assures me, excitement lining his voice. "I think you're going to like this part. The palace is the one place on the island where our ancient ways are required, and that includes your outfit."

I glance down, smoothing the black cotton dress that Hanako insisted I wear. It's a little tight but it's not low-cut, nothing inappropriate.

"Just trust me," Asahi says, and then he disappears into the men's dressing area. Maybe he just wears his nice clothing to the palace, but not actually while he's in the palace?

Within minutes, I'm standing in front of a full-length mirror, and I have my answer.

It's different than the elegant dress of our Chinese court, different still than the few traditional cheongsam dresses my ancestors managed to keep together with siren magic. I think of my favorite one from home, with its deep purple color and white inlaid flowers. Or of the bright red one, the royal dress often used when meeting the mages, a close second favorite.

The style of this is called kimono—that much I do remember from my studies. And it's more gorgeous than anything I've worn in my life. The thought sends me reeling. Am I betraying my people by consorting with the enemy in this way?

And then the even more traitorous thought strikes me. Why are we even enemies with the Japanese empire? I understand that these people's ancestors choose to forgo the siren magic, but it's been generations since then, and maybe we don't have to hate each other. We're not that different. Spending a few days with the people has taught me that much. Perhaps Reo and Hanako are right.

But it's a stupid, foolish thought, to think that we can form an alliance when I know deep in my heart that the majority of these people would kill me if they knew what I was. This kind of thinking will get me killed if I'm not careful. So I put the thought away and smooth the pink silk down around my front, making sure it's tucked in well to the yellow belt-like fabric wrapped around my waist. I raise my arm, feeling the weight of the fabric as it extends to the floor. Yellow, white, and lavender flower patterns are embroidered into the silk. Even under the dim lights, they shine.

The old lady takes my discarded clothing and returns with a pair of matching sandals. She sits me in a chair and twists the hair loose around my shoulders into a tight bun at the nape of my neck, finishing off with a hairpiece of dangling flowers just above my ear, a light brushing of pale powder across my cheeks, and something pink and sticky across my lips. It's my first time wearing makeup. Hanako had wanted to put some on me earlier but I'd refused it. Yes, I'm used to people fussing about my appearance, but having unknown fingers on my face and lips makes my innards squirm. Luckily, it's over within minutes.

I blink at my reflection in the mirror, utterly transfixed.

My blood is Chinese, as thick and as deep red as my ancestors. That is who I am. I am royalty and proud to be siren-blessed. And yet I look like I belong on this island and in this palace, like I'm just as deserving as any human here. I could have just as easily been born a land-dweller princess. Or a commoner, struggling to eat.

"Thank you," I say, my voice numb. I turn toward the woman and smile softly. "Thank you for this." I wonder if she can see through the panic building up inside, the panic born from guilt and shame and the need to prove myself a worthy Chinese princess.

She bows and takes my hand, leading me back to the hallway where Asahi waits. He's dressed in a similar robe that's decidedly more masculine. It's dark gray with a yellow belt that matches mine.

"You look incredible," he says, his eyes amused and his mouth grinning.

I blush and give him a little bow, and then, hand in hand, we enter the palace.

Asahi is the perfect gentleman. He tells me how the palace is made up of eighty-three buildings, all interconnected. That it dates back to the twelfth century and has been the residence of the royal families on and off for years, until the seas rose, and the world was thrown into chaos, when it became the permanent home. He says it was even bombed during World War II, back when all of Japan was above water, and that even then, it still managed to survive.

I marvel at the architecture, understanding why everyone here is dressed as they are. It's an honor to step foot in this building, and I'm becoming more and more aware that not only have I been spoiled for our date, but that the Gods have smiled on me by bringing Asahi into my life. If it weren't for him, I'd never have made it this far alone. My earlier thoughts start to wash away—that this must all be part of the prophecy coming true. I wouldn't be here if it wasn't.

I can feel the siren stone is near, deep in my bones; I know its power is reaching out to me.

"The dungeon is down there," Asahi says, leading me by the elbow to look down a set of stairs. "Don't worry, we're not going there." He raises his eyebrows. "We don't usually have prisoners, but tonight we do."

My breath is lost. My mind spins. Heat burns in my cheeks. "Prisoners? What do you mean?"

Asahi glances around the small drawing room, checking we're alone. We are. He smirks, his eyes bugging out, as he leans in to whisper.

"Technically, they're dead. We found them washed up on shore yesterday. This was the big news I was trying to tell Kyon this morning."

My chest feels like it's closing in, like I can't breathe. "Who?"

"Sirens."

"How do you know?" My hands are two tight fists at my side and all I want to do is push past Asahi and storm down those stairs to see for myself.

"They were dressed like sirens, one even had a spear."

I nod. "Wow." It's all I can manage to say.

"I know, right? They looked like a family. A man, a woman, and a young child. All dead."

Bile rises in my throat and tears burn in my eyes. Asahi is talking about this so casually, like it's just an exciting bit of gossip, and not the death of innocents. I want to claw his tongue out for it.

"How did they die?" I question, finally able to meet his eyes. They light up.

"That's the craziest thing about it," Asahi gushes. "We think they *drowned*."

The air is knocked out of my chest so fast I'm left gasping.

I've taken too long! The siren magic is fading much faster than anyone anticipated. If this siren family washed up on shore yesterday, the only explanation is that they were hoping to seek refuge here and didn't make it in time. And if that was their fate, who else is already dead?

How many of my people have I failed?

TWENTY

ABOVE WATER, MY BODY IS FILLED WITH LEAD. HEAVINESS was the first thing I noticed a few mornings ago when I had to peel myself off that small, hard bed and make my muscles move again. Everything was stiff. Everything hurt. Movement is so much easier below water, where I'm weightless, where I have magic in every pore, every stroke, and each movement.

Everything below the surface is easier. But if I don't do something now, right now, that magic will be lost and I'll be stuck on this island for good, forever removed from my people, my mother, and my beautiful ocean home. The thought sticks to me like a dart and I use it to fuel my courage.

"It's time to go," Asahi says, placing his hand on the small of my back and ushering me back through the halls. "I thought we could get changed back into our clothes and take a walk through the grounds

175

before I take you home."

I nod politely but make sure the disappointment I'm feeling is etched into my face.

"Is everything okay?"

"Of course. It's been lovely. I was hoping we'd be able to go to some of the upper levels, that's all."

He shakes his head. "I wish we could. I just don't know."

I bat my lashes at him. If there was anything I learned from Lei and others of the court, it's that most men see me as a possession to acquire. If I can get Asa to believe I could be his, I know he'll do just about anything to make that happen. "Please? Can't you do something?"

He sighs even as mischief twinkles in his eyes, reminding me of the carefree way he acted when we first met. "Well, I guess I could show you my uncle's office. It's on the fourth floor, but that's all. We can't go into any of the other rooms. And we can't go to the sixth floor where the royals live. Their guards would never allow it."

I nod, gripping his bicep and squealing like a complete idiot. "Oh, thank you! That would be wonderful." I hate having to act this way, but then again, it's working.

"Follow my lead," he says, cupping my hand and pulling me to another set of stairs. There, he tells the guard that he needs to retrieve a document for his uncle. They let him pass, no question. It continues like this until we're on the fourth floor. By now I've started to figure out the layout and feel of the place. There's a guard stationed at every stairwell but most of the corridors and rooms in between are left open and vulnerable. I have to assume the royals have personal guards and that it will be harder to go unnoticed—if I can make it to the sixth floor. I have to try. My people are already dying. I either die here tonight trying to save them, or they die because of my cowardice.

Asahi leads me into a chamber filled with dark oak finishings, a large desk is centered in the middle of the room and rows of bookshelves line the wall, each burdened with thick texts. Many of the books have an ancient quality, reminding me of the monastery. The lower levels of the palace smell musty and dank, but up here, it's all perfumed, reminding me of the flower scent from the gardens. Asahi flips on the desk lamp. I pad across the plush rug to the long window, peering down onto a different manicured lawn from the one through which we entered.

In the center of the grass is a rectangle pool of water. Its still surface glimmers under the moonlight.

"Swimming pool?" I ask before I can catch myself. It's probably a terrible question coming from someone who's pretending to be normal. Swimming pools are one of the things I learned about from my tutors when we studied life from before. Seeing one here uplifts my heart. Asahi walks over to take a look. He stands so close I smell the faint scent of something earthy and unknown.

"Oh yeah, that's the royal's private garden. Nobody is allowed down there. They have a swimming pool because they don't feel safe going out to sea."

I nod, wondering if it's salt water in that pool. I'm beginning to formulate a plan. A plan so riddled with holes that it can hardly be called a plan. It's impulsive and stupid and probably destined to fail. But at least it's something.

"This is a beautiful place," I sigh wistfully. "To think a common girl like me would ever get to set foot in a palace is unbelievable."

Now maybe I'm being unbelievable, given my background, but Asahi loves every word. The lights from the city twinkle below, and the ocean beyond that, almost as bright. He turns me toward him, a knowing look in his eye. I've never kissed anyone and I'm not about to start with someone I hardly know, someone I've just met, whom I'm only using to my own ends. I'm saving that for my fiancé, for the noble man back home facing unimaginable struggles so that I can be here.

And yet it isn't Lei's face that pops into my mind in that moment.

I jump back, shame blurring my vision as I bite my lip. "Can you show me where the nearest restroom is, please?"

Asahi steps back, confusion in his tone. "Are you okay? I'm sorry if I misread."

Why is he being so nice to me? This would be so much easier if he wasn't kind. "No, it's just, this is all a lot to take in at once. I need to freshen up." My voice cracks.

"Uh, sure, follow me."

We hurry back through the office and out into the corridor. The walls are painted a soft yellow, the floors comprised of powdery-colored stone. Our sandals pad softly as he leads me around another corner and then ushers me to a small room. It's made of the same things back at the house, a toilet, a sink, and a mirror. But it's fit for a palace, everything gleaming white.

"I'll wait out here, then we can head back." He steps back to stand against the far wall, his face clear of any emotion.

Once inside, I try to gather my calm in the sea of chaos raging through me. Can I do this? I've had training. I know how to fight. I don't have my siren voice and I haven't fought above ground before. But I'm fast, I'm smart, and with my kimono, I blend in perfectly with the other servants and people I've seen moving about. Surely, some of those same people are permitted access to the two floors above me?

There's no time to question.

I double check that the door is locked and then walk to the window, sliding up the glass pane until there's enough space for me to crawl out. The swooped roof of the level below me isn't more than five feet down. Confident I can handle the drop, I don't let myself think to the next step in the plan. Just take it one minute at a time. First step, get onto the roof.

I crawl out the window on my belly as far as possible before dropping the rest of the way to my feet. A slap of porcelain tile breaking under my sandals echoes through the night and I freeze, pressing myself up against the wall of the palace. If anyone looks up here, they'll probably see my pink outfit and shoot their guns. Sweat pours down my back, and the cool breeze is a welcomed respite, though it does little good.

I take a few more steadying breaths and then inch my way across the roof. One of the first things I noticed about the palace was how the ceiling heights aren't very tall. That makes sense considering how old Asahi said the building is. I'm not that tall either, but at least I won't be scaling twenty-foot drops. I think of Mother, who stands a whole head taller than me, and of Father, even taller than that. To see Father in my mind's eye, my lost protector and closest confidant, the man I admired most in the world, the man I let down, sends another zing of resolve through me.

Keep going. You're doing it for him.

Because the roofs here curve up in so many places, I soon find myself climbing. And my heart rate climbs with it. I tell myself it's a good thing; that anything leading me up is taking me in the right direction.

I come across a window and carefully peek inside. The room beyond is dark and empty, but I still crouch below it as I cross. The roof begins to slant at a much higher degree, leaving me unsteady. I slip off my sandals, then edge carefully down to pick them up. I feel as if at any moment I'll topple over, slide off the roof, and plummet to my death four stories below. My stance is firm as I slip the two thin sandals under the edge of the yellow belt tied at my waist.

I continue, fingers reaching, clawing, until I find grip at the top of the swooped roof above me. I haul myself up, roll into position and reach for the next roof, another swoop of porcelain tiles to begin climbing. Now that I know what I'm doing, I'm much faster. I'm on my hands and knees by this point, clinging to the roof tiles and keeping close to the stone wall. My legs burn with exertion but I scramble from the fifth floor to the sixth and final floor in less than a minute.

From below, the faint call of Asahi's voice echoes into the night, "Senra?"

My heart pounds. My breath catches. My fingers tighten against the wall, toes curling at the cool tiles. I need to move faster. Within a few minutes, he'll alert the authorities. He's bound to.

I find the closest window and peek inside.

It's a sitting room. Couches and chairs of deep burgundy are artfully arranged around the space, ornate rugs tying the look together. On one of the couches rests a young girl, eight years old if I had to guess. Her hair is knotted on top of her head, her face engrossed in the book resting on her lap. She's not dressed like the others here, but rather, she's as casually dressed as many of the villagers I've seen. Her black cotton pants are loose, pooling around her ankles, and the sleeves of her gray shirt are pulled down around her wrists.

I don't spot anyone else in the room, nor do I see the stone, so I move on.

The moment I peek through the next window, I jump back, my heart racing. I take a deep breath and slide slowly back around to take another look.

One curtain is drawn, but the other is pushed to the side, revealing the bedroom inside. The large bed itself sits centered, the carved dark wood bedframe more beautiful and detailed than anything I've seen so far in this palace. A woman lies on top, her head resting on her bent elbow and dressed in silky black pajamas. She's lovely in a way

I haven't seen yet on the island, in a way that speaks of a life lived in luxury, without the sun and salt to age her quickly.

The Japanese Empress.

And at the foot of the bed, a man sits with his face resting between his hands. He too is dressed for bed. His wide shoulders are hunched over and his back is ridged, not the appearance of a man ready for sleep, but of a man with a lot of stress to weigh him down. Have I seen that kind of stress on an Emperor before? My father certainly had his moments, but our people weren't starving, and the monsters and magic didn't start to cause problems until after his death. No, if anything, it's been Mother who I've seen carry the burden. And now it's my turn.

The man begins to speak, and I strain to hear through the glass, catching enough to know I've done the right thing.

"If they seek refuge here, we can't take them. There's no room."

"Don't put this on yourself," the woman replies. "Those *things* are not your responsibility. If anything, we need to keep the magic for ourselves. You know the monsters have been bolder lately. One was spotted just three days ago."

I still, gritting my teeth at her hateful words. Those *things*? Sirens.

"I know," he replies, voice low and defeated. "But to have all those deaths on my hands."

"If it wasn't for them, the monsters wouldn't even be here. Their ancestors did this to themselves when they agreed to be sirens."

"And what if they bring a battle to our shores?"

The woman sits up, sliding down the bed to rub her husband's shoulders. My stomach rolls, sick that she can think so little of us, that it's so easy for her to persuade her husband to show no mercy. But then again, how are we any different? I think of the look Lei had on his face when we spoke of his interactions with the humans.

"If they bring battle," she says, "then we will fight them. We have guns. They only have spears and song. And with their magic waning or completely lost, they're bound to lose quickly."

The man reaches his hand back to clasp his wife's, letting out a long sigh. "You're right. I just hoped that things could be different."

"That's because you're a good man."

His face twists, as if to disagree, then he stands and walks across the room to a chest of drawers. He opens the top drawer and removes a bulky object wrapped in shining blue silk. Unwrapping it, the siren stone sits in his hand. It's larger than his fist and deep black, but it seems to pulse with magic, a slight glow. There's no mistaking this isn't a regular stone. My stomach jumps. I knew he would have it! My toes grip tighter against the porcelain tiles and adrenaline rushes through my entire body, bringing everything into crystal clear awareness. This is one more moment when I feel the Gods' hands directing me in my mission, in fulfilling the prophecy and saving my people. It's as if my ancestors surround me now, urging me to take action. Our way of life is precious and all that stands between me and the stone that will save us is a few feet and a few people. I can do this.

"Will we be able to use it?" the empress asks.

"I don't know." The man sighs. "If we destroy it, perhaps the monsters will disappear."

"Or they don't and things get worse."

"True."

Their eyes are transfixed on the stone until he wraps it back up and returns it to the drawer.

"Come," he says, reaching out to his wife. "Let's go put Aiko to bed. We must pray over our people tonight." They slip from the room, leaving me to make my move.

TWENTY ONE

MY PALMS FLATTEN AND PRESS AGAINST THE COOL GLASS. There's no time to delay. I try sliding the window up but it doesn't budge. Must be locked. It still throws me off that these people lock their homes, an act not practiced in my empire. I glance around frantically, looking for something solid to smash through the window. Of course, there isn't anything. It's dark, and I'm standing six stories up on a roof. What do I think I'm going to find? I don't have a weapon on me, either. I considered bringing the knife but decided it was better not to try to get onto the palace grounds with a weapon. The woman who dressed me in this kimono would have found it, so that was a sound decision. After a strained moment, I hold my breath and slam my shoulder against the glass. It cracks, making a loud crunching noise.

I wince and repeat the action. This time, the glass rains down. I don't think about protecting myself or about trying to get through this unscathed. My blood is still siren, I still feel the call to the ocean, so even though my magic is dormant, I'm certain I'll heal. It might take salt water, but I'll heal. So I dive through the window and roll onto the floor. The layered fabric of the pink kimono shelters most of the blow, though I get a few cuts along my feet. I don't look or let myself think about the sharp pain or the blood as I stand and lunge for the chest of drawers.

I pull open the top drawer, eyes zeroing in on soft blue silk wrapped around a bulky item: the siren stone. I snatch it up, quick, barely able to hold it in one hand. My fingers squeeze its smooth surface, and I press it against my side to get a better grip. It's heavy, weighing at least double what I estimated just by looking at it. Maybe I underestimated it because it's part of an asteroid and not a stone of this earth. I should know better.

The bedroom door swings open.

"Hey." A man's voice pierces through the room. Panic sweeps through me. "What are you doing?"

I don't think, don't answer, don't stall. I rush back to the window, catching a glance of the Japanese Emperor as I move. His eyes are round and wild. His mouth has dropped open and his skin is ashen. I only have seconds—mere seconds to get away before one of his guards follows the noise, rushes in here, and shoots me.

The Emperor's eyes flicker to the open drawer, the discarded fabric, and then to the stone in my hand. "Don't touch that!" he growls.

"This doesn't belong to you," I snap back and then swing one leg through the broken window. He's fast, on me in a flash, gripping the ankle of my second leg as I'm trying to get through. The bone slices against the jagged edge of glass and I scream, kicking out. White heat burns through my wound.

But he doesn't let go.

"Who are you?" he yells. "Are you a siren?"

Our gazes lock, understanding flickering. I see him for the man he is, for the heavy responsibilities he carries, the obligation to put his people above all else. Does he see the same things within me? His eyes soften, grip slightly loosening. I don't stop to consider his reasoning; I just act. I kick harder, and in the process of hanging on, his wrist mercifully catches on the glass. His eyebrows shoot up in pained surprise. He grunts and releases my leg. I don't wait. I roll down the curved roof, smashing tiles as I go.

The serene quiet of this night is broken; the peaceful veil pierced. Hollering voices boom from within the palace walls. I can't think about them. My only focus is on getting off this roof and as far away from this place as possible. My bloodied feet and ankle protest with each hurried step. Tears stream down my face as I push through the ache. My mind clears; vision blurred by tears, tunneling in on this one important task. I sprint from the top of each swoop of roof down to the next, catching hold when needed, dropping down with each floor.

I somehow manage to make it from the royal's sixth floor all the way down to the third before I'm met with more trouble than simply holding on to the stone or fighting against the wounds in my feet. Three men, dressed head-to-toe in black, wait for me.

They have guns, big guns. But as I get a better look, I realized they're not guns at all. They're swords. The sight brings bile to my throat. Who are they? They're not like the simple guards I've seen around the island; there's something about these men that's more practiced, more proud, and much more deadly. My mind scrambles through my lessons with the tutors about the land-dwellers and Japanese history, until it lands on the single word I'm looking for.

Samurai.

The first one comes at me, diving for my middle. How am I supposed to fight with this heavy rock in my hand? I say a silent prayer and toss it off the roof. A thud follows and I offer another silent prayer that nobody else heard it. I'll have to come back for the siren stone later. Right now, I've got to put my combat training to the test.

A flash of the day our party fought the pirates comes to mind, of how I'd gone into that battle feeling ready for the action, and how I was quickly educated on my inexperience. Being a good fighter is more than smarts and practice and training. It takes actual experience, of which I have little. The stab of doubt catches me off guard.

I'll never stand a chance against them.

The man connects with my middle, sending me sprawling. More tiles shatter. I scream and jump up, charging for him this time. It's no use, he throws me back again, and his two companions stalk nearer. One slides the sword from his sheath, a clash of metal that echoes through the night. In the moonlight, its silver edge glints of death. The second man does the same, readying his aim to kill. The third sneers at me, pure hatred darkening his already shrouded expression as his sword arcs through the darkness.

I scramble back, finding the edge of the roof, and swing myself down another story. They follow, silent assassins hell-bent on my destruction. I don't give them the extra time to catch me. I jump up and take off running, a sprint that burns through every muscle in my body. I know where I'm going. If I can just get around the corner, I know exactly what will save me.

Something slams into the roof next to me. Porcelain flies.

"No!" a voice screams, the voice of the emperor.

I don't look. I make it to the edge of the roof and jump. My heart soars as I catch sight of the glimmering surface below me. Water, as black as the sky above. My body bounds into the pool, the water surrounding me in an instant, shutting off the world. Salt fills my mouth and lungs and I smile at the pleasure. I don't know if I've ever been more grateful for the familiar taste of salt as I am in this moment.

I'm not alone for long. The three men dive in after me. But I'm ready for them, my song already pouring from my mouth like liquid murder. The dormant magic springs to life and grows. The ghostly notes send calm through them and yearning through me. I keep singing until the guns and swords drop to the bottom of the pool. As my blood mixes with the water, I keep singing. All three men swim toward me, transfixed. And it's cruel, but I must survive, and so I swim to the bottom and sit and sing and wait.

Death will come swiftly and my assassins will drown in its embrace. From the looks on their faces, they won't mind. It won't be scary or painful. They're grateful for the opportunity to be filled with so much water, to let her inside them as I have. Their eyes begin to glaze over and limbs loosen, hair spreading out like inky fingers. It's almost over.

It is me or them, I tell myself. *Don't feel guilty. Your people are losing their magic. You'll lose yours soon, too, if you don't follow through.*

Another voice rings even louder, *You are not a murderer, Senra. Those men who drowned before, it was out of self-defense and still, you saved Kyon. You would have saved them all, had you been given the chance.*

But what about the man on the fishing boat? I stabbed him. I left him there to die. *And you now know that he was badly injured, but he didn't die.*

And then my mind flashes to my father and harsh tears burn my eyes. What about him? Had I been there to help, I could have saved him. I could have…

This time, it's his voice I hear echoing through my mind, loud as if he were standing right in front of me. *You are not a murderer, Senra. You are not!*

I push off the bottom of the pool and gather the floating bodies into my arms. Together, we break the surface. Water slides down my hair and cheeks, dripping from my lashes as I look around the courtyard. It's empty. I drag the men onto the side of the pool, groaning against their weight. They're passed out, but not dead. Not yet. One by one, I place my hand above their chests and using my siren gift, I manipulate the salt water out of their bodies. It rises to the surface and washes to the grass. The rosy color returns to all three of the men's faces. I watch carefully until they begin to cough.

Satisfied, I jump up, ready to battle, and hoping to leave this palace, this island, to leave all of it behind me for good.

I get my wish. There are guards, but they are running away from me. As they should, now they know what I am and have seen what I can do. It won't be long before they gain courage and turn their guns on me, and I'm useless against bullets. I have to keep moving.

The idea of leaving the safety of the pool makes me want to vomit, but so does the idea of these three samurai waking up. I swallow the fear down and wrench myself onto my wounded feet. They're already beginning to heal. The pain is noticeably lighter, and I practically cry out in relief. Sprinting across the smooth grass, running for the area where I dropped the siren stone, I search for the glow of magic.

"Looking for this?" Asahi steps from the shadows of the palace and into plain view, his voice bitter. Everything about him is different from before. Anger is held tight in his jaw, his eyes are razors, and his stance is as solid as the earth. But most of all, he doesn't look the least bit afraid of me. And in his hand, he grips the siren stone. "You used me," he snaps.

"I'm sorry," I whisper. I reach out for the stone, desperate for this to be easy. "I'm going to need you to hand that over. I will kill you if I have to."

191

But will I? Even as I say it, I know I've made my choice and Asa won't die over the stone. Anger ripples across his face. Or is it the sting of betrayal? My stomach twists, knowing how I used someone who trusted me.

"What the hell are you doing with Kyon's family? You're not his cousin. I knew he didn't have a cousin. But hiding a siren? I knew his parents were sympathetic to the sirens but I never thought they'd do something like this…" his voice trails off.

"They have no idea what I am," I lie fervently, wanting to protect my only human friends. "I tricked them with magic. Don't blame them for this."

The way that Asahi looks at me when I say it confirms everything I need to know. He won't let me go without a fight. And also, Kyon's parents are much different from many of the other humans here. They're special, their mercy and tender hearts are unique. The others harbor a hatred of siren kind that runs as deep as the marrow in their bones.

"I don't know what this is," Asahi says, glowering at the stone as he lifts it up. The black surface shines in the moonlight, the glow brighter now, "but if you want it and if you had to come *here* to steal it, then it can't be good and I can't let you have it."

"I'm only going to warn you once, Asa," I snarl, done with these games. I don't have time for this conversation anyway.

"Don't call me that. And go ahead, try to kill me. I brought you here. I'll probably face death for that mistake. If I fight you, or better yet, stop you, maybe I'll be able to redeem myself and my honor."

I scoff. "You're a foolish man."

Then I lunge for him, knocking him off his center. He's fast. He recovers right away, stronger than he looks. Stronger than me without my ocean. But the salty pool water is still slick on my skin, still dripping from my hair, heavy on my borrowed clothing, and the energy of awakened magic churns through me, readying me for this task.

I throw him off me and release a high-pitched shriek, sending his body slamming into one of the jutting stones of the garden. It knocks him out, his body slumped over as blood oozes from his forehead. An instant pang of regret registers deep within. I push it away. He'll survive, and I have more important matters to attend to.

I snatch the siren stone from where he dropped it, wanting nothing more than to sing my song as I sprint into the cover of night. The music will kill those who hear it, making them long for nothing but the ocean until they find themselves floating in her depths. The fear that's burning me up inside is stronger than reason or mercy, and the song longs to echo from that fear, like a melody unleashed and never-ending death. It would be so easy to give in to the music. I could justify every note, every death, as a requirement for saving my empire and offering my people another chance at life.

But I cage the song deep inside and repeat the words over and over again until they drown out the music: *I am not a murderer.*

TWENTY TWO

WET CLOTHING UNDER WATER ISN'T A PROBLEM. IT EITHER floats or is tight against our skin, moving with us. Up here is a different story. I almost wish I had the nerve to strip naked and release myself from the heavy garment clinging to my body. The kimono dress is dragging me down, hanging awkwardly off my frame, and gathering clumps of dirt along the hem. I long for the black bodysuit in which I arrived at this island. Since it's tucked away under my little bed back at the house, I'd give anything to magic myself there right now.

But magic doesn't work that way and so I continue on, my feet still bare. My sandals were lost in the struggle. At least the siren stone is tucked against my side, on its way to its rightful place. It's smooth and warm to the touch, untold power radiating from it. I squeeze it tighter as I wince, the cuts on my feet throbbing. They haven't healed as much as I had originally thought. They will eventually, but as long as I keep walking on them, stealing through the darkest paths and winding my way down the mountainside, they're going to keep bleeding. I tuck myself against a building and close my eyes for a second, wincing through the pain.

Calm settles over me. It is foolish to let the calm in. I allow it to course through me anyway. It gives me clarity, focus, re-centering me on my mission. I might have to kill some humans before all of this is over, but for tonight, I want to go about getting out of here in quiet, and hopefully without blood on my hands. The more I spark an uproar in the community, the more humans will hate my people, and the bigger the problem I might have to face later.

I wish the Japanese Emperor would have just left the mages alone. I wonder how long he's known about the stone. Why now? Why did they have to come for the stone after all these years? It's not theirs to be had. Siren magic has been alive and well for decades. But then I think of how some kind of strange recognition fell over us back at the palace, how the emperor was going to say something before I kicked him away and ran. It could have been that he was going to answer those questions for me and I ruined it. But then again, his samurai attacked shortly after that, so I can assume whatever the emperor was going to say wouldn't have helped my situation.

I stare into the darkness, eyes again straining against the cover of night now that most of the water has dried up. I don't see anything other than shadows. As far as I can tell, nobody has come after me. Or if they have, they're staying well-hidden. I train my ears, hoping to catch something. Perhaps the crunch of boots on gravel or the release of held breath. But there's nothing. Taking hold of my nerve once again, I peel myself off the wall and run.

I don't know where exactly I'm going but as long as it's toward water—I let that be enough. Asahi walked me up a main road, lined with shops and some of the nicer homes. The street I'm currently on is vastly different. The modest homes have been shuttered for the evening, electricity and candlelight snuffed out. A few trees stick out along the road at odd angles, jutting into the sky. Silence blankets the street, but there's an undercurrent of something else, too. A breath waiting to catch.

My mind races back to just one night previous when I ran along the docks, the floating city shut down. It had the same feeling. I twist my lip, thinking of the bars on all the windows, the heavy deadbolts on doors, the way people here don't seem to like to stay out after dark, especially the closer they get to the water. And that's when it hits me. When Long attacked, there was a battle, and of course, he'd disappeared. And yet, nobody I've met or seen has acted like his attack was all that out of the ordinary. Perhaps the sea monsters venture to these waters often.

Maybe that's why the Emperor tracked down the siren stone.

Maybe he believes it's his only hope in saving his people.

Just as it is mine.

I veer off onto a side path, suddenly feeling the prickle of eyes on my back. It might be paranoia, but if this stone really is that important to the emperor, then there's no way he's only going to send three assassins for me. There's got to be more, perhaps watching me at this very second, waiting to strike.

I wind through back alleys, around houses and gardens, stalking low, quiet as I can possibly be, quiet as the deepest parts of the ocean, but even that doesn't feel like enough. The humidity settles into the creases of my neck. My left arm grows tired from carrying the stone. My thighs rub together and chafe under the pink kimono. The kimono itself is almost dry, evaporating my magic with it. I ignore all of that as I continue to navigate toward the ocean, readying my mind to fight, to kill, to rip limb from limb at a moment's notice.

A distant scream pierces the silence. More screams and shouts. A feral animal snarl skips across the water, across the docks, up the mountain, and right to me. My heart jumps, knowing the reunion is close. And once again, I take off running, this time faster than before. My feet slap against pavement and gravel and dirt and grass, until finally, it's the soft, cool sand I feel slipping between my toes.

I can't help it. I run into the water and dive under the gentle surf. But the nets haven't gone anywhere. I can't risk going very far. I come back up, scanning the beach. It's clear, so I rush from the water and run along it, heading in the direction of noise.

And the noise builds. Voices continue to yell and scream. I make it onto the same dock that leads toward Kyon's home. Hordes of families rush past me, terror lining their faces. They don't pay me any attention. They must be heading for the evacuation zones that Kyon mentioned before. I dodge bodies, get knocked down by a few, but continue on. Running as fast as I can, once again drenched, the magic is back in my veins. I feel it just under my skin, pressing against my heart, urging me on.

"Where are you going?" an old woman I've never seen before questions, grabbing my arm, yanking me back. "You're going the wrong way! There's a sea monster out there, don't you know? You need to get to the evacuation zone or take the risk and board up. I'm staying back; you can stay here if you need."

I sputter, seemingly unable to form a sentence. Who is this woman and how can she be so kind to someone she's never even met? Maybe there are more like Kyon's parents than I originally thought. Or maybe it's because she doesn't know who I really am that she can offer such generosity. I'm about to reply, when a thought strikes me through my core. I was just in the water and my magic is strong. If I begin to talk, it's possible it won't be words that come out, but my siren song. This woman and anyone else near enough to hear would be dead within minutes.

She tilts her head at me, running mossy-green eyes up and down me. She drops her hand, eyes widening and wrinkles deepening. "Why are you all wet?" Her voice is questioning in a way that I can't handle right now.

I shake my head fervently. I have no answer that will satisfy, nor do I have time.

"Are you coming in or not, child?"

I step back, shaking my head. She sighs heavily, muttering something I can't hear and presses herself back into her home's doorway. The door shuts and the sound of the lock clicks into place.

All for the better.

I race down the rest of the dock until I make it back to my temporary home, praying they've left with the others. I expect the lock to be set as is customary around here, but I grip the door handle and throw the door open so fast, it bangs against the wall. Rushing to the darkness inside, I glance around. Finding the space empty, I go right for the bed, falling to my hands and knees and searching the space below. My hands grip eagerly at my bodysuit. I don't delay, unwinding the water-logged kimono and letting it drop to my feet. I'm left with nothing but thin undergarments still soaked through with the sea.

A throat clears and I jump, whirling around. "You came back." Kyon's voice is low. I find him standing in the corner of the room next to the window. He steps from the shadows, his expression unreadable. Then he glances down to my exposed skin and I baulk, holding up the suit for coverage.

"What are you doing here? Where are your parents?"

Kyon ignores the question, going for the door. He closes it and slides the lock in place. Dread pours through me, but considering his back is turned, I quickly slip into my wetsuit. He'll know I intend to go back to the water. I don't have a choice. I'm running out of options. The emperor will want the stone back and Asahi knows where I'm staying. It's only a matter of time before the samurai are back.

Kyon turns to face me and all I can do is stare at the man, wondering what tests I'll be faced with next. Am I going to have to hurt these people to get out of here? I think of Asahi and what I did to him, of the shame I'll have to carry because of it. I don't want to have to betray more people tonight. Kyon returns my stare as if he can see right into my soul, as if I were talking to him like I talk to my siren kind. There's no way Kyon knows what happened at the palace. He couldn't know, not yet. But he suspected something was going to happen and now here I am, dripping wet, while outside, people are screaming. I take a step back, my legs hitting the edge of the bed.

"What's that?" he asks, pointing past my siren outfit and right to the glowing stone. My knuckles are white from clutching it so hard.

My breath catches, and I try to sound relaxed. "Nothing."

"Don't lie." His voice is sharp, the accusation in his tone stinging.

"Why didn't you evacuate?" I change the subject, but his eyes are still glued on the stone, still questioning.

After a moment, he answers, "Father is too frail to make it to the island quickly. We can't be stuck outside at the wrong moment."

"How can you even consider staying back? We're on water."

"We'll take our chances."

And they are terrible chances. I bite my lip and nod.

A snarling roar rips through the night. It's close. I rush to the window, pulling the curtains to the side, craning my neck.

"Senra!" Kyon hisses, grabbing my wrist and pulling me back against his hard chest. His breath is a hot whisper against my ear. "Are you trying to get us killed? The monster is hungry but it won't attack if it doesn't know we're here. Stay still, quiet, and let it move on."

"How did it get through all the traps?"

He shushes me, but then he whispers against my cheek. A shiver runs down my spine and my legs grow weak. "The traps are for our food, not to keep the monsters away. No trap could stop those huge razored beasts. They come every once in a while, find a good meal, and then they leave."

I gulp, trying not to picture it. No wonder the emperor wanted the stone. I would, too. A shadow crosses in front of the window. My already racing heart skids with the effort. What if it's not Long out there? What if it's not my monster, but another hunting for blood? No, it *has* to be Long. He knew to stay close. He must have heard my song earlier. Surely he considered it a plea for help.

Water drips off my hair, trailing down my cheek. Fear burns inside, but so does courage.

Long? I ask, tentatively. *Long, is that you?*

I suck in another breath. The shadow outside the window stills. Everything slows to a pause. Kyon's body hardens, his arms tight around my body. I exhale.

A roar rips through the night and the door is thrown off its hinges.

TWENTY THREE

LONG IS UPON ME IN AN INSTANT, THRASHING THROUGH the opening. The front wall crashes to the dock. His golden eyes blaze, lighting the space as they search the small room, landing on me. I'm frozen to the spot, my hand outstretched in warning.

Don't hurt them, I instruct the dragon. But it's not just an instruction, it's an outright plea. *Don't hurt these humans.*

In my periphery, I catch the bedroom door as it swings open. Kyon is yelling something at his parents, who are yelling back. I don't hear the individual words. I'm too focused on this, on staring into my companion's eyes, on willing him to obey my command. His mouth is bared and growling, muscles tense, and the claws on his short arms and legs are spread wide, sharp as knives.

"It's okay," I say aloud to my human friends. "He won't hurt you. He's here for me."

"Are you crazy?" Kyon growls. "Don't go near that thing."

I nod once at Long. We can do this, him and me. We can get out of here without hurting anyone. He moves closer, his head nearly as tall as I am. His mouth curves in a conspiratorial smile, the little whiskers under his nose bouncing.

"Thank you for everything," I say, turning back to the family.

They gape at me like I've lost my mind. Maybe I have. Six months ago I would have driven a spear through this beast's eye without hesitation and now look at me. He's become my friend. "I must leave now."

I stride to Long's serpent body and crawl onto his scaly back, careful to tuck the siren stone between my legs. I keep one hand on the black stone and put the other on Long, bracing myself.

"What are you doing?" Hanako's voice cracks. I catch her watery eyes and give her a gentle smile.

"I'll be fine."

Kyon steps in front of his mother. "You got what you came for, didn't you?" Our gazes collide like fire and ice. "Go, then, Senra. Go and don't come back."

My heart splits.

He doesn't know what I've been through or what I have yet to endure. His judgment has no place here. He's just a common man, trying to survive. He only has two people to look after, but I have thousands. Long stirs beneath me, as if sensing my anger. His body tenses, and he stands. The house is ripped open now so it's no trouble for him to move about. I wince, regretful and wishing I could

203

do something to repay these people's kindness. What will they do without this home? Will someone help them repair it?

Long paws at the ground, snarling at Kyon—Kyon, who's still glaring at me.

It's okay, buddy. I pet Long's side and talk to him through our link. He's still wet from the ocean and it sends a tiny thrill of anticipation through me. I can feel his lungs exhale underneath my palm. He's beginning to calm. *My friend is angry that I'm leaving like this. Truth be told, I feel guilty about it, but regardless, we do need to leave.*

And then Long does something I never could have imagined. He lunges at Kyon, snapping at him with his razor sharp teeth. Kyon falls back, arms up in a block. But Long doesn't bite Kyon, doesn't kill or injure him. Instead, he gets ahold of Kyon's tan canvas jacket and flings him up into the air. He hits the ceiling, then falls, eyes and limbs wild, when Long jumps up and catches him on his back. Kyon lands right behind me. He grunts and grips the side of the beast.

Long's body swings around and pounces. He takes off so fast I can hardly hold on. He's off, past the horrified calls from Hanako and Reo, past the low hanging roof of the broken home, past the docks and splashing into the water.

Kyon can't breathe underwater, I cry out to Long. But the dragon must already know because he stays on the surface, swimming faster than I've ever seen him go before. We're racing across the top of the water. It's slapping us in the face, coating our legs, pelting every inch of exposed skin. Long's claws are extending, teeth out and thrashing, cutting through any kind of ropes or traps or anything that falls into our path. He makes quick work of them, like they're little more than string.

Kyon's wet arms grip around my waist. "What's happening?" he calls out, his voice overcome with sheer terror.

It's the first time I've ever heard that emotion from him. I've seen many of his sides in the short time I've known him. I've seen his hate and his tenderness, his friendship and his suspicion. I've witnessed the care and the resourcefulness, the laughter and the calm, but I've never seen his fear. And I don't want to. So I don't look back. I allow him privacy as Long races us across the spraying water.

We're too fast for anyone to follow. No boat could make it in time, even if they tried. Within minutes, the outline of the island bleeds into the dark of night. All that's left is the three of us riding an endless horizon.

Long keeps swimming along the top of the ocean at breakneck speeds for a couple of hours, but after a while, he begins to slow. I sink into myself with relief. Kyon has been gripping me so tight, I fear I'll have handprint shaped bruises on my abdomen. His hands loosen and then let go.

"Senra, what the hell is going on?"

I scoot up on Long's back, flip a leg over, then turn myself around so I'm facing Kyon. Our knees touch. I don't pull away. Neither does he. I sigh and glance up to study his hardened face. It's still dark out, in fact, if it weren't for the glow of the moon, it would be pitch-black. But the stars are innumerable and the moon is bright and Kyon's face is lit enough for me to tell he's still soaking wet, still afraid, still angry.

I clear my throat. "I don't really know what to say."

"How about starting with the truth."

There's nothing out here but the rolling water against the night sky and the three of us. My dragon is fixed on some unknown destination and Kyon and I are along for the ride whether we like it or not. Would it be so bad to tell him? He's part of this now. Maybe he's always been part of this.

"Seriously, Senra," Kyon growls, "I'm about ready to lose my mind. Just tell me." He holds up his hands in exasperation, pointing to the endless ocean in either direction. "It's not like I'm going to run off and tell on you. My parents are now homeless and I'm stuck out here instead of helping them. I deserve to know why."

He's right.

So I tell him. Somehow, it all tumbles out of me. The truth comes so much easier than lies, it's light instead of heavy. I tell him of the siren stone, of who I really am, of my life as a princess and what I think it all means. My voice shakes, hot tears threatening to burst free, as I explain what's been happening to my people and why I had to journey to his island in the first place.

"Any questions?" I ask, releasing a pained laugh.

"Why didn't you tell us this from the beginning?" He inches closer, his hair covering one eye. His usual guarded expression is gone, washed away by my confession. He's so earnest, it's impossible for me not to laugh again.

"I didn't know if I could trust you." I shrug, cheeks burning.

He nods slowly. "We're not all bad, you know?"

"I know." And it's true. It's so true, that it leaves me feeling empty, knowing the way I've treated the humans I've interacted with. I assumed the worst in them at every opportunity.

"And I hate to admit it, but you sirens aren't all bad either." He's turned serious, reaching out and placing a warm hand on my shoulder. Despite the heat, I shiver. "I understand why you've done what you did, Senra. You're not a bad person. It's amazing that you got that stone without killing anyone and I sincerely hope you can find a way to save your people."

I swallow the lump in my throat and look away. "Me, too." He thinks I'm a good person? Somehow, hearing that from him makes this whole situation feel better.

"So, tell me about your parents. What was your father like?"

I smile, this time, the tears really do break through. I don't wipe them away. "He was amazing. He taught me so much." My voice catches. "I miss him."

We continue talking into the night. Reminiscing about my family and his family, about siren life and what it's been like for his people to try to stay alive. We discuss the sea monsters and the prophecy, looking at it from every angle, but neither of us are able to come to a definite conclusion about what's next. Then we talk about the silly things, the stupid non-important thoughts and feelings and likes and dislikes that somehow feel like they matter more than anything else tonight. We chat until our voices are hoarse and our eyelids droop, until there's nothing left to say.

Hot sun presses down on the back of my neck, prickling my outstretched arms and legs. My hair twists around me like a net. Kyon's heavy body is draped across my back and the siren stone digs into my hipbone. My eyes flutter open, and I start awake.

I elbow Kyon. "We fell asleep," I mutter. "How did we fall asleep?"

The last memory I had I was fully awake and alert, teasing Kyon about his pirate life.

The man had listened to me better than I could have ever expected, better than anyone ever had, with his silent pondering way that held no judgment. Once I'd started, it was like I couldn't stop myself. I needed to tell someone of the burdens I've been carrying; I feel so much lighter now. Perhaps that was why I had revealed my truth to Kyon, perhaps it was my need and his proximity, and not the way he made me feel so safe. Even as I think it, I know it's not coincidence. It's Kyon. Nobody else could have helped me open up like he did.

Last I remember, we were laughing, the sun was beginning to rise and then … nothing.

Kyon stirs but doesn't open his eyes. "Wake up." My voice cracks, and I lean against him, trying to get his body off mine so I can stretch. Finally, he stirs and sits up. Blinking, he looks around confused. He must not remember falling asleep either. It's beyond sunrise now, the morning long gone. The sun hangs high in the sky, its rays blazing hot. He lifts his hand to shield his eyes as he takes in our surroundings.

"What happened? We just fell asleep?" he asks. His tan canvas jacket, black t-shirt, and jeans are soaked through. Red blotches his cheeks, and his black hair sticks to his forehead. "That doesn't make sense. We were laughing…"

"There's only one explanation," I groan, realizing the truth. "Magic."

Something dark flickers across his face. I can't read what it means, but I can make an educated guess. I sigh and twist around, searching in all directions. The horizon is an endless line. It's still the sea against the sky, blue on blue, with Long's slithering, black, snake-like body the only thing to break it up. And then it changes. I blink and rub my eyes, just to be sure.

It's as if Long swam through a protective barrier or invisible shield, and has now brought us to the other side. A world spreads in front of us, and my heart races.

It's another island, with homes twisting around the base and a monastery. The architecture closely resembles the island I've visited every year since birth, the only island I thought the monks had. I was wrong. And they've been keeping more secrets than I ever could have imagined.

"What is this place?" Kyon asks.

"I don't know," I say, "but I can guess it's Tibetan. They've kept it hidden for all these years."

"This isn't the island you've been to?"

"No, this one is different. It's much larger than the other and covered in at least three times as many homes. The monastery positioned on top is like the other."

"That's where they worship?"

"And do magic." We stare at the earth-toned building, the red roof, and the strings of colorful flags fluttering in the wind. The place stands like a beacon for all those below, a reminder of what they'll find should they look up, a reminder that their Buddha is watching over them. Their history is strong here, their Buddhist and shamanic teachings intertwined with the supernatural, carried through the centuries.

"Why do you think they've brought us here?" Kyon's body is still pressed against mine, and he shifts to wrap his arms around me. I can sense the protectiveness in the movement and my thoughts drift away on the breeze. Why is it so different with Kyon? Every time Lei tried to protect me, I found myself annoyed. But this, this feels dangerous and electrifying and like I might never be able to forget him once it's all over.

I take a couple deep breaths to steady myself. "I didn't know this area even existed. They must have used their magic to shield it from all others."

"Until now."

I nod, shuddering. "Until now."

"And they want the stone."

I nod again. "I'm sure, but something doesn't add up. Why didn't they take the stone with them when they fled the first time? Why did they flee the other island and leave the siren stone behind?"

"And why have they brought *me* here with you? A human?"

"Exactly." I lean into him. He gets it. This is the kind of easy talk we had during the night. Part of me regrets how everything is about to change again. I know Kyon is eager to get out of the water. He hasn't complained, but I can tell he's ready. Meanwhile I'm dying to dive in. I've stayed perched on Long out of both courtesy and curiosity. And maybe also to stay extra close to Kyon, not because I enjoy the proximity but because I don't want to be held responsible if something should happen to him.

I inwardly groan, knowing I'm spinning lies in my head that could very well entangle my heart. Somewhere down below, Lei waits for me. I made a promise. And the mages here know about the engagement. I can't entertain anything with Kyon but friendship, even if he brings out emotions in me I've never experienced before. I glance down at the stone. I have bigger obligations.

Long swims like he knows exactly where he's going. He's either been here before or he's being directed by strong magic. Maybe both. After all, it was a mage who brought Long to me. Those monks are orchestrating much of what's happening. Could they be behind everything? Why?

I intend to find out.

Long's speed increases as we near the island and instead of slowing once we reach the shore, he jumps up on it, using his short arms and legs to run along the winding pathway. The two of us cling to his back, shocked and watching the island as it rushes past. I catch sight of people, of men and women and children, as they go about their duties. They smile and wave, not the least bit concerned by our presence. There's a sea monster running through their streets, for heaven's sakes!

"What is going on here?" Kyon mutters against my ear.

I shake my head, unable to form a coherent sentence. This is not what I expected either, and it's left me feeling like I'm standing on unstable ground. I don't know what to do, how to act. Should I call out? Should I jump off? I'm lost. I have no plan for something like this.

Within a minute, we're on top of the mountain, the monastery spread out before us. Monks in deep burgundy robes line the pathway. They're chanting in succession, a low rumbling sound, incantations not of my language, not even with the siren magic. This language must be ancient. Their heads are shaved, the scalps shining in the sunlight. The earthy smell of incense wafts and drifts on the breeze.

Kyon and I don't speak, but intuitively, we slide off Long's back at the same time. The sea monster stands and stretches, nuzzling his face against my legs, and then steps back, curling in on himself to rest. I clutch the smooth stone between trembling hands, once again feeling the weight of it, the weight of the prophecy and this moment. It's a weight heavy with responsibility and I don't know how much longer I can carry it alone. But I'm not alone anymore, am I? Kyon takes my other hand and the two of us walk down the worn stone pathway.

Together, we enter the monastery.

TWENTY FOUR

THE AIR IS ALIVE WITH MAGIC. I CAN'T SEE OR HEAR IT. I FEEL it so deep that it rattles my bones. My breath catches. Kyon grips my elbow. I straighten my spine, finding my strength. Whatever is next, I'm ready.

There are three monks sitting cross-legged on the floor, facing each other, eyes closed, and deep in meditation. Besides them, the room is empty save for a couple of tapestries on one wall and a shelf filled with scrolls on the other. The floor is made of weathered white stone. It's beautiful in a completely different way than my Chinese palace or the Japanese one across the ocean.

It's reverent.

I step closer, recognizing one of the three men to be the Dalai Lama, the head of the mages, and the same man who appeared out in the ocean with Long. His calmness, oneness, it radiates outward. It feels like love. I'm foolish to have ever questioned the monks. They're good people. They may have secrets, they may be different from me, but I'm certain I can still rely on them.

A stream of light cascades down from one of the windows, making his bald scalp shine brighter than the others. He doesn't seem to notice or care. His stillness is beyond time and space, and I don't want to interrupt his worship, but we were summoned here. So I do the only thing I can think of. I quietly stride forward, kneeling just outside the three men's circle, and place the siren stone in the center.

And I wait.

The chanting continues outside, long notes not too unlike siren song. The magic presses in around me, a warm tingling pressure, more powerful than anything I've experienced. A bead of sweat drips down the back of my neck and settles against my bodysuit. My knees ache against the hard stone but I don't get up. I stretch out my hands, squeeze them into tight fists, and release them again.

"Remember what I said? You must learn to love what you hate," the Dalai Lama's gentle voice breaks the silence. His eyes stay closed, his aged face serene. "You must learn to trust."

I think of all I've done to get here. Of my initial hatred of Long and his kind, and how we've since become a team. I think of Kyon's family, and of the way the man standing behind me makes me feel like I'm not alone anymore.

"I have."

The Dalai Lama's eyes pop open and he smiles. "Perhaps."

I sigh and glance expectantly at the piece of asteroid that has been the cause of my entire existence. Now it's my turn to continue the legacy. "I've returned the siren stone to you. What else is left? Please, I beg you, restore any lost magic and allow my people to continue living as sirens in peace."

"Peace is what all of this is for," he says. "It's why you're here."

"I know," I agree. Why doesn't he see that we want the same thing?

He picks up the stone, studies it for a moment, and hands it back. It's heavier than ever. Confusion drowns me, dread rising to the surface. Why won't he just take it?

"It doesn't belong to us," he says simply.

"I know. It's siren. But you're the ones who wield its magic."

He shakes his head. "You still don't understand. But you will."

I jump up, anger spreading through me, hot tears prickling my eyes. "Do you have any idea what I went through to get this? And now you're just going to deny me?"

"As I said, *peace* is what all of this is for."

I scoff, any ounce of patience long gone. "Peace? Is your idea of peace letting thousands drown? Is that what you mean by peace?"

The other two men are still in a trance, oblivious to my raised voice. Something about that makes me even angrier. Don't they care? Do my people matter so little to them? Do I matter so little?

The Dalai Lama stands and steps toward me. His gaze levels with mine and he smiles. "There is always another way, dear one," he says. "You must learn to find the other way. And if it can't be found, find

216

the next one."

He chuckles, and I bristle. If only it were as simple as that, but I know it's not. How else are our people going to survive if not with this stone and these monks? They've had magic for centuries but it wasn't until the asteroid that their magic was enhanced. Defeat washes over me and the tears slip loose. I wipe at them, furious.

"Come now," he says. "There is little time and much to learn."

He glides silently past me and out the door.

I turn to Kyon, wanting nothing more than to sink into his arms. I don't. His expression is as alive with frustration as my own. "Much to learn about what?" I grumble.

The Dalai Lama's voice rings with the answer, "Magic."

We advance through the square courtyard. It's comprised of large sandy stone and planter boxes with vibrant flowers in every color. The monks still line the main pathway. Their chanting has subsided and has been replaced with the low rumblings of a nearby gong. It stands on a base, as tall as I am. Someone bangs it, loudly, and the bass sound sweeps across the entire island, until it slowly fades to silence, and then is repeated. Who knew worship could be so noisy? But there's something spiritual about the gong and the chanting that actually isn't noisy at all.

"Everything vibrates at different levels," the Lama says. His teacher tone suddenly reminds me of my tutors back home, and a pang of homesickness bursts within me. I hold it in, trying to focus on him. "Magic is the same. It's a vibration."

I nod like I understand the wisdom he's trying to impart. It's all lost on me. He leads us around the side of the monastery where the courtyard opens up to a fruit orchard. I've never seen one in person before, but I've studied about them, about the way the earth used to be alive with Gaia's life-giving force. My jaw falls open, and for the first time since landing here, Kyon speaks.

"You have so many fruit trees," he says in wonderment. "How do you have so much vegetation?"

The Dalai chuckles, and we follow him to the closest tree. It branches out above us, casting a shadow over our party. He plucks a fleshy round orange ball from the branch and peels off the outer layer.

In one hand I'm still holding the siren stone, and in the other, he places a piece of the fruit. "Try it. It's called an orange."

An orange? How original. I roll my eyes. The juice leaks onto my hand and the aroma is pure heaven, certainly there's nothing underwater with this kind of fragrance. I'm used to fish and seaweed. And I like fish and seaweed. I tentatively bite into the fruit and am shocked by the taste. It rolls across my tongue and down my throat like sweet nectar. I moan. It's like biting into paradise.

"Our magic allows growth because we don't practice with the dark, we only engage with the light. And where there is light, there is growth."

Again, the monk's poetic words make little sense.

He leads us through the orchard, with its sweet aromas, shady trees, and earthy pathways, letting us gorge on as many oranges as we'd like, while he explains. "I'm going to start from the beginning. I know you are aware of most of this, but it's important you understand everything."

I nod as I take it all in. The sky is bright blue, the green leaves dance in the breeze, and everything smells of the oranges. I can't imagine a more perfect place in the world, including my home. If it takes him ages to explain, so be it, at least I'll get to stay here.

"When the seas rose, billions on this planet perished. Those left scrambled to survive but sadly, most did not. And then the asteroid came." He points at the stone in my hand. "When it hit the Earth's atmosphere, it broke into thirteen pieces, raining down all over the earth. That's when the vibration changed."

I raise an eyebrow and let him continue.

"Another way to say it is, that's when the magic came."

"But I thought your people always had magic?"

"In a way, we did. But this vibration was different. It was much stronger. It broke the earth into thirteen territories. Have you ever tried to leave this territory?" he asks.

I shake my head. "It can't be done."

"No, it can't." He sighs. "It cut us off from each other. We only have rumors of the plagues of the other areas."

"And what's our plague?"

"The remaining land dried up. The oceans became more dangerous. And even fewer people survived. During all of this, our Tibetan Buddhist magic grew. We became stronger as others around us weakened. That's when your people came to us, begging for asylum. But we had nowhere to house so many people for the long term. So we sent a party to find the stone, having heard rumors of its possibilities. Once they brought it to us, we used the enhanced magic to grant you the power to live under the ocean. It was an offer we made to all the people in our region, but the Japanese empire refused, finding the idea of magic evil."

I look at Kyon, who's busy staring at the ground. He runs his boot along the dirt, drawing a line around him. Clearly, he's uncomfortable. His ancestors had enough land above water to survive. They didn't have it easy, and still don't. They didn't want the magic. Not until recently, not until things started to get worse.

"So why is the magic fading?" I blurt.

"It was foretold, and it's all part of the plan." That's all he says on the matter, and he turns and leads us from the orchard back into the monastery.

Long is still taking his nap on the front steps. His whiskers flutter up and down with each snore. The gonging has ceased. The area is clear, and we're quiet as we enter the building. The two monks we'd left earlier are gone, and it's just the three of us in the large, open, simple room.

"You have powerful magic, Senra. Do you not?"

I nod, remembering my father's death, thinking about the monsters attacking my home, about all the times I have used my magic, or failed to use it, and the consequences of each.

"It is a great responsibility. Tell me, do you use it for good?"

I stiffen, drawing my eyebrows in. I want to challenge him on that question, but I've softened to him and I finally let out a sigh.

"I try to," I mumble.

"And what's the most powerful thing about your magic?"

"The fact that I can breathe underwater is pretty special." I laugh.

"There's that, of course, and there's also the telepathy," the Dalai Lama adds. Kyon's eyes spark with questions and he stares at me. This is news to him.

"And then of course the siren song," I say, getting to the point.

"Oh, yes. The song is what you use to defend yourselves and gather food, is it not?"

"That's correct." Where is he going with this?

"What if I told you that was never our intention?"

I pause, confused. Is this a trick? I search his face, trying to figure him out, but he's the same honest man now that he was when I first got here. He's the same gentle spirit he's always been.

"Explain."

"As I said, magic is simply a level of vibration. And what better vibration than that of a song? We used our magic for peace and our remaining islands flourished."

Islands? I wonder just how many they've been keeping hidden all these years but don't say anything. Now is not the time.

"Had you done the same," he continues, "you could have created greater peace for your people as well. Instead, you've used it to fight your enemies, often times, *killing* your human enemies. And so, the magic has eroded, and the sea monsters, as you call them, have gotten worse."

It all clicks into place. We are losing our magic because we are losing our humanity.

"But you, dear one, have proven yourself worthy to change history."

The world seems to slow as I take it all in.

"You had many opportunities to murder humans in cold blood and yet, you have not." Heat prickles across my face. My palms grow sweaty. I'm lost for words, as he continues. "We know about the act of self-defense when you saved this young man, but others drowned." I gulp, knowing it's true. I am a killer. "That responsibility lies with the siren warriors and not with you. When you were alone and put to the test, you had ample opportunity to murder, but your spirit remains unblemished. You never killed anyone. You are clean."

I blink at him, transfixed. I shake it away and ask the question burning me up inside. "How do I fix the siren magic?" I pray it's not too late.

He smiles, a conspiratorial glint lighting his watery eyes. "You learn to sing."

I tilt my head at him, and he chuckles, the wrinkles around his eyes deepening.

"I already know how to sing."

"Do you really?" he teases. "Maybe it's time you learned again." He puts a hand on Kyon's shoulder and one on mine. "Like I've been saying all along, Senra, you need to learn to love your enemy for any of this to work. Love is the root of true magic. Love is the mate to peace. There is no room for hate."

As if on cue, the doors open and monks stroll in, row after of row of them, their burgundy robes barely swooshing above the floor. They gather all around us.

"We don't sing as your people do. But we do make magic out of our music. Let me show you our way and perhaps you will be able to find yours."

The monks each have a golden bowl resting on one palm and a thick, short, stick in the other. The bowls are all different sizes, some gleaming in the sunlight, others dull and ancient. One by one, they use the sticks to rim along the outside of the bowls. The music fills the room, each bowl creating a different tone, a different sound, a humming vibration. It fills me, fills every part of me. It lifts and washes away all the anxiety and pain, all the doubt and anger that I've been holding on to for so long. It's not forced. It's not manipulation. I let it go of my own volition. My freedom is my choice.

Kyon and I stand in the center of these men as they play their symphony of peace, each of us transfixed. And finally, for once in my life, everything makes sense.

TWENTY
FIVE

THE FOAMY SURF ROLLS UP AND DOWN MY LEGS, THE SAND
tickling my skin. I'm lying down, half in and half out of the water.
Maybe it's a metaphor for my life. For my heart. I sigh joyfully and
close my eyes. The sun kisses my face, but this time, I relish the heat.
I let it blanket me like the friend I never knew I needed. I've changed.
I can see that now. As was pointed out to me, I chose not to kill the
humans. I chose not to kill Long. I'm different now. How is it possible
that so much about a person can change in such a short amount
of time? Yet here I am, enjoying something I never expected with
someone who I once intended to drown with my song.

Learn to love your enemies...

I roll to face Kyon. He's hunched over with his elbows draped
across his legs, staring out into the horizon, eyebrows drawn in
contemplation, black hair flopping over his eyes. I know he's worried

about his parents, but he doesn't say it. He probably doesn't want to burden me with any more concerns. I sit and scoot to him, gathering enough courage to rest my hand on his. The tips of our fingers barely twist together but it's enough to ignite a fire inside me.

He's changed, too. Or maybe, it's just that we see each other in a different light.

"They'll be okay," I say. "This will be over soon and then everyone will be better." I try to believe the words I say, but a small part of me doubts it.

He nods and stands, brushing the sand from his shorts. He's not wearing a shirt and his bronzed chest glistens with salt water and sweat. He stretches and his muscles flex, and I'm sinking into the sand like a puddle of water. I try not to stare, but I can't help myself and he catches me with a smirk. Blood rushes to my cheeks and I look away.

"What do you say, Senra? Should we get started?"

I jump up and nod vigorously, joining him in the stretch. My black suit is gloved to my body and I'm able to move freely. It cuts off just above my knees and runs all the way up into straps that cover my shoulders. It's not fancy. And I'm covered, modest enough, but the way Kyon looks at me right now makes me feel like I'm the most beautiful girl he's ever laid eyes on.

"Yes, I'm ready," I say. "Are you sure about this? You don't have to—"

"Yes I do. And I want to. I trust you, Senra. I know you'll be gentle."

The teasing way he says that makes me question if we're talking about the same thing and I'm alive with the thought.

I take a deep breath, refocusing. "I'm just glad we have a beach here."

There wasn't a beach on the Tibetans' other mountaintop island, and it wouldn't be a lot of fun for Kyon to do this work on a cliff face. The mages lent us this space and made sure everyone knew to stay away for the afternoon. It's been two days since we landed here. Two days of learning everything the monks know. And now, with time running out, I must apply that knowledge.

"Now or never," I say. "This is your last chance to back out."

"I'm not backing out." His voice and gaze are solid. Again, I'm struck with the thought that he's talking about something besides testing magic; that he's talking about his feelings for me.

I back down into the ocean; our eyes stay locked the entire time. Water laps at my ankles, then my thighs, my waist, my chest, my neck. I drop my gaze and dunk under for a moment, letting the magic consume me. Then I pop back up and unleash my song.

His face slackens, eyes glaze over, and he rushes toward me, arms outstretched. He's under the water within seconds, sucking it in. I rush to him, hauling him out of the water and back onto the beach. He coughs water and then fights me, eager for more ocean.

"Kyon," I yell in his face. "Kyon, stop!"

His chest rises and falls with heavy breaths, but finally, his eyes clear and he shakes his head, sending water in all directions. "Guess that didn't work."

"I'm so sorry," I say. "I was too rash. I didn't think..."

"It's okay." He runs a hand up my arm. "Let's try again."

I don't want to, but I have to. We both have to try. It's the only way. And so we continue. Over and over again, I sing and one way or another, he is pulled into the ocean by my song. He doesn't complain. Even when he nearly drowns, he doesn't say one negative word. He just encourages me to keep trying.

The day goes on like this until I'm about ready to give up. Again, I find myself in the water. I've tried my song in all the ways I can think of, and the result is the same for him. He rushes me, and if I get out of the water, he wants to stay. He wants to be under it, full of it, one with the waves and the tides and the murky depths. I don't know how much more I can take.

"Do it," he calls out over the beach. He raises his hands. "Come on, Senra. I'm fine. You need to keep practicing."

And so I concentrate and sing again, this time making my pitch the highest it's been so far today. Kyon's body reacts the same as before, rushing into the water, lapping in the waves. I'm upon him in seconds, dragging him up the sand. Something is different this time, though. Panic settles over me as I realize he's passed out.

I press on his chest, trying to force the water from his lungs. "Kyon!" I scream, shaking him. "Wake up." Tears stream down my face and everything tunnels in on just this one thing, just him and me. He's pale, his face tilted to the side, lips bluing, hair a wild halo around his head. "No!"

I slam against his chest, harder this time, looking around frantically.

The beach is empty, of course. I could go for help but would they get here in time? I remember how I helped those Samurai and will the salt water to leave his body.

Kyon coughs and spits water. His eyes flutter open, and I sob, dropping onto his chest. "Thank the Gods you're okay," I cry. His breath is shallow but after a minute, it starts to even out. "I thought you were dead," I mumble into his warm skin.

He runs a hand through my hair and pulls me to him. "So did I." He searches my eyes, finding an answer to a question, and then his lips are on mine.

It's my first kiss and it's nothing like I'd imagined. It's more. It's more than words or daydreams or betrothals or entire kingdoms. It's more than the call of the ocean or the spark of magic. It's more than prophecy or religion.

It's everything.

My whole body radiates from within, a molten fire that prickles and burns and caresses and soothes. His hands are everywhere and everything is his mouth, his lips, his tongue and teeth. There's water and salt as our kiss deepens. Our kiss, the result of everything unsaid between us. I don't ever want to pull away.

But eventually, he puts space between us and grins wickedly. "You have no idea how long I've wanted to do that."

"I might," I giggle, and then press my lips to his again. He tastes like the ocean and it only makes me like him more.

After a while, I lean back, gazing into his bronze eyes. Up close,

I notice the tiny dimple on his left check, and three dark freckles clustered next to his right eye. His black hair is messy and perfect, and he smells even better than the orange orchard. I've never felt like this before. I don't know what to do with this wild emotion; it's so big, so raw and consuming.

"Are you ready to try again?" he asks. "The song, I mean, not the kiss. Though, I'd be happy to kiss you all day."

I laugh, incredulous. "Are you serious? You want to try again? No, Kyon, I almost killed you."

"I believe in you. I believe if the monks can change their magic, you can change yours. You can use it to create peace just as they did in that monastery. But, Senra, do you believe it's possible?"

"Yes." I say it with certainty because I do. I have to.

"And do you believe in yourself?"

That question stops me. "I'm not sure."

"You need to believe in yourself for this to work. It's *your* magic, Senra. It has to come from you. It can't just come from me, even though Gods know I think if anyone can do this, it's you."

"But what if I fail? What if I make things worse?"

He smiles, running a hand down my face. "You won't fail. You can do this." He kisses my nose gently then gives me a knowing look. "Now, we're going to try this again. This time, you need to not only focus on what you're trying to create, but you need to *believe* in yourself like I do."

I take a steadying breath and nod. "Thank you."

Then once again, I back into the water. I dunk myself under and sit on the bottom for a moment. The dark blue water glitters under the sun, which has now begun to set. It paints the sky orange. Everything changes. There are cycles in all life. Maybe this is mine.

I swim back up to the surface and sing, letting my song stretch outward, an ethereal call of peace and love and magic and most of all, belief. My eyes focus on Kyon, watching the way he stands with such confidence. This time, Kyon doesn't come rushing into the water. This time, his face doesn't slacken.

He stays standing on the beach, the biggest smile stretched across his cheeks. He places his hand on his heart and laughs, joy radiating from him.

At the same moment, we run for each other, clashing in the surf. He lifts me up, spinning me around. "You did it! I felt that. It was peace you were sending me, right? I felt every bit of it."

I scream with excitement, more alive than I've ever been in my life. Free.

And in love.

Love? The thought of it sends a shockwave to my core. How could I be thinking that word already? I barely know Kyon and it's only been a few days since he warmed up to me. But still, that word reverberates inside so intensely that I know it's my truth. It's a terrifying thing to hold in my heart. And yet it's there and I couldn't remove it even if I wanted to. I don't want to.

He lowers me down to my feet, wrapping his arms around my

weakened body. My heart pounds, my thoughts zeroed in on my newest realization. I have to say it. I can't hold this in, not with my future in question.

I gaze into his eyes, no longer the slightest bit afraid. "I love you." Even as I say the words, I can't believe they're coming out of my mouth. But it's true, this love. It's as real as the ocean at our feet.

His face lights up, something dark releasing from his gaze, opening him to the words that whisper from his lips. "I love you, too."

And then we come together again, clashing bodies and mouths, clashing worlds, so very different, but then again, maybe not different at all. I don't know what's going to happen to us or how we're going to make this work, but I'm certain now that we've found this love, we're never going to let it go. Even as I think these things, burning in the back of my mind, are thoughts of Lei, of my promise to him, and of the beloved world still waiting for their princess to return.

TWENTY
SIX

THE NEXT MORNING I JOIN THE MONKS IN MEDITATION.
Sitting cross-legged on the stone floor, I keep my eyes closed and attempt to clear my mind. It's useless. All I can think of is the day ahead. Now I've figured out a new way to use my magic, I can't stay here. This peaceful island is a safe haven in a cursed world and I hate to leave it behind. The low rumbling gong rings through the room and my eyes flutter open. I stand with the others and wait as they disperse. I find the Dalai Lama and bow to him.

"Your Holiness."

"Princess Senra." His voice is overflowing with delight. "You're ready," he states like it's a fact, even though the state of my readiness could be up for debate. I don't feel ready, I just feel called.

I nod. "Thank you."

I take a deep breath and make one last attempt to get him to take this burden from me one more time before I go. I lift the black shining siren stone and my tone turns to begging, "Please, Your Holiness, please take it. I fear I can't succeed without you. My people are blessed with your magic but we do not know how to create it for ourselves. I beseech you, take the stone back and continue to keep our people strong. I will do as you've instructed with peace magic, I will teach them all. But please, I can't return home with this stone when I know nothing of its use."

His eyes turn compassionate as he shakes his head. "My people can no longer be steward to that stone. As I've said before, it doesn't belong to us."

"But we made a covenant," I challenge. "Your ancestors promised mine this magic."

He steps close, gazing into my eyes, and places his hands on either side of my face. They are warm and wrinkled and it takes everything in me not to cry. "Trust yourself, dear one. You'll know what to do with it when the time comes."

The rejection burns deep. I let out a tear and step away.

"You must go now," he says. "Long will take you and your young man where you're most needed. Time is running out."

Then the sage old man turns away from me and walks out the door and out of my life.

This time Kyon rides up front and my arms wrap around him. I press my face into his back and let my hands roam across his chest as we journey across the ocean. Long's scaly body wiggles under us and every so often, I pet his side affectionately. My anger at the monks is a battle within me. Because even though they won't take the stone, they taught me a better use for my song. And they gave me Long. I hope whatever spell they've cast over the dragon lasts and lasts, because he's become my friend. I can't imagine what will happen to him if he turns back into a monster.

Just as I can't imagine Kyon returning to his home without me. Based on the direction we're headed, I'm guessing that's our first stop. It makes sense. Kyon needs to take care of his parents.

I push the thoughts of goodbyes to the darkest parts of my mind and focus on the rolling sea. The color has started to change from dark to light, and the temperature has begun to warm. We must be nearing land. Kyon's body tenses, his hands tight around mine, as if he senses the difference, too.

"Whatever happens to me," he says, "I want you to fulfill your prophecy and save your people."

I bite my tongue, not entirely sure what he means by that, but not liking the sound of it. If something bad were to happen to him, I couldn't live with myself.

"I'm going to save everyone," I snap. "You included."

He nods, not a bit put off by my defensiveness. "I know. But you come first, Senra. You and your people come before me."

"Why?"

"Because I love you," he says simply. My heart catches and warmth floods me. It still feels surreal to hear those words directed at me, words that, against all odds, are genuine. I kiss the back of his neck and breathe him in. When I open my eyes to peer out into the distance, I catch sight of something orange glimmering on the horizon.

"Is that ... fire?"

"I think so."

Hurry, Long, I say through our telepathic connection. *I need you to get us there as fast as possible.*

He jerks forward and the three of us soar over the waves, wind and foam whipping through our hair and pelting our skin. The siren stone burns hot against my thigh, and I move one hand over it to make sure it holds firm. My only choice is to take the stone to the Elders. Maybe they'll know what to do. But that's not what matters right now...

The familiar outline of the Japanese island takes shape. Kyon is almost home. But as we near the island, it's plain to see that something terrible has happened. The savageness of battle has torn it up in places. Some of the docks have sunk; pieces of rubble float on the ocean current; and a fire rages on one side of the mountain, taking more homes with it. Black smoke billows into the sky like a clawing hand.

Kyon's entire body stiffens. His energy is dripping with fear. I squeeze his hand with mine, wincing when his squeeze back is as tight as a steel trap. He must be thinking of his parents. It was so easy to reassure him when we were back on the monk's island, when this reality wasn't spread out in front of us. Now, there's nothing I can say. I can't bring myself to give him false hope, even if he is the one I love and to see him afraid wrecks me. My eyes scan the docks, looking for the one on which his family lives. If I can just locate his home, then maybe…

That particular deck is completely gone. My heart drops.

"What happened?" His tone is both accusatory and grieving.

He points at the water and that's when I see them. My people. Their heads bob on the surf all along the edges of the island. A few are singing. Many more are fighting the humans. I see warriors mixed with families; even children have come to fight. Terror rolls through me. This was never what I wanted!

"No!" I scream, my voice screeches through the air but is lost to the noise of death and battle. I can't let this go on. This is my job.

"Stay safe," I hiss at Kyon. "Keep Long away from these people, they'll kill him on sight."

I don't give him a chance to respond or argue. I know what I have to do, the plan formed in my mind the moment I saw the fire. I grip the siren stone in one hand and jump from Long's back, diving under the water. The cool liquid surrounds me but my heart doesn't settle. I have changed. I won't go back to the way I was before. I won't value the ocean over innocent human life ever again. Something about being with the monks opened a space in my heart that I refuse to let close, especially now.

Most of the booby-traps have been dismantled by this point in the battle. Still, I veer in and out of what remains, swimming as fast as my arms and legs will take me. I come to one of my people, someone I don't recognize. It's no matter. I'm their princess, they'll know me.

You, stop! I call out. The woman turns to me, her face a mix of confusion and fear. She has a cut on one arm and a spear in the other. I grimace.

Princess? Her voice is high. *You came! We need you!*

Spread the word of my command. I rush in. *Do not kill the humans. Do not let them drown. If they come in the water, do not let them drown. Stop hurting them. Do you understand?*

She blinks at me a few times, her mouth dropping into a frown. Her black hair spreads around her face like a halo and she tilts her head at me. *But, we're losing our power. We need their land if we're going to survive.*

I inwardly curse. It's no wonder so many of these land-dwellers hate us. We're the ones that opened up the ability for the sea monsters to return. They went on without us, surviving against all odds. And now that we're in trouble, we're just going to kill them and take over their homes?

Bile rises in my throat. No, this cannot happen.

I mean it, I scream through the link. *Do not hurt the humans. Do not let them drown. Go! Spread the word to all you can find that this is my command. Go now!*

She falters for one more second and then nods, taking off.

237

I swim toward shore, spreading my message, praying they'll listen. I tell every siren I meet the same instructions. Satisfied enough that they know what to do, I swim back to the surface, bursting with song.

The music that pours from me is rich and lovely and devastating. But it sounds right. It sounds how it did yesterday on the beach when I finally succeeded.

I believe in myself. I can do this.

I banish the dark thoughts and think only of my love for Kyon, of the humans who showed me kindness, and of what our people can be if we adapt the same mindset of the mages, if we focus on love and peace instead of simply survival. I remember all those special moments between me and my father, knowing that this is what he would want, too. This is my way to honor him. I sing and sing until my throat is raw, but still, I continue. I sing under the water, I sing above the water. I swim the perimeter of the island as I go, singing my song so that all can hear its melody. I get as close to the docks and shores as I possibly can. I stay in the water where I know I am strong.

And nobody bothers to stop me. Any humans or sirens who come near are transformed by my music. I see it in their faces. I see it in the way they move. In everything about them—I see the peace. Their hatred and anger and fear, all the fight left inside of them falls away.

A few times I come across humans *with* sirens in the water. And my people are doing as I asked of them; my people are keeping the humans afloat. They're keeping them alive. My eyes prickle with tears, grateful for their love for me that they would follow my instructions, even with everything they must have gone through these past few weeks.

Around the island I go for as long as I can possibly stand, until the sun begins to lower toward the horizon, until song softens on my lips and my throat burns and all I'm left with are my thoughts, and then even those are washed away. Once I'm sure I can't go any longer, I cease any noise and find the same cove I'd swam in not long ago, the one I know has a soft blanket of sand and a long welcoming beach.

I stumble up it. Somewhere in the distance I think I hear Kyon's voice calling to me, but I can't be sure and I'm too tired to focus on it, anyway. Exhaustion has overwhelmed all of my senses, and my knees buckle underneath the weight of my body.

Why am I so heavy?

I'll just lie down for a minute, close my eyes and let them rest. It won't be long, a few minutes only. The darkness of sleep pulls me under just as men's voices yell and unknown hands grab me, and I'm carried away.

TWENTY
SEVEN

I WAKE WITH A START, SITTING UP SO FAST MY HEAD
spins. I'm not on a sandy beach but in a warm bed. I breathe fast,
taking in the surroundings with frantic eyes. The bedroom is small
and exquisite. The walls have a papering of thin white texture and
lace curtains of the same white hue hang next to a large glass window,
a starry night beyond. I run my hands along the plush midnight-blue
blanket, its velvety texture soft against my fingers. I lift it up to find
I'm no longer in my bodysuit but in a modest black silky nightgown
that reaches all the way to my ankles. I bite my lip, mortification
prickling across my skin.

I jump up and dash across the carpeted floor to get a better look
outside. A courtyard with a rectangular pool of water shimmers
back at me, and I know exactly where I am: the Japanese Emperor's
palace. My heart thuds against my ribcage as I race around the room,

searching for the stone. I pull open drawers and lift blankets and even throw a pillow across the room.

It's gone.

I steel my spine and charge for the door. I expect it to be locked up tight, but it opens easily and the movement gives me pause. Am I not a prisoner? I glance back to the room. No guards. No chains. No samurai or guns or anybody at all. And I know they have a dungeon underneath the palace, Asahi showed me the entrance. So why am I not there, locked away where I can't do any more harm?

I pad out into the hallway, then to a room I've seen before: the royal family's sitting room. It's empty and dark. I walk the perimeter and recall the young girl I'd seen sitting on the couch, curled up with a book. I run my fingers along that same couch and wonder if she's okay. I hope she wasn't harmed in all of this. I inwardly curse myself for not stashing the stone somewhere before stumbling up on that beach. I'd been too delirious for coherent thought. How long have I been out?

"Oh, mercy, you're awake," someone says, flipping on the lights. I know that voice and I whirl around, joy bursting through me.

"Mother!"

I rush to her and we embrace, arms clinging onto the other for dear life. I nearly sob. I'm so relieved to see her.

"Are you okay?" I step back, patting her cheeks. "What happened? What are you doing here?"

She smiles, a knowing glint in her eye. "Come." She takes my hand and leads me to the couch. "When you left on your mission, things started to get worse for our people. All over the kingdom, siren power has dwindled. It got to the point where people started to drown."

I frown and look down, ashamed at my failure. I knew about that possibility, about the family of three who washed up here, but I can't seem to utter a word.

"How many?" I finally ask, the question coming out in a whisper.

"Since you left, we've lost over sixty innocent lives to drowning."

I let out a breath, a shockwave reverberating through me. I had no idea it had gotten that bad. Sixty innocent people. The number seems too high to fathom.

"And so we left," she says, her voice trembling. "We didn't know what else to do. Some of our people went to the abandoned Tibetan island and some came here. We didn't have many options. We needed to get to ground."

"Where would everyone live? This place is overcrowded."

Shame crumples her face. "I know. I made the call after enough pressure from SunYu. We attacked."

I nod. I saw as much. None of this should come as a surprise but it still does—my mother has never been a warrior. But she is fiercely loyal to her people, and perhaps anyone would have done the same thing.

"Senra." She runs a hand down my arm, ending at my hand. Hers is cold in mine. Cold as the sea. Cold as death. "You saved us all from killing each other. How did you do that? I never knew song could change people's hearts that way. The battle was turning deadly when you showed up and calmed us all with that beautiful music."

242

"The monks showed me." I smile.

"The monks?" Her eyes go wide. "Where are they? Are they safe?"

"They're safe… I'm afraid we may never see them again. They've used magic to hide themselves from us. They were kind to me, but believe we've used them as a crutch, that our empire has become wicked over the years, killing more and more of the land-dwellers. They don't want any part in magic being used to harm innocent lives. The covenant is broken."

Her face falls, her hands dropping helplessly to her sides. Her hair is loose and for the first time, I notice that the gray is more predominate than the black on my otherwise timeless mother. It's the kind of thing that grounds me into the moment, that makes me realize just how much has happened to us. "But what of the magic?" she asks.

I close my eyes for a moment, overcome with grief. "I think we might lose it for good. I don't know. I retrieved the stone but when I woke up in here, it was gone."

A throat clears behind us and a shadow crosses in the doorway. The Emperor enters the room, purpose in every stride. Three guards follow. They're armed, but I'm not even a little bit afraid. I stand to meet him. He's dressed in black silk robes, the air about him brimming with authority.

"Perhaps I can answer that question for you," he says, stepping forward. His lips curve up into a gentle smile. He reaches a hand from behind his back, holding out the stone. I gasp, eager to steal it again. I don't have to. He places it in my outstretched hand and steps back.

I'm stunned speechless. The stone practically vibrates with its magic, glowing even brighter than I remembered. Is the power increasing?

"We've been trying to find information about the magic in our territory for ages but have had little to no success," he says. "We knew of the stone's existence, we even knew of the Tibetan monks keeping it for you. But we didn't know if we could destroy the stone or use it for ourselves."

He goes to the window, gazing out at his land. "We're a series of islands, in case you didn't know. There are more that survived the rising seas than just this one, though this is the largest. It's up to me to keep these people safe and alive."

He turns to my mother and me. "I'm sure you can relate to that?"

I nod. "Chinese land isn't as elevated as it is here. We didn't have the same luxury and so we agreed to the siren covenant."

"I know, nor do I blame you."

Once again, I'm stunned. He doesn't blame us? If that's true, then how come so many of his people hate us?

He chuckles and walks back to the sitting area. Relaxing into a plump armchair, he gestures politely for me to return to my seat on the couch. I don't want to relax, but I follow anyway. The tiny hairs on my arms are standing on end, my heart is racing, my muscles are primed to pounce. I pray this isn't a trap. Mother's hand finds mine again.

"Don't get me wrong," he says. "I have blamed you in the past. The monsters have gotten more aggressive in recent years, especially over the last six months. And so my wife and I blamed your people for taking the magic."

"You believe the sea monsters are a result of the siren stone?"

His eyes flash to the mound of black shining asteroid in my hands and he nods slowly. "I do."

I twist my lips—maybe there won't be peace between our people after all.

"Let me continue," he says. "We became desperate and so I sent out a party to retrieve the stone. When they arrived on the island, however, it was empty, but the stone was still there. So my men took it and brought it to me. I didn't know what to do with it. Some advised I should destroy it, others said we should try to harness that magic for ourselves. Both of those choices made logical sense, but neither was the one I wanted to take."

I'm not sure I believe him. I heard the conversation between him and his wife, and while he was regretful to harm my people, she was not. Not only that, they'd seemed intent on doing one of those two things. Either use the stone for their own gain or destroy it. I fold my arms across my chest and sink further into the couch, studying him, searching for lies mixed with truth.

"There's a third option," he says quietly. "An option I didn't think I'd ever have the chance to take. But now"—he looks at me—"with you here, it could be possible."

"What is this mysterious third option?"

"You know of the prophecy?"

I still, heat burning at my cheeks. "Which one?" I question.

"The Dark Ocean Princess?"

I flick a glance to Mother and she nods.

"It's okay, Senra. You can tell him."

"Yes, I do," I say.

"Then you know what you need to do with the stone."

My lips part and my eyebrows draw together. "No I don't. It's vague."

He shakes his head. Standing, he hurries to a chest of drawers and removes a scroll.

"My men found this with the stone," he says. "The answer is right here."

I roll open the faded paper. It's so old it nearly crumbles under my touch. There are drawings and text written upon the parchment, the same as what was etched into our walls down in the temple below the water.

But as I scan the document, I see more to the poem. I turn toward Mother. "Did you know about this?"

She shakes her head. "The mages only gave us part of the prophecy. I know as much as you do." I pass her the paper, and her eyes scan it, the blood draining from her face.

"No," she breathes. "No, we can't ask her to do this."

"We have to," the emperor says. "It's the only way we all survive this. The monsters are only getting worse. I've received word of more attacks. They're becoming bolder. Only she can stop them." He narrows his gaze on mine. "The monks left this with the stone for us to find. I believe it wasn't coincidence, but so that we could save each other."

I take the scroll back from my mother and read the prophecy a second time. It all makes sense now, the truth settling over me with finality. The peace of which the monks spoke, and why he kept asking me to love my enemy. The Dalai Lama said the stone didn't belong to him, and I'd assumed that meant it belonged to the siren kind. But it isn't either people's to possess. And if I'm to complete this task, it's because I have learned to love my enemies, to the point that I would die for them.

I read the complete prophecy for the third time, committing it to memory.

The water rose and the asteroids hit.
Earth Mother slumbered and Gaia recessed.
The magic swelled, the people blessed.
They became the sirens and made their bet.

And all will be well for the first century
The people will flourish in ocean's prosperity.
But magic always comes with a price,
And only a royal heir will suffice.

The ocean is cursed. The monsters are real.
But she is far worse. She is the siren heir.
Her reign is life and her song is death.
They will call her, Dark Ocean Princess.

When her people perish, the magic waning,

And her enemies take dominion, the order of Kings.

She, and she alone, will enact Gaia's retribution.

For she is the chosen one and in death she will save them.

With the stone in hand, following her dragon companion,

With love for the enemy now changed in her heart,

She'll return the stone to the earth, bring it back to Gaia,

Restore it to the place where it was meant to be from the start.

The scroll slides closed with a whoosh of cool air and I stand. This time, it is I who crosses to the window. It's not just the island I'm surveying but the vast ocean beyond. It's all the lives that have been lost so far, all the bodies left to the bottom of the sea. It's my father I think of, and his men, and the countless others who will also die if I don't fulfill my destiny. I touch my fingertips to the glass, my eyes refocusing on my own reflection. My hair is loose and brushing past my shoulders, my skin pale and smooth, just like my mother's. My eyes are dark and steady and sure, my shoulders set back, just like my father's.

"What does this mean for my people?" I ask, spinning on the emperor.

"You have my word that I will give them safe harbor."

"Even if this means we lose our siren magic for good?"

"Especially if that's the case. We're overcrowded, as you know, but we'll find a way. And with the dragons gone, it will be easier. We can build more dock homes on our other islands."

"Senra, don't." Mother comes to stand at my side. "You don't have to do this."

My smile is soft. "It's the only way. If I don't, we'll lose our magic anyway, but the sea monsters will only get worse."

I think of Long with his black lethal body and his golden eyes. He's the one monster who didn't turn out to be a monster at all. He's meant to go with me, to lead me. He's always meant to be my companion for this.

Love your enemies...

"Do you know where I'm taking the stone?" Even as I ask the question, I'm sure I have the answer. It must be some place under the water, some place of which Long knows. And when I return the stone, it could mean the end to siren magic and the end to me.

The emperor joins us. His eyes flick to the window, searching the endless horizon. "I'm not sure where the stone needs to be placed but I think your dragon companion will know. I suspected, and the moment I heard you'd left on the back of a sea dragon, I knew for sure it was you, that you were the Dark Ocean Princess come to retrieve your stone. I prayed you'd complete your task. I will still pray for you."

"And will there ever be retribution for my people's attack on your island?"

He shakes his head. "Blood has been spilt on all sides. But you

Senra, you could have killed my family and my men, but you didn't. You showed mercy. So you have my word, Princess. If you complete this task, if you heal our world of those terrible beasts, I will take care of your people as if they were my own. Nor will I take your throne. Our kingdoms will unite and we can work together to bring about a new way of life."

I nod and stretch out my hand. We shake on the agreement that means life for him and for so many others, but likely not for me. The line from the scroll comes back to my mind, loud and feral and as terrifying as it is redeeming...

...and in death, she shall save them.

TWENTY
EIGHT

"YOU MUST HAVE A THING FOR BEACHES," I SAY AS I STEP

out onto the cool sand. Kyon is sitting with his toes in the surf. He

jumps up when he spots me, his hair flopping, his smile widening. My

stomach flips. I skip to him and we embrace in a tight hug, soaking

in the feel of each other.

"Actually, I have a *thing* for you," he whispers against my ear. "And

I figured this beach was the best place to look." I can't get over his

amazing smell, still unsure how to describe it other than spicy and

earthy and uniquely *him*. I breathe it in, willing it to stay with me

forever, even in death.

I smile softly, warmed by his sweet words, but still, I'm torn up

inside. "Did you find your parents?"

"Yes," he replies. "They're okay."

Relief floods me, and I hug him tighter. "Tell them thank you for me, please?" I should do it myself, but I can't bear the thought of it.

He stills. "What do you mean?"

It's the dead of night. I can't waste any more time. I can't stay here with him for long. I also can't imagine saying goodbye. My mother saw me off back at the palace and the emperor chose to stay back with his family. He wanted to send some of his guards to escort me to the shore but I asked to go alone. With the peace magic still flowing through the island and the time of night, I didn't expect to face any problems.

And I was right.

Above, the moon is cut down the middle, the beginnings of a waning crescent. The night is darker than it's been since my journey began. It's hard to make out Kyon's features. I long to see the gleam in his eye and the smirk in his smile, the small dimple or the cluster of freckles, but maybe this will make our goodbye easier. I find his lips and kiss him with everything I have left. His hands run up my arms to find my face, deepening the kiss. We go on that way until my thoughts return and the burn cools to embers. Finally, the tears I've been holding leak from my closed eyes and roll down my face, snuffing out the last of the kiss.

"I have to go," I say, anguished.

"What's wrong?" He steps back, trying to see me in the darkness. It's no use. It's hard to make out anything tonight. "Senra, what happened? Tell me."

I don't want to do this to him but I know I must. And so I do. My voice catches as I speak. "There's a final part of the prophecy, something that ties everything together."

His body freezes, rooted to the sand. The persistent crash of the surf fills the space between us.

I go on, rushing the words from my lungs, "I have to follow Long down into the ocean and return the siren stone to Gaia."

Gaia, the energy of the earth herself. She's been waiting…

"What are you talking about?" he growls.

"It's the only way to heal the land and sea."

"And what of magic?"

I don't say anything, my words snuffed out.

"Senra?" Panic builds in his tone. "And what will happen to the magic?"

"I don't know," I confess. "It might be lost."

He shakes his head. "No, you can't. You'll drown."

"I know."

He takes several gasping breaths, his hands fly up. "This is not what I meant when I asked you to fulfill your prophecy. It's too much. It's not fair."

"I know," I say again. The truth pulls me to him like a rope. I wrap my arms around him once again and cry and gasp the confession into his warm shirt, "But I have to do this, Kyon. I have to. The sea monsters are only going to get worse and my people are drowning as our magic wanes. How are we to fight them when they follow us here? To this island?"

"What about your dragon, Long?" he challenges. "If he's good, can't the others be turned, too?"

"He's been magicked by the Dalai Lama. But he's only one monster and the mages can't possibly have enough magic to stop the rest of them." I steady my sobs, calming myself. "I made a deal with your emperor. He's going to protect all siren kind should anything happen to the magic, so long as I do this. I'm doing it for *all* of us."

"You owe me," he blurts out. "Remember when I first brought you to this beach? You were acting crazy and were willing to do anything to get in the water. And I helped you and you agreed to a favor, any favor at any time. Remember?"

"Kyon…" My voice cracks. "Please don't do this."

"Well, I'm calling in that favor now," he continues, bending slightly to glare into my eyes, talking over me. "I mean it. You can't go. It's too much for one person. You'll die if the magic is lost! We'll find another way to stop the sea monsters."

"You would do it for me," I say. "You would do it for your family, for your people. Don't pretend you wouldn't because I know you would."

"You're right. I would, but I can't," he says, defeated. He drops to his knees, gripping my hands. "I'd give anything to take this from you but I can't."

I lower myself down to my knees as well, wrapping my arms around him. "And nor would I ask you or anyone else to do it. This is my burden to carry."

He pulls me back in for another kiss, his arms now circle me, caging me in. This time it's a kiss laced with the bitter taste of regret. It's a physical representation of the love between us and the unfairness of this prophesied life. If I could stay in his arms forever, I would. That's impossible, so I end the moment and step away. It's time to go.

"Hey!" an iron voice booms over the water. "Get your hands off her!"

I spin to find someone tall and lean bounding up the shore. He emerges from the water like a warrior charging into battle.

"Lei!" I call to him, raising my hands. "Stop!"

But he's on us, ripping Kyon and me apart. "Don't lay a finger on my fiancée, you filthy human!"

"This is your fiancé?" Kyon asks me as he glares at Lei. "This is the man who's trying to force you to marry him?"

I'm struck with panic, remembering the way I spoke of Lei and his father when I first met Kyon's family, how I acted like Lei and I weren't compatible and I wasn't happy with the match. Truth be told, I could marry Lei and live a comfortable life. But I'd never be satisfied, not when I've experienced the real love that's possible with Kyon. None of that matters now, anyway. Not when I'm leaving. But Lei doesn't know that I'm leaving, does he? To him, this is a fight for my honor and his future. His hands become fist and he growls.

Sand and water fly as the men jump at each other. Kyon is valiant in defense of me but Lei is a trained killer. Even above water, it shows. They're both fueled by a passion stronger than reason, not hearing me as I cry out and beg for them to stop. They roll across the sandy beach, punching and grunting as fists and knees pummel into each other. A bone cracks, and Kyon cries out in pain, followed by a battle cry as he dives on Lei.

I need to stop this. I look around frantically. Is there anybody here to help? No. The beach is empty. Water licks at my heel and then relapses into the surf, giving me an idea. I follow the rescinding water and slip into the surf, letting the water surround me, the magic of my power build. When I burst through the surface, I sing my song of peace as loud and as sure as I ever have. The men don't seem to hear me at first, so intent on hurting each other, they continue to grapple in the sand.

I press on and after a minute, the riving form of limbs ceases movement. I run from the water and land on my knees beside the men. Lei sits up, rubbing his head, hurt and confusion reflecting in what little I can see of him. But it's not really Lei I care about.

"You're with someone else? A human? What about us?" he asks the questions in rapid succession. His eyes are glazed over with my magic, but confused just the same.

I can't answer those questions now. They don't matter, not when Kyon isn't moving. I shake him but he's nothing except for flesh and blood and bone. Where is his breath? Where is the smile on his lips or the flutter of eyelids?

"What did you do?" I snap at Lei. The water on Lei's suit glints, and I catch the flash of something metal as he slips it into a pocket.

"I defended your honor," he replies simply, sitting back on his heels.

"What's that?" I point to the area where he's returned some kind of weapon.

"A dagger," he replies mechanically, the peace of my song still in effect. "I used it in self-defense."

My fear is blazing hot and sharper than any blade Lei could possibly wield. I run my hands over Kyon, looking for the wound. "How could you do this to me?" I sob.

I look up at Lei, noticing the way his eyes are clearing. He's returning to himself.

"Don't bother." Lei stands, brushing the sand from his sleek bodysuit. "He's dead. I stabbed him in the heart."

I cry out and press on Kyon's chest but don't feel anything. There's no cut or blood ... or heartbeat.

"It's not on the front. I stabbed him through the back," Lei says, stepping away. "You would know a thing about that, wouldn't you, Senra?"

Pure rage envelops me, and I jump to my feet, charging Lei. He doesn't expect it when I slam him to the ground and tackle him, angry fists flying at his smug face.

"I'll kill you," I sob. "I'll kill you for this."

"Stop!" Lei's hands fly up in defense but he doesn't fight back. "Don't make me hurt you, Princess."

The sobs become too much, overpowering the rage, and I fall against him. The pain is so intense it's as if Lei has stabbed me through my heart as well. I ache with it, ache with the loss of Kyon. I continue for a while and then roll off Lei, crawling back to Kyon's body. I cry into his chest, pleading with him to come back to me. He doesn't move.

"I loved him," I shoot back to Lei. "How could you kill him?"

"How could I? How could you love a human? How could you betray our engagement? You've only been gone ten days. How could you possibly know him enough to say you love him? You're a foolish girl."

I shake my head. "You know nothing of what I've been through. You know nothing of love. You're the fool."

I should kill Lei for this. I should avenge Kyon's death right here and now. I can't. That's not who I am; it's not the siren I want to be, nor is it how I want to lead my people. I'm not like Lei. And if murder and hate is what it takes to be a strong siren warrior, then I'm more human than I ever thought. My heart cries out with the grief. I should have sung my song sooner. I should have stopped Lei. But it's too late. It's over.

I haul Kyon's body onto my back and drag him toward the sea, praying his parents will forgive me for what I'm about to do. I'm sure they'd want to give him a proper burial. It's what he deserves. And yet, I can't bring myself to leave him here, not like this, not with his murderer standing over his body to gloat. I'm most likely heading to my death anyway. He can come with me. Our bodies can rest at the bottom of the ocean for eternity. At least we'll be together.

I stop to pick up the siren stone where I'd dropped it in the sand and step into the water.

"Where are you going?" Lei calls after me, his voice accusatory and possessive. I was right about him. He knows nothing of love.

I don't bother to answer or to look back. Not at him, not at the island, not at anything. Kyon's body lightens once we're submerged in the water. His limbs spread and his head floats on the waves. I swim further and call out for Long who comes quickly. He's been waiting nearby. He's ready for this, too.

He lets out a whine when he sees Kyon's limp body, and it takes everything in me not to break down again. *Time for one final journey together, old friend*, I say to my dragon, to my friend. He waits as I climb onto his back, pulling Kyon up with me. We take off and when the three of us drop down into the watery depths, my tears are absorbed by the salt of the ocean.

TWENTY NINE

IT'S ALL I CAN DO TO HANG ON TO KYON'S BODY, LONG'S scaly back, and to keep the stone tucked between my legs. We race deeper and deeper toward the ocean floor. My eyes adjust to the darkness. There are remnants of the past here; whole cities that have been left to rot and ruin and fall to pieces under the cruel current. What was it like for the people who didn't make it out in time? In their last moments, did they cling to their accolades and titles and wealth, or was it their families, their loved ones that mattered most?

As I hold Kyon's body to mine, I know my answer.

I will go down in history as the Dark Ocean Princess, as the one who saved them all. They will remember me for that accolade, but I hope they tell the story as it really was. That all of this was born from love. I love my people and I love the humans and I love Kyon. I want their civilizations to thrive, for them to work together to not only survive but to thrive. And so I'll make the ultimate sacrifice, I'll do it, because nobody else can, because my love is greater than my fear. I'm ready to trust.

I lay my cheek against Long's back. I've gotten so used to his sharp scales that I know exactly how to position myself to keep from getting cut. I don't see him as a monster anymore. My heart aches that he'll be destroyed in all of this. I'd give anything to be able to magic all the sea monsters to be just like him. That would solve everything. We could all live together in peace. But I know the dream is useless. The siren stone doesn't belong to me or to any of us.

I'm so sorry, I say to Long. *I wish there was another way.*

He twists his long neck to look back at me, golden eyes gleaming. He nods his head once, and then his forked tongue slips from between puffy lips. It slides against my face, rough as coral. The affectionate move makes me laugh.

You're a good friend, Long, I say between the giggles and tears. *I really needed that right now.* His head twists further so that he's staring me down with both of those magical glowing eyes. I stare back. *Do you understand what you're sacrificing?*

He blinks once and licks my other cheek, then turns and swims on. I sigh. I don't know if he understands what's happening and maybe I never will. Maybe it's okay for me not to know. And maybe it's better if he's simply a puppet. A small part of me is convinced he's known the truth all along, that he willingly agreed to this journey and it's not only magic at work here. Perhaps he really is the reincarnation of the ancient emperor, sent to guide me on my path. I'll probably never know the truth. Either way, he's my friend, and I'll always be grateful.

The tears grow in number as we continue deeper and deeper and deeper. I no longer care to hold them back. They flow freely as I cry for Kyon, for my father, for Long, for all those lost in the battles and bloodshed and those whose magic faded too soon. I cry for the vibrant world of decades past and all the souls who were lost to the floods. But most of all, I cry for myself, for my vanishing future and the love I'll never get back.

After a while my tears dry up, and I'm left with nothing but a peaceful numbing sensation. I twist from side to side, trying to identify the area in which we are, but Long has taken me somewhere I've never been to before. We're long past the territories that used to be above water and are now closing in on the deepest crevices of the ocean floor. Even the sirens don't journey this deep. We can, but the worst of the monsters live down here and the temperatures drop to further than we can stand. Long doesn't slow, and the weight of the water crushes down around us. The black is so thick that even my siren eyes struggle to adjust. The prickling cold fills my every pore with ice. It climbs deep down into my lungs and then beyond, ravaging my bones and blood and sinew.

I can hardly move. My joints ache, but I keep hold of Kyon and the stone anyway, pushing through the searing pain. I can do this. It's almost over.

We drop into an earthen canyon of jutting black rock. A shadow darts past, and I jerk up. Another hulking figure whisks overhead, swooping in low. Then more appear, circling us.

Sea monsters. Dragons. Ancient myths come to life.

They're made of every color and size, all with open mouths of razor sharp teeth and clawing arms and legs. There's too many too count, at least a hundred. Maybe two hundred.

And they're hungry.

My heart pounds, and I squeeze Kyon tighter to me. So it's true. The monsters are getting worse, much worse, growing in both size and number. But I never imagined it would be like this. *They're everywhere.* There are far too many beasts for my people to battle, especially with our newly struggling magic. The humans wouldn't stand a chance against this many, either.

Fear washes through me. Should I sing?

It might work. I might be able to subdue them. But for how long? And with so many, what if it doesn't work? Singing will alert each and every monster to my location. The thought strikes me that we might not be able to return the stone to Gaia after all. I never considered the possibility of failure.

A body of gleaming alabaster juts toward us, swiping out at Long with razor sharp claws. Another follows, a smaller but faster blood-red beast. Its mouth is open, snarling with hunger. Long growls and swipes back. I have my answer.

He can't do this alone. He needs me.

So I fill my lungs and let out the music, my sound reverberating through the water. I sing the song I've always sung for ocean life, the kind that draws them in but makes them malleable to my will. My voice has succeeded against these monsters before. It should again. *It has to.*

The alabaster dragon relaxes. The crimson beast does not. He charges, screeching and angry, claws thrashing. Long narrowly dodges out of the way, and I almost topple off his back. I tighten my grip and continue singing, desperation lacing the undercurrents of my song.

It's not working.

Many of the dragons are subdued but still, more are not. And they're circling, hungry for their prey, eager to get a bite. Long is still caught by the tail and he thrashes, his armored scales the only thing keeping us alive against this wild, ravenous predator.

I catch the eye of a brown monster lurking. He's slowly winding up from below, his mouth open and almost grinning. His black eyes twinkle, and his forked tongue juts out. It brushes against my ankle and latches on tight. I scream as it yanks at me with nothing but an icy tongue, a muscle so much stronger than it looks.

I squeeze my eyes shut and dig into that place of peace I know is within. I'm flooded with the memories of my journey so far, of my newfound ability to change my song. I need to keep singing, to keep trying. But if I'm going to use siren magic one last time, I'll let it be to create peace and not more death.

So again, I sing. This time the tone shifts; the notes longer and lighter. They pour from me like liquid magic, like pleas for peace, twisting and spinning and spreading through the den of beasts.

The tongue at my ankle slackens. The crimson beast with his

massive jaw clasped around Long's tail falls away. All around me, the sea monsters relax. They calm, one by one, the frenzy of water and thrashing scaled bodies slowing to a stop. My insides burn with gratitude. My heart pounds even harder. As I continue to sing, the beasts swim alongside us, companions to our cause.

I'd burst into tears if I had any left to give. Instead, I smile. I can feel it deep inside me, deep where the magical part still lives. We're almost there.

Down we go, further into the belly of the earth. My song attracts them all, each and every dragon follows in our wake. And I can feel it, too. That peace. That calm. We're doing the right thing. *I'm* doing the right thing. I will die to let the others prosper. I won't just subdue them, but I will rid our part of the world of these ravenous monsters, even if that means I have to go down with them. If there really is such a thing as an afterlife, I pray Kyon and I will get to spend it together.

The thick expanse of black sea is broken by an emerald light. My eyes widen as we draw near. Down below, Gaia is beckoning. She calls out to the basest part of me. She wants the stone, her stone sent from the heavens. We dive further until we come upon a sight more beautiful than anything I've witnessed in my short life.

In the deepest, darkest part of our ocean, there's a glen.

It grows wild with green swaying grass and tall trees and vibrant flowering buds. It emanates pure life, each plant glowing from within. This is nothing like the dredges of vegetation I saw above the surface. Even the monks' fruit orchard pales in comparison to this glen.

We land at the foot of it. I slide from Long's back to step into the grass. It's soft against my bare feet, caressing. Holding the stone in one hand and Kyon's hand in my other, I slowly walk toward the center of the glen. Kyon's body floats next to me. I turn to him one last time. His eyelids are gently closed, his shiny black hair floating around his beautiful face. His pale pink lips are barely open, as if he were sleeping and nothing more.

I place a final kiss on those lips, my heart ripping in two.

Then I kneel. The grass grows brighter, pulsing at the proximity of the siren stone in my hand. It's alive with magic, too. I can feel the frenetic buzz of it between my fingers. No, it's not the siren stone any longer. The stone belongs to no man.

I find an opening in the earth, a place just large enough for the smooth stone to fit in its embrace. The peace I've been singing again and again, finally settles over me, filling every inch of my being. It's a calming embrace. It's a whispered promise. It's faith. Taking one final steadying breath, I press the stone into the earth, returning the magic to Gaia and fulfilling the prophecy at long last.

THIRTY

THE LIGHT BLINDS AND TRANSFORMS FROM BRIGHT EMERALD to searing white. It flashes and expands, eating everything up, swallowing me whole. Heat prickles across my entire body, sweeping down into my core, thawing the ice. I'm jerked back, the light burning through me. I strain against it and reach for Kyon, gripping at his floating arm. And then the light grows even brighter, unimaginable, and I lose thought. Something is shooting through me, rushing past me, pushing me, up and up. I'm flying, body whipping, heat still searing, tossing me like I'm made of nothing.

Is this what death feels like? It's so encompassing… so *bright*.

I still can't open my eyes. In my hand, I fiercely grip onto something. Kyon. No, that's not right. If I'm dead how can I be holding his body?

I'm shot through a barrier, my body going from heavy to light, flying further, further, further. The heat falls away. A gust of wind whips through my hair. I push open my eyes but something slams against me and again, I'm lost to the brightness.

I'm floating. Something tickles at my ears. A hand squeezes mine. "Wake up," a voice says from somewhere much too far away. "Senra, wake up." The voice is familiar but still too distant to place.

There was green and then white.

There was cold and then heat. I was flying.

"Senra," the voice says again, closer this time, harder. My eyes flutter open, and I cough, water sloshing in my lungs. I search for the source of the voice and find him. Kyon.

He's clinging to me, floating with me.

"Are we dead?" I ask, grappling for him.

I already know the answer. If Kyon is here, then I must be dead. Joy bursts through me anyway, realizing it was worth it if we get to spend the afterlife together.

Water splashes across my face and I start, fully awake now. I try to sit up, only to sink further with nothing to hold me. I look around, startled to find Kyon and I are floating in the middle of the ocean. The morning sun peeks over the horizon, turning the whole world rosy gold. It reflects off Kyon's smiling face, and I forget about our location and squeal, pulling him to me. We kiss, legs kicking, trying to keep afloat, but lips sealed together.

Can I breathe underwater? Do I still have siren power? Am I really dead?

The questions spin through me as we cling to each other.

"You did it," a playful voice calls out over the waves. We both turn. The Dalai Lama floats on his rudimentary raft. It's the same vision of him I had when he brought me Long.

No, not a vision. That was real…

Realization grips me. It's too good to be true. "So we're not dead?" I breathe. I share a glance with Kyon and then peer up at the monk. "How?"

He floats closer. In his right hand is his long wooden staff that he's currently using for an oar. The bottom of his burgundy robes are soaked through but he doesn't seem to care or even notice. His smile is infectious, and he laughs loud, a deep belly laugh that echoes across the water.

"You're not dead," he confirms.

I sputter, still not understanding, "But Kyon, he was gone." I choke the final word out and squeeze myself closer to him.

"She saved you," the monk says. "Gaia must have found your heart pure and worthy of saving." And then he winks at me, laughing once again. "Kyon, he was in the right place at the right time."

None of this makes sense.

Once his laughter settles down, the monk explains, "When you gave the stone to Gaia, you gave her the magic and she not only chose to heal the land left on our territory, but to heal both of you, as well."

My lips part, the breath light on my tongue. "She saved us?"

"Yes."

"And you say she saved the land? What do you mean?"

The monk grins again. He lifts his staff from the water and points it at us. "See for yourselves, dear ones."

And then in a flash of sparkling gold light, he's gone. He's gone, and we're flying across the ocean's surface, gripping onto each other, screaming over the crash of waves and wind. It could have been a few seconds or a few minutes, but before long, Kyon's island appears before us.

It's different.

It's bursting with life, as green as the emerald glen below the ocean.

We're thrown from the ocean and washed up onto our beach, rolling across the sand before we come to a stop. Kyon is on top of me and now he's laughing. I can't help it. I burst with laughter as well, the weight of the prophecy replaced with the weight of him sends my heart soaring.

"I can't believe it," I breathe, "you were dead. I should be dead, too."

He points to the vibrant green island behind us, the dead scorched land is completely gone. "Apparently I'm not the only thing brought back to life, Senra."

He gives me a quick kiss, and then pulls me to standing. We're running up the side of the mountain, hands clasped together, running for the emperor's palace, to share in the news.

We're welcomed with cheers and hugs and tears from both the land-dwellers and the siren people. The celebration is only beginning and one that will probably last all day and night. The people are pouring in from all over the island, their eyes alight with the possibility of a new and better world. They bring with them fragrant food, joyful song, and it doesn't take long before most of them begin to dance. My smile is so wide that my cheeks start to ache, but I can't help it, nor do I mind, not with everything that's happened, not with Kyon by my side. He and I stay close, our story rushing out to anyone who asks.

At one point Asahi appears from across the courtyard. His dark eyes travel over the protective arm Kyon has wrapped around my shoulders. I freeze, expecting a hateful exchange. Did I ruin their friendship for good? The idea of it turns my stomach to knots. But then Asahi laughs, shaking his head and sending a playful "thumbs up" motion toward Kyon. Both men grin at each other as we stumble further into the crowd.

When I find Mother, her downturned eyes blink up at me, disbelieving. Then she runs for me, pushing through the thick mass of bodies, arms flying, all pretenses of queenly decorum vanishing. "Senra!" she yells, wrapping me in her thin, strong arms. "You're alive! How did you do it? How are you here? When the island transformed, I thought for sure it meant you'd drowned."

I laugh, shaking my head. "I can hardly believe it myself. But I'm here, Mother. I'm alive."

"And you're not the only one." The Japanese Emperor joins our little group, his expression alight with both disbelief and excitement. "Anyone who was killed in battle yesterday has miraculously come back to life, healed of injury. I don't understand how that's even possible. But you did it, Senra, you saved us."

"It wasn't me." I shake my head, my voice cracking, tears gathering in my eyes. I assumed it was just me and Kyon who were healed. This news is better than anything I could have imagined. "It was Gaia. When I returned the stone to her, she returned our lives to us."

It takes a week for us to sort everything out. It's the best week of my life.

"Come on," Kyon says, tugging at my hand. We're back on our beach. Today I'm going to show him how to hunt. I didn't always use my song to catch fish; hunting without the use of magic was a sport in which all siren partook from time to time.

We run through the surf and dive under the cresting waves together. I watch him under the water as he takes it all in, watch as he pulls in a deep breath of water, as it fills his lungs and doesn't harm him. He laughs, and large billowing bubbles rise to the surface. Our legs tangle together and we kiss. We can't help it. Mother says it's new love. She's worried it will wear off, but she's agreed to end the engagement with Lei so I can follow my heart and be with Kyon. Nobody put up a fight about it, not even Lei or his father. I think after the earth healed and the stories were passed around, everyone was stunned by the sacrifice I made. They're giving me this happiness.

And as for Lei and SunYu, they left the island and returned home without argument. It's a new world, after all. Everybody must decide what to do with this new reality in his or her own way.

All right, we can't kiss forever, I say to Kyon through the telepathic link. *We'll go hungry!*

He laughs again but we swim on, hands still tangled together.

The siren magic was the biggest surprise of all. We were sure Mother Gaia was going to take it all away. Instead, she distributed it evenly between all the people. Now everyone can breathe underwater. The only difference is the song. We can no longer use it to control or manipulate, not even with the sea life. The peaceful music is still within us, but that's all.

So now, we have to hunt for real.

Kyon and I swim deeper into the ocean where the fish are plentiful. When our earth mother healed the land, she healed the sea as well. The abundance of life now swimming through our sea is dizzying. We may have to hunt without the aid of song, but we'll never go hungry again, of that I'm certain.

I think I could live down here, Kyon says completely out of the blue.

I spin to look at him, to see if he's joking. His adorable face is as serious as ever, his eyes boring into mine. We still haven't talked about where we're going to establish our home. Mother wants me to return to the palace and rule as Empress. But she says I have a choice. I can stay here.

Everyone has a choice now.

The Japanese Emperor has stayed on his island. His people have taken both paths with his blessing. Most have chosen to remain in their homes or to rebuild what was lost, but there are others who are trying life in the ocean. There's more room to spread out, more spaces for them to build something brand new, and hopefully, something lasting. Last I heard, some of the land-dwellers had even chosen to join my people in the cities forged by our first siren ancestors. Same goes for the sirens, some have taken to life on land, wishing to taste the sun on their skin.

But Kyon and I...

I wouldn't want to take you away from your parents and friends, I say. *We can stay on land. Or we can stay underwater and build a new home near your island.*

He squeezes my hand. *I know it will take some getting used to, but I'd like to see you in your element. I can only imagine how attractive that will be.* He winks. *If there was ever a person meant to rule an empire, Senra, it's you.*

I stop to look into his bronzed eyes, to see the earnest expression on his face. He means every word. His lips pull up in a wide smile.

Are you sure? I draw my eyebrows together, hoping he understands that we don't have to do any of that. *We could start a new life together, one free of obligation. One just for us.*

He cocks his head, the light from the surface reflecting off the planes of his face. *We could. And it would be wonderful. But I like you the way you are. I like the princess in you. You're selfless and full of love for your people. They need you. I can't take you away from that. I wouldn't want to.*

So you'll come with me?

He nods. *I'll happily come with you. I love you.*

I gasp and pull him to me, kissing him all over again. *I love you, too.*

Besides, I'm pretty sure my parents will love life underwater. You know how much they were interested in sirens. And I can't imagine anything better for Dad's health than to be weightless.

I squeal aloud, the bubbles tumbling from my mouth. I'm burning up with the joy of my life, with the future we're going to share.

I promise to make it amazing for all of you. Now come on. I break free and race deeper into the sea. *I bet you can't catch a fish before I do.*

He laughs and rushes past me. My eyes trail him as he attempts to grab a shiny silver fish with his bare hands. He fails, the fish easily darting away, and my heart bursts with love for my man.

When all of this started, I never thought it would end this way. I never thought I would grieve the loss of the sea monsters. I do. I think of Long's memory with nothing but gratitude. I never thought I would fall in love with a human, either. But I have. I never thought I would be confident to go on without the guidance of the Tibetan Monks, but I am. And I certainly never thought I would grow into the kind of Empress that could save not only her people, but thousands of land-dwellers as well.

I have done all of those things, and have many yet to do. I have my whole life ahead of me, a whole world to explore, and the best part is

I don't have to do any of it alone.

Come on. I catch up to Kyon, intertwining my fingers with his. I nod toward the school of fish swimming in the distance. They weave in and out, a glimmering dance of silver against cobalt. *Let me show you how it's done.*

ACKNOWLEDGEMENTS

I have so many people to thank for *Dark Ocean Princess*. First, I have to thank Rebecca Hamilton for inviting me to join this collection. This project has been so fun and I really appreciate the opportunity to be a part of something so special. And thank you to everyone behind the scenes of the OTOH team who set this up for us. Many hugs go out to my fellow authors. Thanks for all the collaboration and inspiration. I can't wait to read all your siren stories!

My biggest thanks goes to my husband, Travis, for supporting me while I wrote, edited, and published this book in a short amount of time. It was a sacrifice for our family, one that you made more than anyone else. Thank you, babe. I love you.

A giant thank you goes to my extraordinary editor, Kate Foster. You saw all the things that this book needed to be and helped me get there. I can't thank you enough for everything you've done for me.

Rebecca Frank, thank you for this incredible cover and for seeing my vision right out of the gate. I love it so much!

Molly Phipps, thank you for the beautiful paperback formatting.

And to my proofreaders, Chelsea, Kate, Ailene, Sarah, and Travis, many thanks for putting up with my typos and helping me polish my books.

And to my Advanced Reader Team, thank you for taking the time to help me launch this book, for dropping your TBR list and jumping into Senra's story with such enthusiasm.

Thank you to all my friends, my family, and my Mom, for your extra love and support.

Thank you, readers. Thank you for buying books and supporting authors. We're real people with lives and bills and feelings and it means so much for us when you love our books like we do. Seriously, you make this all possible.

And finally, thank you to my Heavenly Father for giving me the strength to follow my dreams and the courage to see them through to the end.

ABOUT THE AUTHOR

NINA WALKER lives in Utah with her husband, two young kids, and three fur-babies. She's very active on Instagram and Facebook and loves to connect with other YA fanatics. Find her on instagram @ **ninabelievesinmagic** or in her reader group at **www.fb.com/groups/ ninasreadingparty**. She's looking forward to meeting you!

WWW.NINAWALKERBOOKS.COM

www.ingramcontent.com/pod-product-compliance
Lightning Source LLC
Chambersburg PA
CBHW020648030726
47498CB00002B/413